SHARENE

SHARENE

DEATH: A PREREQUISITE FOR LIFE

A NOVEL BY

ROCKY WILSON

iUniverse, Inc.
New York   Bloomington

Sharene
Death: A Prerequisite For Life

iUniverse books may be ordered through booksellers or by contacting:

iUniverse
1663 Liberty Drive
Bloomington, IN 47403
www.iuniverse.com
1-800-Authors (1-800-288-4677)

Because of the dynamic nature of the Internet, any Web addresses or links contained in this book may have changed since publication and may no longer be valid. The views expressed in this work are solely those of the author and do not necessarily reflect the views of the publisher, and the publisher hereby disclaims any responsibility for them.

ISBN: 978-1-4401-1785-5 (pbk)
ISBN: 978-1-4401-1786-2 (cloth)
ISBN: 978-1-4401-1787-9 (ebk)

Library of Congress Control Number: 2009920628

Printed in the United States of America

iUniverse rev. date: 01/22/2009

DEDICATION

This novel is dedicated to Karola, who taught me how to love; my best friend, Roy, whom I hope to join in heaven one day; and Edna, my Hawaiian Mom, who taught me how much fun being a Christian can be.

Acknowledgments

Thanks to my mother, Eileen Wilson, a former high school English teacher who stirred my interest toward fine literature at an early age.

Thanks to George Venn, an instructor from what's now Eastern Oregon State University, who said, "How do I know what I think until I've read what I've written?"

Thanks to Will Pitkin, a former instructor at what's now Western Oregon State University, who was the first person to indicate to me that I had a true talent to write. On a paper he graded, Pitkin wrote he'd give me a nickel if I developed that talent. I hope one day to again cross paths with Professor Pitkin, who'd moved to teach at Brigham Young University at last account, and collect that nickel.

Thanks to Pastor Joe Slawter, a passionate, knowledgeable man of God, who read the text and said he's of the belief that the content of Sharene, though written as fiction, is theologically accurate.

Thanks to Richard Ripley, Paul Read, and Kim Crompton, all editors at a business newspaper in Spokane, Washington, who honed my writing abilities. Though I wasn't always the most appreciative student at the time, I now realize the value of their lessons and thank them for their patience in dealing with me. The only thing I'd change if I were to repeat that experience would be to supply Kim with a rubber stamp at the outset of my employment there to save him from writer's cramp and the loss of pens discarded because they'd run out of ink. The stamp would read, "Don't split your verbs, Rocky."

But, most of all, I'd like to thank God, Jesus Christ, and the Holy Spirit—the Holy Trinity—Who've carried me through some perilous times to reach this juncture in my life. I can do nothing to earn favor, yet I offer this novel as a humble form of thanks for all They've done and continue to do in my life.

"I tell you the truth, unless a kernel of wheat falls to the ground and dies, it remains only a single seed. But if it dies, it produces many seeds."
Jesus Christ

CHAPTER 1

The sun, the bridegroom coming out of his chamber, was melancholy and the roof steep. The two met regularly on early spring mornings when the sun's first rays embraced the lofty eastern exposure of a rural church which towered over the Appalachian burg below like an old cotton gin neglected in a southern farmer's vine-covered field. The church and the gin were landmarks, almost relics.

The western exposure of the gabled church saw little of the sun this spring because, even with freshness in the air, the sun routinely chose to follow its bright, daily ascendancy with a feigned withdrawal behind wind and thunderclouds, behind rain and coolness.

Thus was the sun's melancholy. It knew the suffering, the sacrifices many must make before it would withdraw from sight and call it a day.

The roof had been constructed and shingled many years before by men of God, and sometimes not men of God, who had wrapped ropes around themselves, made two-by-four footholds in steep wooden scaffolding, gritted their teeth, and squeezed their butts tight to hammer nails into high, slanting wooden planks. Then they'd covered those planks with the same shingles that today, weathered and covered with lichen and moss, now host the afternoon rain.

The efforts of those roped workers initially had been heralded by pretty women who brought hot food and coffee through crowds of sore-necked onlookers who, in 1913, had time to watch and analyze this brave Christian endeavor. Others, educated nonbelievers, laughed about the "Tower of Babel."

But the workers weren't heralded for long. Seemingly within days those same workers merged with the crowd without accolades, just memories. Some felt as if the hot coffee wasn't enough, that they had risked their lives for nothing. Others, over the course of many years, died willingly.

In the spring of 1981, in Northern Alabama, it didn't make much difference what those roped workers had thought about the rewards for their efforts 68 years earlier. What they'd built remained solid and, just as it had in 1914 when the building was completed, the morning sun continued to bring warmth to it on a daily basis. There always would come a time when God's gift of sunshine would warm the seasonally shaded side of the roof, but that didn't necessarily happen in the early spring.

Inside the church on this warm April day was, primarily, a homogeneous assortment of White worshippers, working-class people of God who quietly scattered among the hard, wooden pews. They either waved at new arrivals or piously stared at the seven-foot-high wooden cross that normally hung on the wall above the preaching pulpit. Made of locally produced pine plywood, the pulpit was equipped with wheels and could easily be rolled from its position of prominence to accommodate special events such as guest drama, a well-attended baptism, or a funeral.

Today, the pulpit was rolled aside.

Speaking clearly from where the pulpit normally stood beneath the cross was a middle-aged man of God wearing a vestment. He exhibited skittish mannerisms, and sported a frayed, multi-colored beard that covered hard years of pockmarks and wear. The voice that boomed throughout the chapel, belying the unconventional look of the man who spoke it, was unclouded, almost crystalline. And Carol Marsena, surrounded by family near the front, left-hand side of the sanctuary, wondered for the umpteenth time how Pastor Dale Hemri could project so bravely before the congregation, yet so humbly in everyday life.

"Jesus Christ never lost his focus," said the man of God from behind the multi-colored beard that covered years of perseverance and pain.

Carol Marsena and her son were the only ones with actual bloodlines to the roped roofers whose efforts long ago had built the ceiling above them, the walls around them, and the mossy, steep surfaces that now provided coolness and shade. Her late grandfather had been a pioneer laborer, an architect of sorts, who, according to stories relayed by her mother, had died without conflict before Carol was born.

Carol's husband, Jake, only 42, had no bloodlines to the roped roofers, but maybe had bloodlines to the one for whom they roofed. He wasn't positive who that was, but knew somewhere deep within that his own heritage was soiled. Unlike, or maybe like, many of Jewish origins, Jake Marsena neither had nor wanted a clear picture of his role in the cosmos.

When Carol had entered his life and asked him to forsake his past for Christianity, he had acquiesced like the water he was dipped into, putting she, and later their children, on the pedestal of his life.

He looked upon the cross this morning, this fine, bright morning with the sun now gracing the church's steep, eastern roof, with most of his family by his side. Jake Marsena, a grocer by trade, saw the simple, wooden crucifix as a powerful symbol of pain and suffering, but had no cognizance of the true personage it stood for.

"Jesus Christ died for our sins, not His ..."

Peter Marsena reluctantly sat on the outside of his mother. He was young and didn't want these memories.

Beside Peter sat the only nonfamily member of the immediate party, twenty-one-year-old Jordan Norton. He certainly was no stranger. Jordan had been constantly at the Marsena household from breakfast until after dark on weekends, and at least in the afternoons during school days. He was an admirer of Peter's sister, a friend who laughed and cried and shared and raced and read and stumbled and played with the abandon of Romeo running from below the balcony and into the trees, or grunion leaving the ocean to deposit their eggs.

3

His eyes would sparkle in her presence, his heart pump madly at her smile, her touch.

But she wasn't there.

"And from the final verse of Galatians, 'The grace of our Lord Jesus Christ be with your spirit brethren, amen.' "

What can you say about a beautiful woman who dies young? Can you say she was a blessing, smile sadly at her mother, then go home to fix lunch for your family? Can you follow the procession to the cemetery and pray for her soul? Can you remember her beside you at an earlier time, the sensual thrill of touching hands during a sermon? Can you remember a daughter who exceeded your dreams for her, yet died without explanation far from home? Can you remember a sister who was always there for you, only to be replaced by an unimaginable void? Can you remember a gentle Christian woman who imparted a freshness of life, a special trust in the future that must never be allowed to die?

This is the story of Sharene Marsena, the beautiful daughter, sister, and friend for whom the funeral was being held.

"She deserved so much more," said Mrs. Newton, shedding tears as she sat in the back row. "Take my Richard, but not her."

Mrs. Newton had been in the same church only a week earlier for the funeral of a friend and mentor, Claudia Bohna, but that had been a different experience. Claudia, at age 92, had died in her sleep, and, lying in her open casket had the look of a woman who'd accomplished her mission.

Sharene Marsena's coffin, on the other hand, was closed, only fanning mysteries that this Black mother couldn't comprehend.

Next to Mrs. Newton sat a woman with strong, bare arms and short-cropped hair whom no one in the church knew. The unknown woman stooped forward with her eyes cast down toward the floor in an apparent posture of prayer.

Pastor Dale Hemri spoke from behind the casket, through a flood of his own tears. His voice was strong, but so too, was his will to not stop the spontaneity of his personal love for Sharene. So the tears flowed. No one saw their destination on the carpet behind the casket, and on his shoes.

The casket was piled high with colorful, fragrant flowers, and shut firmly.

Everyone present had different memories of the beautiful, hometown girl.

In her youth, Sharene had been likened to a dolphin.

"To say Sharene Marsena is beautiful is like saying a dolphin can swim," an admirer once said on the streets of Plateau, Alabama. "You're totally accurate in either case, but you darn sure fall short of the point. That girl is a gift from God."

The admirer had been surprised that his tiny audience hadn't readily vocalized their agreement, had instead looked at him stoically as if wanting further explanation.

Then he'd added with absolute conviction, "And dolphins swim real good."

Sharene's physical gifts had been great, almost flawless, and her mother sometimes had rued not having named her Sarai, or Rachel, or Esther. Sharene's skin was soft and touchable; her eyes quiet, trusting, and intelligent. Men's hearts melted at the child's respect for all whom she met, and Carol Marsena, good mother that she was, accelerated lessons to prepare her for the world beyond her childhood. Values and patience were stressed, plus a certain degree of wariness.

It's not that Sharene was a goddess or the cherished one to hold the lamp, but she was closer to such celestial grandeur than most. God obviously had smiled when he made this child, and her purpose, whatever it might be, would impact many.

Jordan, the would-be lover left in the pews, momentarily forgot a painful, misunderstood separation, and remembered a scene on the same seats many years earlier. He remembered Sharene's left hand, with no ring on it, gripping the wooden pew beside his right hand.

He remembered wanting to reach out and touch her hand, almost being compelled by an outside force to do so while the words of Christianity had flown beyond his consciousness. Jordan had sneaked a peak at her cheek, her neck, and then back to the hand that had disrupted his morning in church. They must always be like this, he had thought, and cemented his musings by brazenly placing his young hand on Sharene's, all the time watching Carol Marsena, the mother, sitting nearby.

Sharene had started for an instant, dragged her left hand away as proper etiquette would dictate, then plopped down her sunbonnet to cover the boy's eager reach, to cover its well-intended vulnerability that had been left naked on the pew. She had thought of his inexperience, his clumsy attempt to solidify bonds at an improper moment, and smiled almost sadly, as if she were a widowed woman in her thirties swatting away overtures from a well-meaning teenager. She had carefully determined that her mother was still concentrating on Pastor Hemri's words, then continued their little pantomime to its conclusion. She'd slipped her left hand under the bonnet and into the grasp of his right hand, and then—for only the two of them and omnipotence to ever know—had slapped his hand meaningfully, yet playfully, with both respect and an overtone of finality.

Then she'd pulled away.

Jordan smiled from the memory and brushed away a tear.

The congregation readied for the trip to the cemetery.

Sharene's great grandfather, from an elevated balcony seat among the saints, applauded her purpose as well as her beauty. He alone understood the love, pain, death, and spiritual correctness that had marked the life of Sharene Marsena. He knew Sharene had been destined to throw herself into the fire, refine, and one-day sit upon the judgment seat. He had no fears for her now.

Carol Marsena, dressed in black, stood with dignity, while Jake Marsena slouched in resignation. He didn't yet understand.

At the door, Pastor Hemri asked Mrs. Newton about Richard.

"He says he never knew fear until those doors closed behind him," she replied. "Keep praying, Mrs. Newton," he said. "God loves Richard just as much as he loves you, or me, or even Sharene."

The woman with strong, bare arms, who hadn't signed the guest book, tried to squeeze by without addressing the pastor but, by instinct, Pastor Hemri reached out and touched her arm. Their eyes met, and the man of God understood more than she was willing to tell.

"You loved her, too," he said, and, without speaking, the woman turned her back and started to walk away. Then, after a short retreat, she paused, turned, and walked back to the pastor, who still was looking her direction.

"You know, pastor, Sharene Marsena taught me there has to be a God," said the woman. "Someone up there has to know just how many lives she impacted during her lifetime. You know some and I know some, but only God has a true count that goes far beyond the people Sharene even met."

And this time the woman, bypassing maps placed on a desk by the door for the purpose of directing outsiders to the cemetery, walked away for good.

It was then, looking down, that the man of God first noticed the spattered tears on his shoes.

"I'll see you at the cemetery," he said to anyone who might be listening.

CHAPTER 2 (1974)

The hunter left the main trail and, crouching, eased his way into a stand of trees. He sighted down the barrel of his gun, anticipating the moment he would slowly, very slowly, squeeze the trigger and know blood.

He was dressed in camouflage fatigues, multi-colors of brown and green designed with care to allow one to blend unseen with the environment, to sneak point-blank upon an unsuspecting foe.

He tested the wind by putting spittle upon his thumb and forefinger, gauging the coolness of his fingers as he lofted them into the gently passing air. No edge was too small, too unimportant to overlook in this game.

And it was a game to him. Of life and death there was no doubt, but his interest lay with the game. It had to. Victories may come his way, and kills, many of them in fact, but this hunter knew that one day he would lose, be caged for longer than he could imagine, then loosed for a short spell to renew hunting until his true and final end would come.

But for now, he smiled in anticipation. It was an eerie smile on lips that spoke in nearly every tongue. He reveled in the powers he possessed, the art with which he now stalked his foe, his unsuspecting foe that darted in the sunshine without a care, without any knowledge of the hunter creeping into her life. It had been like this for countless moons, and the hunter couldn't soon foresee a lessening of his strength, his manipulative craftiness that he routinely employed on the creatures around him. He was their master, their tormentor, who could wreak havoc as easily with acid words as the gun he now dragged in the dirt behind him.

He carefully surveyed the immediate surroundings, seeing the high grove of trees, the gently moving, high grasses. He saw the new-growth wildflowers and weeds, the dip in the landscape that led to a sizable, mirrored body of water just beyond. Then he went into a crawl, an unencumbered flow of snaky purpose that, like the hint of wind, moved the grass.

And he tugged the weapon behind him.

He knew the terrain like a landlord off to collect rent, and smiled grimly as he glimpsed his target frolicking by the water.

The hunter could kill from this distance, could kill from many distances, yet preferred a more personal slaying where he could view the horror in the eyes of those who feared him. He lived for those powerful moments, when his prey realized their end had come and that he was no gentle executioner, but one who also could administer pain after death.

Halfway down the slope, moving like a leathery lizard, he stopped and readied his weapon.

But it was still a game.

He sat up in the grasses, adrenaline flowing, and was totally invisible to his foe. Like a demon, he once again sighted down the cold rifle barrel with no thought to time or place. He wanted the female now, the one whose energies were an irritant to his world, his existence. He sighted carefully, with calculated hatred, and effortlessly, methodically, began to administer his dark brand of justice.

Were others to fall in her wake, he cared not. The hunter was focused.

So focused was he that he failed to notice his dreaded rival monitoring his actions, slipping a slim parcel of time between the hunter's forefinger and the trigger mechanism of his weapon. The target would be granted a few more days to share her gifts.

On another plane of time, in the everyday life of 1974, a little boy dressed in camouflage fired his BB gun and yelped with glee when the tiny finch quit fluttering, then splashed without life into the Tagwell's family swimming pool.

"Frankie Spindler, get out of here," yelled Bobby Tagwell.

Bobby and Peter Marsena had been wading on steps at the far end of the pool. They knew the young hunter, didn't like him, and liked even less the prospects of fishing a dead bird from the midsize swimming pool.

"Don't ever bring your gun around here again," yelled Bobby.

The hunter walked away without fear, toting behind him the trusty weapon that had served him well on this mission. He vowed to return.

Bobby and Peter soon forgot Frankie Spindler as they gazed, perplexed, at an uncanny quirk of nature. The dead yellowish-green finch had not been alone. A second finch, a male with bright yellow colors on his breast, refused to acknowledge the death of his mate. Frantically, his fluttering wings dipped into the pool next to the dead bird, splashing water upon her body as he valiantly tried to revive her.

But she remained lifeless, her light form floating in the chlorine-rich liquid.

Bobby and Peter, at their young ages, thought they recognized a danger to the yellow-breasted male and yelled for it to fly away. But the American goldfinch ignored their pleas. His roots screamed an affinity for one he'd so recently flown with, and the miniature-sized bird so precious to God continued flailing its wings wildly, as if hoping the water he splashed had restorative powers.

He wasn't relinquishing his own future, in fact could still fly away at any time, but the boys didn't know that and reacted quickly.

Like trained paramedics, they responded in seconds to what they thought to be a life and death drama. Bobby grabbed the extended pool-cleaning pole with nylon netting that ordinarily dipped debris from the pool, while Peter raced to the closest point he could get to the live bird without diving in, and encouraged it to choose life. It didn't matter that the would-be rescuers were humans and the one thought to be drowning a tiny, almost insignificant bird, or that the saviors were merely children. A universal language transcends even the barrier of species when the topic is survival. Tones of love, of caring and support, can be translated even to a tiny bird with scared, darting eyes.

"You'll be all right. Bobby will get you out in just a minute," said Peter, as if he were a fireman coaxing a toddler to jump from a burning building and into his arms.

The male with a yellow chest, now treading the pool's water, was beside his dead mate, and Bobby Tagwell netted them both with the first swipe of the nylon net. He dumped the birds on the concrete walkway beside the pool, watching both life and death with innocent curiosity. The male finch continued to beat his wings instinctively and was ready to fly away, but Bobby held the net tight.

"Let him go," said Peter.

"I will," said the assumed co-rescuer. "I just want him to know what a stupid thing he did."

Bobby proceeded to counsel the tiny-brained fowl in eight-year-old talk, explaining that the loss of one bird was not worth dying for, that God would bring him another bird friend. "Just wait and see," said Peter Marsena's neighbor and good friend before opening the mouth of the net and encouraging the tiny bird to fly, to begin life anew.

The finch hesitated as if fearing a trap, and Peter reached across to jog the bottom of the net. The bird still held back from flying away, and Bobby gently toppled him onto the manicured green grass that bordered the concrete walkway. The bird then took flight away from the boys and his dead mate, never circling back to verify what he already knew.

Bobby and Peter scrounged around and found Mrs. Tagwell's gardening trowel, and used it to bury the female finch under a row of verbena bushes, maybe ten feet from the pool.

They forgot to say a prayer.

Peter rushed home to tell his mother, to brag about the successful rescue mission he and Bobby Tagwell had undertaken. Carol Marsena was politely respectful when she heard the tale, and most interested in the male bird's willingness to, as Peter explained it, risk his life to save hers.

Then Sharene walked in fresh from a confidential visit with Pastor Dale Hemri, where the ramifications of touching in church and first love had been gingerly charted.

The eager, vibrant younger brother found a new audience.

"And the stupid yellow bird kept flying and dipping until he was caught in the water next to the bird Frankie Spindler shot," Peter said.

By this time Sharene, mature for one in her early teens, was washing carrots, looking carefully to remove any traces of dirt from the fresh vegetables. She, too, listened politely to Peter's exuberance; even nodded once or twice as she concentrated on the work of her own hands.

Too, she fantasized about a young lover risking his life for her.

"The male went free and you buried the female?" she asked.

"Of course," said the eight-year-old indignantly, as if she'd piqued the limits of his tolerance. "That's what I'm trying to tell you, Sharene. We saved him, but the girl was dead when she hit the water."

Peter marched out of the kitchen with a feeling of conviction much like Elijah must have experienced after proclaiming a drought to Ahab. Nothing more needed to be said.

Still standing in the kitchen, Carol looked at her beautiful daughter and smiled sadly while thinking of the male bird. Hadn't she, too, long ago kindly been introduced to the mysteries of love? The memory warmed her.

"Tell me, Sharene," said the mother, selecting her words carefully. "Do you think the little bird was grateful for being pulled from the water by your brother and Bobby Tagwell?"

The daughter's response startled her mother, both by its content and its unpretentious brevity.

"It would depend on whether he knew God or not," said Sharene.

CHAPTER 3

Jordan Norton was a patient young man. Although he saw his future in Sharene, the young lady he expected to spend his life with, he never pressed or pressured her. She would come to the same realization one day, of that he was confident.

In ways, the carefree youth was mature. In ways, he wasn't.

When it came to the courtship of a pristine beauty, he displayed a patient gallantry bred in the South. Yet, when it came to maintaining his first automobile, he was neither patient nor gallant.

His middle-class parents purchased Jordan a '61 Bel Air for his 16th birthday and he drove it on his and Sharene's first official date. That was the second summer after she had discovered a strange fluttering in her soul, two summers after Peter claimed to have saved a lovesick bird from drowning. They had gone to the Drive Inn on Summit Street near the church, and Sharene had ordered a grilled cheese sandwich. He'd ordered fish and chips, and she'd pulled gum from her purse to share with him.

Their second date, also in the Bel Air, took them with two other couples to the closest bowling alley, located miles away across the county line, and all six had laughed with innocence, seemingly oblivious to the red, white, and blue banners waving at the entrance to the bowling alley. The young people in the lane next to them giggled and waved small American flags mounted on wooden sticks.

It was early July, 1976.

All were aware of the time's significance (hadn't the Declaration of Independence been reproduced that week between the sports page and classified section in Plateau's struggling weekly newspaper?), but on this trip down the two-lane highway across the county line, messages of love seemed to supercede flags and national colors.

Or maybe they were synonymous.

Sitting on the plastic bench waiting for another turn to bowl, Jordan awkwardly placed his left arm around Sharene's shoulders and was rewarded with a smile. The action was repeated many times when he returned from rolling the black ball down the lane, and, by the completion of three lines each of bowling for six people, he was cupping her bare left shoulder with sensitive fingers.

The bowling wearied Sharene, and, as they drove home with young kissing and touching going on in the back seat behind her and Jordan, Sharene's thoughts wandered ahead to her annual reunion with an elderly loved one in South Carolina.

Jordan, thinking of Sharene, mastered the auto and looked unusually handsome, even radiant.

In her eyes, Jordan maintained that aura of Southern gallantry over much of the next year.

When together, which practically was on a daily basis, they perused what little social life was available to them in a small Alabama town, talked about everything under the sun while "cruising the gut" in Jordan's Bel Air, and laughed with little thought beyond the present.

They were young, and they thought of love.

When away from Jordan with girlfriends, Sharene often spoke of Jordan Norton in glowing terms, her already beautiful eyes sparkling from pleasant memories.

Jordan, a year older than Sharene, thought frequently of her when they weren't together, yet also spent time developing a friendship with an unusual transfer student from New York City. That young man's family, in an effort to remove him from the big-city temptations he'd begun succumbing to, had relocated him to Plateau to live with distant family members.

Jordan was attracted to the youth from New York because of his worldliness, cocky demeanor, and apparent fear of nothing.

On one evening in the spring of 1977, Jordan and Sharene attended a party thrown by Mr. and Mrs. Norton, who socialized occasionally with food, alcohol, and friends. As anticipated, Jordan and Sharene were the only minors in attendance that night and, following perfunctory greetings and salutations to people Sharene and Jordan both knew, they exited, and Jordan boldly drove to a popular wide spot along the highway west of town.

Where Jordan parked, the car was near a bright night-light, and the two saw sides of each other they'd never seen before. They talked and laughed, and paused at length to look into each other's eyes, wanting, yet afraid to think of what the future might hold.

Jordan was on his absolute best behavior and Sharene's insides felt guilty for wishing he weren't. Like Charlie Chaplin swooning in one direction, then listing in another, did Jordan and Sharene spend those moments misreading the other's desires.

Still without a first kiss, they drove away from the wide spot along the highway and parted as even better friends.

Their next date, only a week later, drew them together like none other, but it didn't come without a price.

Jordan began the evening in the company of three male friends who were jovially jealous about whom he would spend the coming hours. While cruising in Jordan's Bel Air, the three lingered around an ill-gotten bottle of wine, bragging that it would be a big night for them as well.

Jordan declined overtures to imbibe. They knew he wasn't afraid to drink, in fact on occasions had led them on adventures into his parents' liquor pantry, but on this night, he maturely opted for a higher priority.

"John Riggs' parents are gone and Pavo owes me another trip to the store, so it's gonna be a big night," said the shaggy-headed, blond transplant from New York, named Corey, before tipping the bottle of wine for another drink. "If you and the little lady want to catch up, that's where we'll be. And this," he said while touching his lips to the bottle once more, "is what we'll be doing."

The three boys, as did Jordan, laughed.

Then the others turned thoughts to the beautiful Sharene, boyishly lamenting her poor taste in men.

"I bet she moans good when you rub her up, Jordan boy," said one as the wine stirred his imagination.

Another normally quiet youth, one seldom listened to even when he did speak, spoke gutturally with rare excitement is his voice, "Bet she French kisses like a Russian racehorse," and the three laughed hungrily as if they were forming a small line to test Sharene's merits on the score.

And the hunter—out of sight, out of mind, and hearing every word—nodded with approval.

Jordan lightly cautioned his friends about the tone of their conversation, fearing above all they might learn that he and Sharene had never touched lips. The Southern gentleman was suddenly feeling remorse for his chosen course of patience and valor, his willingness to wait decades if he had to for the right time to kiss and hug, to rub Sharene's contoured body. Their words intoxicated Jordan Norton as readily as the wine he didn't drink, and he willed in his being that this would be a night to be remembered for he and Sharene, that some physical needs would be addressed.

"We'll be at 'ol Riggsy's place, so bring her along. Lots of room, if privacy is what you want." And Corey from New York ended his words with a taunting laugh, a challenging laugh that had been intentionally formulated years before, for the sake of survival, in the public schools of a much larger city.

Jordan laughed, too, but not the same kind of laugh. He didn't laugh out of disrespect, but, without conscious thought, wanted Sharene to share tonight on his terms, the terms created by his friends.

He drove the Bel Air up Ollicut Road to the house where John Riggs lived. It sat back a distance from the county road near a small stream filled with leaves and periwinkles. Many of Plateau's youth had at one time or another donned tennis shoes and explored the stream. But that was in the past for Jordan and his friends. These were young men with other interests.

"Maybe I'll see you later," said Jordan as he dropped off the three boys and their wine.

"You won't be back," said Corey with conviction. "You're pussy whipped."

And the other two laughed as if they understood what had been said, as if they approved heartily of the damning slur thrown at Sharene and her boyfriend, as if they cared enough to damn.

Jordan wanted to spin his tires as he pulled from the driveway, to accent the power he possessed with an automobile of his own, but the surge of power wasn't there. His '61 Bel Air with an automatic transmission, although user-friendly, had its limitations. His parents had given much thought about what car to buy their son. Unless the gas pedal was pushed to the floorboard for a good amount of time, or alcohol was consumed to alter one's thinking, Jordan's '61 Bel Air was relatively safe.

Thinking of a showdown with Sharene, his youthful hormones racing, Jordan played with the accelerator of the car, lulling to twenty-five miles per hour, then punching the gas as quickly as the car would allow to forty, and even forty-five. He illegally coasted through the stop sign where Ollicut joined Topu Avenue, and drove a short distance farther toward Plateau High School, where only a handful of track athletes could be seen working out on the adjacent football field.

It was starting to get dark.

Too early for their date, Jordan stopped at the Drive Inn and, once inside, saw Penny Davidson looking like Rahab the harlot. Her mouth turned half way into a smile when Jordan looked at her, then he broke eye contact.

He ordered a Coke in a paper cup and laughed with classmates who were playing The Rolling Stones on the jukebox, listening to Mick kicking folk off of his cloud.

"You taking Sharene out tonight?"

The question made Jordan feel important, look almost invincible in their eyes, and he responded with more bravado than caring. "We'll be having some fun tonight, I guarantee it," he said, and the classmates unanimously voiced their approval as Mick Jaggar eased into another selection of poignant rock 'n' roll.

Jordan Norton sat and talked with his friends for two more jukebox tunes, then left for the nearby Marsena home, passing the towering church as the day's final rays of sunshine departed from the steep western slope of its roof.

When he saw her, Sharene was radiant and loving, and Jordan inwardly was shamed by his recent words of bravado. Yet, his loins felt alive, almost giddy, and he sensed some physical progress soon must be made in their relationship.

Jake Marsena, always the protective father, carefully and pointedly itemized his rules for the evening, noting that this was his only daughter, a fact that shouldn't be treated lightly. He ordered an 11 o'clock curfew, and Sharene smiled at Jordan's visible grimace. Even at age fifteen, she understood the competing interests between her father and Jordan Norton.

After all, she was the topic of their discussion and a woman in the making.

Jordan politely opened the door of the passenger side of the Bel Air before walking around to the driver's side, opening his door, and sliding behind the wheel. He started the engine, turned on the radio, and pulled away from the Marsena driveway.

Sharene tentatively scooted to the middle of the front seat, and Jordan Norton again felt important, wanted.

They "cruised the gut," driving repeatedly up and down the main street of Plateau, waving at the occupants of most cars they passed, even at baldheaded Mr. Corning who was driving home later than usual from his hardware store.

Jordan's '61 Bel Air surely wasn't the newest car on the strip, but it had redeeming qualities. The body was straight and the beige paint job more than respectable. The ignition routinely started its engine on command, and, tonight, the whitewall tires were clean. Too, and most importantly, sitting next to the driver was the prettiest girl in town.

The streetlights, the colors, and the looks from others all were intoxicating to a sixteen-year-old in his first car, and Jordan looked toward his best friend with young love and a misguided sense of power.

"Let's not go to the school," said Jordan after considerable thought, as he made yet another U-turn at the west end of the town's main street, pulling into the gravel parking lot of the Farm Supply Store.

"Riggsy's having a party and I thought maybe we could go for a little while. Not to drink, of course," he added quickly.

Sharene balked.

"We told my father we were going to the school. Would you lie to my father?" she asked.

"No. Not intentionally."

Jordan frowned. "Maybe we could make a quick run by the school, then jog up to Riggsy's. It would give us a chance to spend some time together."

"What do you think we're doing now, Jordan Norton?" she asked suspiciously.

"Well, it would be different up there," he responded in a pouting voice.

This special woman he thought he loved frustrated Jordan Norton. His hormones had jumped unnaturally when he'd dared to mention Riggsy's party, and she was again quashing his male thrusts before they could even materialize.

"What do you want at Riggsy's party, Jordan?" she asked. "Couches, beds, alcohol?"

Jordan backed off a notch, feeling hurt by what he perceived as her lack of faith in him. He'd done nothing wrong, he thought. Wasn't he simply suggesting an alternative to the rote boredom of school functions? Couldn't she see that the world went on outside the parameters of her mother's Christian church? Couldn't she trust him, her best friend, to protect her from the perils of a simple high school party? Couldn't he, at age sixteen, take his girl out to be with his friends on a Saturday night?

The boy's jaw muscles tightened.

"Sharene, be real," he said. "There's nothing at that party to be afraid of. We're the same as adults. Would I do anything to hurt you? Come on. Let's go for just long enough to say 'hi'."

His voice now carried an unnatural tone, a whining inflection Sharene hadn't heard since years before when he'd gotten stubborn on the playground and taken his ribbed, black-and-white soccer ball home, leaving a field full of kids with nothing to kick but grass and air.

Jordan's power play years before had stopped the game, and Sharene had cried.

Not this time.

"No, Jordan. I will not tell my father I'm going to do one thing, then do something else," she said.

They made the turn on the east end of town, about two hundred yards past the Drive Inn, and returned back toward the center of the small town, continuing to wave at people in nearly all of the cars they met.

Their waves now lacked smiles.

Jordan became petulant. "We've been best friends for over ten years, and yet you never let me do what I want to do. It's always us doing what your father wants us to do."

Then he raised his voice. "Well, I'm tired of it, Sharene. Every once in a while a man has to do what he wants to do, and not always what 'The Father' wants."

He said 'The Father' irreverently, with intent to ire, and Sharene bristled.

"You have no right to speak of my father in such tones, Jordan Norton. Take me to the school or take me home," she said firmly.

"Why is it that what I want to do isn't even an option, Sharene? Why do you have to control every minute?" he said, again in a whining tone. "And another thing, Sharene, you've never even kissed me. You sit right next to me in my car, sometimes put your hand on my thigh, but you've never even kissed me. What are you afraid of? Will one kiss ruin your perfect record? How can we spend all this time together and never even kiss? Every guy in town has kissed his girl, but not 'ol Jordan. Sure, I've been kissed by other girls, lots of them, but not by the one I really care about."

Jordan drove past P&T Grocery, then the Farm Supply. He next turned right on to Johnson Road.

She cringed at the turn. A vital crossroad in their relationship was nearing. They passed the aging pool hall and the theater that seated less than eighty Black and White patrons who came every Friday and Saturday night to immerse themselves in another world, to leave their cares at the door and live vicariously for a few hours.

Jordan turned right on Topu Avenue and, one block later, made a left turn onto Ollicut, which led to John Riggs' house. Sharene pulled away to the passenger door, grabbed the handle, and said, "I'll jump before you take me to Riggsy's party."

He pulled apologetically into the parking lot of a small nursing home, and turned the car around.

"I wasn't really going to take you," he mumbled. "I just wanted to scare you."

Then Sharene, uncharacteristically, let the outer fringes of her human side surface. Suddenly his turning around wasn't enough. Even recanting wouldn't have been enough at this point in time. She wanted to return a scare for a scare.

"I'm sorry, Sharene," said Jordan. "I want to do what is best for you. I only …"

"Maybe," she interrupted slowly and deliberately. "Maybe, Jordan, I need another man that 'My Father' will approve of." She said the 'My Father' thickly, sarcastically, wanting to be blunt, and even hurt, without risking eternal offense.

But she was only fifteen, and the cry for another man didn't go well.

Jordan Norton gasped in a pain that enveloped his entire being, his soul. He began to bleed inside, to hemorrhage from tiny capillaries in his heart too small for anyone but God to detect. No human physician could have assessed the damage done by Sharene's harsh words.

Anger from a kind soul bites deeper.

Jordan pushed on the gas pedal, taking the Bel Air off of Ollicut and onto Topu, heading this time toward the school. He refused to look at her as he drove, and she remained by the door, trying to read his response to her outburst. Her unnatural words had achieved their temporary intent, yet Sharene was troubled. All she wanted now was God's peace and warmth.

She refrained from commenting on the vehicle's increasing speed until Jordan ran a stop sign by the school and the Bel Air careened onto Summit Street.

"What are you doing?" she asked in dismay. "You could run someone over!"

Students stopped to watch the fast-rushing car, commenting on whom was driving and speculating on why he was driving fast.

Sharene's emotions vacillated between anger and regret.

On his most recent pass, Jordan had driven, excluding the crucial block out of his way up Ollicut Road, in a rectangular pattern that started and ended near the Drive Inn. While waiting at the red light near that popular hangout, they caught a glimpse of Corey from New York as he paraded by as a passenger in someone's father's Ford station wagon. He brazenly waved a brown paper bag out the window at Jordan and Sharene.

Neither of them spoke.

When the light changed, Jordan drove straight through the intersection at a normal rate of speed. Sharene knew she was being taken home at an early hour and wanted to repent. The Bel Air was guided past the east end of South Street from where night-lights illuminated the church grounds. Jordan slowed the vehicle to a crawl and looked to Sharene for the words of apology he longed to hear. She remained by the passenger door, frozen in confusion, wanting to make peace with her first love, yet, too, wanting somehow for God Almighty to speak through the moment.

Jordan pulled the Bel Air into the church parking lot, a deserted church parking lot, and parked between two of many diagonal white lines. He shut off the engine.

Placing his battered heart on the line, the sixteen-year-old boy said, "Sharene, I love you more than the wind and would do nothing to hurt you. It's just that sometimes we see things differently. Let's work it out."

He abandoned the big steering wheel, swung his feet over the floorboard divider hump, and approached a wary fifteen-year-old beauty that had perfection, or the appearance of such, to lose. Trust was in their eyes, yet Sharene chanced a quick look to gauge the church lighting all around them. She sensed that nothing would be hidden.

Jordan misunderstood her look toward the church and hurried the moment. He stopped an inch from her face, her smooth hair pressed against the window behind her, and waited for permission for a first kiss. She looked initially weak, afraid, but their eyes continued to share trust, and Sharene, with a faint smile, reached to him for that pivotal moment in the Bel Air in the church parking lot.

Blissful. Tender skin on tender skin. They shared tentatively for long seconds, and broke into a hug and major sighs. She remained, by her own volition, pinned against the passenger door.

Being sixteen and more experienced, Jordan became more aggressive, kissing through to her teeth and pushing roughly against her body. She liked it, or, as a classmate might say, "loved it," yet was tensely fearful at the same time. She wanted to let go and enjoy, yet was attentive to his every move, his every motion, his every advance.

Jordan, moved by instinct, forgot the razor blades that so recently had pricked his heart, and proceeded as if this beautiful creature was Penny Davidson, or a lonely, widowed woman who had wantonly consumed five beers after stepping into a bar for a night of forgetful solace.

His hand cradled Sharene's budding, sensitive left breast, and her wariness revolted. She reacted tensely, scrambling to unhand his advance, and he, being sixteen, failed to understand her youth. He proceeded with his mouth forced against hers, and what had been bliss for her was now fear.

She looked away from him to the church lights and felt strangely ashamed, dirty. She wanted to return to her former self and fumbled to open the car door.

"What are you doing?" Jordan asked in dismay.

In haste, Sharene pushed him away to pull the door handle and regain the clear Alabama night.

She opened the door and backed out of the car, Jordan following with questions. Had he done something to offend her? Were his actions too familiar? Didn't she trust him?

Sharene retreated away from the Bel Air and farther into the church parking lot, the well-lit familiar lot only three blocks from her home. She was confused and wanted someone to talk to, probably her mother. She was filled with nothing but intense emotions and love for Jordan, yet was unable at this moment to share them.

She looked toward the three lights situated high in the church gables and told Jordan she was walking home. He was incredulous, took steps to follow, and she altered her course to walk at an angle closer to the church. Then Sharene proceeded to the sidewalk along

Summit Street, where she turned right in the direction of her home.

He followed at a distance, more hurt than angry, yet sensed not to forcibly intercede. She had marched away once or twice as a child, and he knew no antidotes to her stubbornness.

Yet, he tried with the weakness of an adolescent.

"Sharene. I'm sorry if my being a guy makes you angry. Don't put this guilt trip on me. Let's talk for a few minutes and I'll take you straight home. Don't do this," he pleaded.

His high-pitched words characterized the strain he was under, his own youthful vulnerability, and Sharene Marsena marched away from him mired equally in intensity and confusion. She wished for a moment that she could be like other girls, could put sensations, emotions, and fun ahead of what she had been taught. But that brief thought had no chance of reaching fruition.

Jordan, from a distance, watched Sharene enter the door of her parents' house, then returned to the parking lot to lean dejectedly against the Chevy's hood. He ran his hands over the cold, smooth metal, and swore beneath his breath. Bewilderment was fast giving way to an anger that eclipsed the earlier moments of blissful contact, the memories of a first kiss that, unknown to him, would bolster Sharene's spirits in the trying days ahead.

The hunter, still attired in camouflage, willed the turning of the Bel Air's key and fanned the young man's anger from where he stood in the night shadows of the tall, Southern church.

Jordan drove sanely from the church parking lot to the Drive Inn, and caught a green light onto Main Street. Plateau's traffic was moderate this Saturday night, and sixteen-year-old Jordan Norton didn't hit the accelerator seriously until he reached the westernmost end of the business district, with Mason's Auto Parts on the south side of Main Street and the busy Round-Up Pub immediately across from it to the north.

He gained speed as quickly as his slow-accelerating auto would allow, hitting sixty miles per hour as he bounced over the hump that marked Johnson Road—poverty to the south and Riggsy's party to the north. Because of Jordan's speed in a regulated traffic zone, some approaching vehicles respectfully pulled to the side of the road as if the Bel Air was a red-and-white ambulance with lights flashing and sirens blaring.

Jordan concentrated intently through two forty-five mile-per-hour corners just west of town, braking on the second turn to keep the Bel Air under control on a brief stretch of state-owned, two-lane highway that carried he and his car past the brick home of Pastor Dale Hemri.

Then he made his next mistake.

Now exceeding sixty mph, Jordan looked too long at the pullover where he and Sharene had studied eyes a week earlier, and failed to brake in time for a sharp right corner in the road. It was a turn where highway engineers had failed, years before, to either acquire enough right of way or condemn private farm land to provide for a safer, more sweeping corner than the thirty mph one built there as an unwelcome compromise on the old state route.

Jordan knew the road well, but not as a driver, and suddenly sensed the inevitable when he looked back from the pullover.

He instinctively hit the brakes, his tires locking on the pavement, and, had he time to think about it, Jordan would have assumed he was never more alone. A ditch, and behind it a sloping bank covered with briars and colorless weeds was fast approaching beyond the sharp asphalt corner his Bel Air wouldn't make.

His speed was slowing, but not nearly enough.

Focusing on the immediate, fleeting as that was, he felt no fear. A flashing thought of Sharene, their first kiss, and Jordan was smiling as his screaming black tires left the pavement and lost what traction they had, then crossed the narrow gravel shoulder of the roadway. He gripped the steering wheel with the strength of Samson, and pointed the car toward the thickest clump of briars and weeds visible in his headlights.

But before hitting that foliage, the Bel Air struck the far side of a waterless irrigation ditch and more than a ton of metal stopped instantaneously. Glass flew, and a twisting momentum resurrected life into the ditched Bel Air, easing it into a slow, then faster roll that took the car beyond the ditch, up the weed-infested dirt bank, and beyond it into a field of snow-white cotton. The crush of metal was deafening in the quiet night, and Dale Hemri, not far away, was roused from his meditations.

Watching from the shadows was the hunter, who had willed the turning of the Bel Air's key, fanned Jordan's anger, and years earlier stalked, then killed a fast-hearted, tiny bird. He watched and smiled as Jordan Norton's legs were mercilessly and painfully ripped from their position below the dashboard. Jordan's face and body were scarred and slashed by glass as he was ejected through the windshield and deposited roughly on the cold earth. The twisting automobile narrowly missed crushing him on its second revolution, and continued to roll into the cotton and the night.

With attentive eyes, the hunter watched as the Bel Air's mirrors were shattered, and the boy's body, maybe lifeless and maybe not, hugged the loam soil made for cotton and okra and beans; not for human sacrifices to a God who wanted no such thing.

The hunter waited.

Neither to his surprise nor his dismay, the hunter watched as his rival, radiant and alone, appeared from nowhere, gently touched the crumpled body of Jordan Norton, breathed in a glow of life no other being could instill, then ascended back to another realm.

The hunter envied the other's powers, always had, yet clung stubbornly to the belief that the rival's love and patience for humans such as Jordan Norton would give he, the enemy, an eternity of his choosing to advance a discordant cause. Did not such weaknesses as those displayed this night by Jordan Norton help extend his parole, allow more time for him to shoot female birds and tantalize the world with temptations?

In her home, near the tall church in Plateau, Alabama, Sharene Marsena pleaded to be alone when questions arose about the unusually early return from her date with Jordan. Saying little, she retreated to the confines of her bedroom and promptly got down on her knees to pray for understanding, to be understood, and for the protection of the one she loved.

God answers prayer.

CHAPTER 4

It was only natural that Sharene be sent to South Carolina to care for her paternal grandmother the summer after Jordan's wreck. She'd visited many times over the years and she and her grandmother were more than friends. Jake Marsena himself couldn't leave his business, and Sharene's mother, realistically, had a few more pivotal years to devote to Peter's upbringing.

And so Sharene, with sadness in her heart, packed her clothes only days after finishing her junior year in high school.

She wasn't sad because she had to leave her immediate family to stay in her grandmother's big house in rural South Carolina, but instead because Jordan had graduated and would be away to college in the fall. This should have been their most special summer together, a summer for future plans and love.

Now she was going away.

Jordan had recovered quickly from the wreck, his slightly damaged lung the only physical reminder of what could have been. He couldn't play basketball as competitively or as long as in the past, and his tennis game lacked stamina, but Jordan Norton had learned a valuable lesson. He pinned a photograph of the demolished Bel Air on the bulletin board in his bedroom and genuinely was thankful to be alive.

Both Jordan and Sharene had tried to apologize for their actions the night of the wreck and been drowned by the other's love.

Sharene practically became a live-in nurse during his time of recuperation, and strictly enforced the doctor's order for immobility. Jordan's pain, though initially great, in no way compared to its antithesis, the love flowering in his heart.

Young Peter Marsena, whom no one expected to comprehend the growing relationship between his friend and his sister, came twice to the hospital to visit Jordan. On the second visit, only he and Jordan were in the room.

Peter felt important and laughed eagerly like the child he was. Too, he picked up and read a confidential letter, written by Sharene to Jordan, after the injured youth had excused himself and gingerly walked from his bed and into the bathroom.

The ten-year-old was anything but coy when Jordan returned from the bathroom, giggling excitedly and quoting portions of the letter out of context.

Jordan was chagrined. He didn't want Mr. and Mrs. Marsena to know what had been shared in confidence, and urged Sharene's little brother to remain silent on the matter. A bribe of a certain tropical fish from the town's only pet store elicited a solemn oath of silence from Peter Marsena.

When Sharene came to visit that evening in the hospital, a conference was held between the two young lovers. They agreed that the damage was done, but shouldn't ever be repeated. Their solution was a simple, personal code to be used on all future confidential correspondence between them. Any important messages of a personal nature were to be placed in the second paragraph of a letter. In that paragraph alone, the letters of the alphabet from the author's initials would be used to trigger a code with deeper meaning. They played with it, laughing more than Jordan's ribs would comfortably allow for, and found it workable. No one would pilfer their mail again.

She had kissed him that night in his hospital bed.

But that was earlier.

Jordan Norton had since recovered and Sharene was to leave by Greyhound bus the following morning.

Jordan picked her up after dinner in his father's Plymouth station wagon. He now held new respect for the deceased Bel Air.

"Can I stay in your grandmother's house if I come for a visit?" he asked.

"It's a long trip, Jordan."

"It's not all that far. I could make it in a day. Would I have to stay in a motel?" he asked, not knowing how a Jewish grandmother would react to her granddaughter's suitor staying under the same roof.

They cruised down the same Main Street and waved to the same people as the day's sunshine waned, sharing less and less light on the western side of the big church's roof. They were upbeat in their smiles and dialogue, and saddened at the base of their stomachs where tomorrow's inevitable loneliness already was seeping through. They were closer now than they'd ever been, yet faced the biggest chasm of their relationship. Jordan would be off for an East Coast college in the fall, and neither of them knew whether his exit would precede her return from South Carolina.

"I've got to come see you. That's in stone unless you come back early," he said. "Tell you what, Sharene. If you're not back by the middle of August, I'll just take the bus myself and visit on my way to school."

"Wouldn't you rather take the plane to school?" she asked quietly.

The Mason Auto Parts store's sign flashed outside the passenger window. She sat next to him in the Plymouth with her left hand placed on his right knee.

"What about Mr. Adamson?" she asked, as if she needed to protect every interest but her own.

"He'll be fine. He knows I have to leave, and a couple weeks one way or the other won't make much difference," Jordan said.

He casually, indifferently glanced toward the liquor store, then Corning's Hardware, as he approached the familiar Drive Inn, whose patrons now seemed younger than ever before.

"Besides, Sharene, he did fine for thirty-five years before I came along," he added. Jordan smiled a sad smile, and Sharene nodded.

He drove his father's car past the Drive Inn, through town, and found a gravel side street, a familiar one, as he left the highway. He shut off the engine and the headlights. It was that gray time of the evening when one person would call it night and another person would call it day.

She looked at him with trust and wonderment.

In the partial light they kissed and hugged gently, like the closest of friends willing to trust their futures to unseen tomorrows.

Then he held her at a distance, marginally visible in the twilight, and began to speak.

"Sharene, please don't talk. I've given a lot of thought to what I'm about to say, so please be still and listen."

Then the new man of the world, the recent high school graduate who soon would be off to a distant college, spoke with elevated maturity about love and commitment, about the future he foresaw for he and the beautiful young lady sitting beside him. Jordan was careful not to pressure the one he loved, demanded no commitment on her part, yet outlined a scenario of love and happiness and college degrees and babies and incomes and houses and parental visitations that made a seventeen-year-old girl's head spin.

Her silence wasn't indicative of the wellspring of jumbled emotions radiating from her heart.

Jordan talked at length, almost abusing her silence, reassuring Sharene that he had no intentions of rushing any commitment on her part. Yet, he said he wanted to be first in line to say he was committed and ready for an eternal relationship whenever, if, she could ever feel the same way about him.

"I want to speak now," the beautiful virgin finally replied, flashing a gentle, caring smile, the memory of which Jordan would carry with him to college and for the rest of his life.

Sharene paused before addressing her best friend with thoughts from deep within her soul, receiving strength from silent, impromptu prayers she'd just offered to Jesus, her avowed Lord and Savior, while listening to Jordan's confession of love. The words she was about to speak were byproducts of silent prayers made earlier, long before the man she was to love, to her human comprehension, even had an identify. These were the depths from which her words were drawn.

"I pray that you will understand, Jordan," she began.

"I will," he responded in earnest, and Sharene pressed her right forefinger to his lips to signify the need for his silence.

She moved slightly further away from him, enough for Jordan to mentally note the shift, and said, "Now it's time for you to listen."

He didn't understand the sadness that surfaced quickly from hidden depths within him as she pulled ever so slightly away from their physical closeness. He felt a knot fast-forming in his throat and fought off the unmanly desire to cry. He said nothing, yet waited, hoping he might still have a role in her future.

"I love you Jordan Norton, and I always will," she said. "Yet, at this time, our love isn't enough. You know that as well as I. Life is a matter of priorities."

And Sharene Marsena slipped into a teaching from Pastor Dale Hemri, her Christian mentor, a non-Biblical doctrine from him that she'd swallowed as gospel. She'd blindly assumed Hemri's teaching to be God's Word without a thought to the far-reaching perfection of The Almighty's omnipotence, the thousands of human years sometimes required for change.

"Our priorities are different, Jordan, which is neither good nor bad. I'm different from you in that I don't put a high priority on myself."

She knew he wanted to respond, and said, "No, you mustn't argue. It's true. My priorities are more of a spiritual nature. My top priority is God and what He has in store for my life. My second priority is family. Very simple, but at this time, Jordan, you don't fit into either category. Maybe someday you will, but not now. That will depend on whether God wants us to be together. Can you understand?" she asked, looking imploringly at him with crystal clear, light blue eyes.

"Is there someone else?" he asked, and the words immediately sounded foolish in his own ears. He yearned to call them back with the urgency of a circuit court judge instructing a jury to disregard testimony not intended for their ears, yet lacked the authority of a judge.

"Only God," she said innocently, with finality in words, if not tone.

"Where do I fit in?" he asked.

"Pray for me, Jordan," she said. "Pray for us. If God wants us to be together, we'll be together. But the time is not now. I'm only seventeen. I have to discover how God wants me to share the gifts and talents He has given me. That may take a year or a lifetime, I don't know."

"But what do you want to happen between us, Sharene? I need to know."

Sounding like a missionary in her response, the young, but mature-beyond-her-years woman replied, "Don't misunderstand, Jordan, but my wants mean nothing."

He understood to a point, but never fully understood her words until short years later when he buried his face in the dirt of a foreign country and cried himself clean.

They abandoned their gravel hideaway and, surprisingly upbeat, drove to town where they walked the streets of Plateau. They danced above the sidewalk cracks, waved laughingly at friends who envied their wanton gaiety, and window-shopped at Corning's Hardware.

Their love seemed to be on a higher, purer level, and Jordan Norton vowed as he kissed her goodbye and dropped her off for a pending trip to South Carolina that he would never stop loving this special lady, no matter what God had in store for either of them.

Sharene slept soundly that night, with no dreams to dampen or enhance the patient hope she held for her future.

Jake Marsena drove his only daughter to the bus depot the following morning. He had arranged for an employee to open the grocery store.

"Take good care of Mom, and follow what the doctor says in regards to her diet exactly. And don't forget to eat well yourself," he added, speaking on behalf of Sharene's mother as well as himself.

He parked the car a short distance from the bus depot and walked her inside. They checked in her luggage, then, uncharacteristically for one who often had trouble expressing intimate emotions, Jake Marsena pulled his daughter aside to a bench with no one seated nearby, and spoke softly to her, earnestly pleading to be understood.

"You need to understand, Sharene, that your mother and I don't want to send you away for the summer," he said. "It's just that there is a great need in the family, and you are the only one who can be spared. Please don't look at this trip to South Carolina as punishment, Sharene, but as an opportunity to serve those whom you love, all of us."

Then her earthly father smiled warmly. "Remember, my love," and she never forgot that her father called her 'my love' at that moment, "remember that no matter what experiences may befall you—sadness, pain, whatever—that love from your mother, myself, and Peter will always be with you. Think of our love as being in your hip pocket—out of the way, but always there when you need it."

Sharene blinked back unanticipated tears. She'd always loved and respected her father, even had grown comfortable with his reserved demeanor. Yet, he seemed unusually tender at this moment, as if Jesus had come down from the cross and momentarily perched on Jake Marsena's Jewish shoulders. She felt a bonding for her father she'd never felt before.

Then she kissed him on the forehead and started to walk, wearing jeans and a light blouse, to the bus. On a whim, she turned to him one more time and, prompted more by timing than having anything specific to say, said, "Tell Peter thanks for saving the second bird."

She felt slightly exposed as she walked up steep, metal steps onto the bus, as if those final words to her father had come from the lips of another.

Jake watched his daughter through the bus windows as she walked down the aisle and chose a seat for a long ride. He scratched his forehead where his only daughter had kissed him, shrugged his shoulders, and went to work with a question mark nagging his soul.

That night, he relayed Sharene's message to Peter, and neither of the males understood. Carol Marsena, listening from a distance, remembered an incident in the past, frowned, then proceeded to provide sustenance for the members of her family who still remained at home.

The trip from Plateau to South Carolina was long, with two bus changes. Sharene slept minimally, looked out the window with sometimes-distant eyes, and thought about Jordan, her family, and where she was going.

One highlight of the summer ahead of her, she knew, would be her reunion and time she'd spend with Nora Okatee, an Ugandan exchange student she'd met on a brief visit to Grandmother's the previous summer. Something mysterious about Nora had drawn

Sharene to her like a butterfly to a lantana bush, and a strong friendship had bloomed. Each had written many times in the past year, and Nora had said in one letter that she and her new boyfriend would meet Sharene when her bus arrived.

Nora came from a distinguished ruling family that had been brusquely tossed aside by the emergence of a new Ugandan ruler, Major General Idi Amin. Half the world away from her home land, Nora spoke little about Idi Amin. Minimally in their late-night conversations in South Carolina, and never in her letters did Nora Okatee speak of the militant ruler who was terrorizing her family and millions more in Africa. It seemed to Sharene that Idi Amin was very much on Nora's mind, but she said next to nothing about him to her new friend.

At one point, Sharene boldly had asked about her past in Uganda, and Nora had replied without emotion, as if shooing flies away from raw meat, "Sometimes wisdom says not to say."

Sharene had made the three-legged bus journey to rural South Carolina more than once, and this trip found the buses to be only half full. Across the aisle from her for the first one hundred miles sat a soldier in uniform with wired plugs in his ears and a cassette player on his lap. The young man with short-cropped brown hair grooved to music only he could hear, looking occasionally Sharene's way. Sharene smiled at the young man as the two of them exited the first bus, and prayed silently for his safety, wherever life might take him.

After a brief wait in a small, poorly lit waiting room that reeked of smoke and poverty, Sharene boarded the second bus and claimed a seat next to the window halfway to the rear of the bus.

Gazing, on a sunny day, toward a lazy retail strip across the street, she was startled mildly when a well dressed, about 50-year-old woman asked, "May I sit by you?" The woman hesitated, waiting for Sharene's permission to sit down.

"Sure," said Sharene with a kind smile, and the woman who'd bypassed dozens of unoccupied seats to sit next to the young traveler, placed her purse on the floor of the bus between them, took off her light sweater, sat down, and began to talk. She talked freely, like a Texas preacher on a hot day with no distractions in sight; a preacher only slowed in midsermon by a brief pause to gulp some soothing water or iced tea, then begin anew.

"My family doesn't appreciate any of the things I do for them," were the opening words of a personal purging that, as the bus proceeded down the tree-lined, two-lane highway, evolved into a harangue on Sharene's ears.

Hours later, when the bus mercifully completed that second leg of Sharene's journey, the woman thanked Sharene for 'our talk,' and said, "I certainly feel better for having met you."

Sharene, somewhat burdened by the one-sided conversation, said in parting, "God bless."

The final leg was Sharene's favorite as the bus crossed over into South Carolina and wound its way into the beautiful interior of a state that had always maintained its southern heritage. It was a white and black southern heritage, with white mansions withdrawn from the highway protecting their White occupants and Black preachers rhythmically preaching to flocks normally, but not always, confined to color barriers. The souls those preachers reached were sometimes made clean, yet it made no difference to God if those believers, or even the look-alike nonbelievers sprinkled among them, were of Black heritage or White heritage. He loves them all.

"God wants you, not your color," would say one massive Black preacher on a day so hot that Blacks would show white sweat lines and Whites black ones, "because, my friends, who you are includes your color."

Tunnels of sun-swatted southern trees, their leaves green, funneled Sharene and the Greyhound bus along the way; lined the highway like tall flower tossers from Jerusalem. She watched it all from her window seat, noting the contrast between the tree-lined highway, the rolling fields of cotton, and the distant stands of loblolly pine trees.

Sharene reached her destination suddenly. One minute, with patient endurance, she was squiggling toes within her shoes to release the tensions of a long bus ride, and the next minute she was reading the population sign of the small city where Grandma lived. The bus cruised by whitish-beige businesses and churches, then slowed to a stop at the Greyhound depot in a rural town just south of the North Carolina border.

Nora Okatee was by the metal step as Sharene descended onto South Carolina soil. The two beamed, studied eyes lovingly, then hugged tightly. They spoke of surface things and laughed. Anyone watching would have thought the two had been friends for many years.

Anyone, that is, except Evon Trask, who was viewing the reunion from the midday shadows of a gray building that shielded him from the sun. His eyes focused solely on the fresh-looking seventeen-year-old from Alabama, Nora's friend; and something unnatural kindled within his soul. Seeing the African lady he knew so well hugging and kissing a vision of purity made him want to participate as well, but on his own terms.

He was twenty years old, good with words, and strong. Nora yearned for his strength, his manliness, sometimes against her expressed will.

Evon, tossing aside a half-smoked cigarette, walked from the shadows into the afternoon sunshine and approached the two women who were engrossed in exuberant conversation. Sharene saw him first, seemingly focused on her from a short distance, and was startled. She felt a negative energy force as if she were being hunted, and she recoiled.

"Who are you?" Sharene asked less than cordially.

Nora Okatee turned, grabbed her White boyfriend by the arm, and said, "This is Evon, Sharene. You two will become good friends."

His first words to Sharene were in a kind, sincere voice. "I am quite pleased to meet you. Nora speaks highly of you."

Sharene looked at Nora's friend in a new light. She wasn't in the habit of judging others, and maybe her initial reaction was wrong. Evon now looked to be the perfect gentleman, yet her instincts urged caution.

The three of them loaded Sharene's luggage into the trunk of Evon's battered Bonneville, and drove, three in the wide front seat, to the home of Grandmother Marsena.

The house was huge, with enough semikept grounds around it to warrant a weekly gardening service. Seven-foot-tall briar bushes and berry plants contoured the grounds, towering over edges of the green lawn that tried, but couldn't quite cover all of the hard, orange-red dirt that gave it life. The back yard was a large jungle that the gardeners, because of time and money constraints, rarely touched. In that back yard, surrounded by overgrowth, was a miniature second quarters, an African hovel that would have been demolished had there been any need to hack through the vines and reclaim the land it occupied.

Grandmother Marsena represented the old rich. She owned all but two lots on the block. She was Southern, Jewish, and now stood leaning against the front doorpost as the one she equated with the future, her granddaughter, stepped away from Evon Trask's car. The old woman craved the respect, the honest friendship, the love, that Sharene brought so freely into her life: the respect, friendship, and love to a lesser degree that she'd so wantonly taken for granted in her younger years of schooling and romances and affluence. The affluence remained, yet its pleasures had waned through the years with few comforts to replace the charming yard parties and suitors she'd once known.

She'd found no replacement for her late husband whom she'd loved for many years before a long-ignored stomach ailment hospitalized him, weakened him to the point where he spit blood, and then he'd died painfully. Grandmother Marsena had been present at the passing of Jake Marsena's father, her own husband and friend, yet always had regretted the fact that he'd died in the hands of nurses who, though skilled, didn't know who he was. At that time, she'd trusted others to give him comfort, when he'd most needed something much more valuable from her; the culmination of years of love and friendship shared in gentle touches and kind words.

When he'd died was the one and only time Grandmother Marsena had doubted the presence of God in her life.

But now, the loving light from a new era was coming to see her, and the old woman suddenly felt young again, refreshed, as she stood at the doorway of her elegant southern home.

Sharene, all smiles, led the way up the long, curved walk with Nora and Evon, holding hands, following behind her. Evon watched the natural fluidity of Sharene's backside, her butt and legs, and was inwardly aroused like a duck hunter on a cold Oregon morning.

Sharene ran the final steps to hug her grandmother, to ask the obvious questions of greeting. Grandmother Marsena eagerly hugged her back and, for an instant, closed her eyes and forgot about her fading health, about estate responsibilities, about her deceased husband, and her own Jewish roots. And, for that instant, Sharene's pure youth surged through the veins of Grandmother Marsena in mutual love, and the latter knew happiness, youth, and innocence once more.

The visit had achieved its objective.

"Where's Junior?" asked Sharene with heartfelt enthusiasm as they broke away from the hug.

"That old dog's around somewhere," said Grandmother. "He's getting old like me. His eyesight is getting bad and his hearing will be the next to go."

Grandmother Marsena then greeted the Black girl at her door, one she'd met the previous summer. She greeted Nora Okatee with more courtesy than her upbringing as a Southern belle would have allowed. After all, she was a friend of Sharene's.

Evon stepped forward and took the elderly lady's hand in greeting.

While Sharene and grandmother talked, Nora and Evon carried Sharene's luggage from the dusty Bonneville and placed it on the wide brick porch. Over the good-natured objections of her friend from Alabama who said she had the information tucked away, Nora Okatee jotted down the phone number and address of her host family on a piece of paper, then encouraged Sharene to call her soon.

She and Sharene hugged once more, and Evon, in parting, met Sharene's eyes for an instant. Sensitive to the pain of another, Sharene was strangely saddened by the look.

The Black and White couple returned on the curved cement walk that led to and from the front of the house, then drove away as Grandmother, with a little help, tottered back to her deeply cushioned recliner.

Sharene served hot tea, and they talked story into the night.

"Your mother is one fine woman," said Grandmother Marsena. "There is no way, other than through the grace of God, that my son could otherwise have a daughter as beautiful as you."

"You're too hard on Daddy," responded Sharene.

"Let's just say I know him far better that you," said the aging southern lady whose eyesight was failing.

Junior, an overweight basset hound, wandered into the room with water-bowl excess dripping from his jowls. He padded unobtrusively to Sharene's feet and plopped down, his chin resting on her right shoe. The two had been joyously reunited earlier, and this was an old dog's encore of love.

Junior had been dubbed Jake II at an earlier age, only to have the name mercifully changed when Grandmother Marsena had ruled that the upbringing of Jake and Carol's children was appropriate.

Grandmother tired noticeably as that first evening progressed, but Sharene chose on this occasion not to insist she go to bed. There would be plenty of time for that. Although getting on in years and relatively frail, Grandmother Marsena had no verifiable ailments other than loneliness. Her strength seemed to fluctuate proportionally to the kindnesses expressed to her by those she encountered.

Sharene finally tucked Grandmother into her bed, kissed her on an old-woman's wrinkled cheek, then proceeded to begin unpacking her belongings in the room that would be hers for the next few months. It was the same guest room in which she'd always stayed, and nothing of merit had changed.

Grandmother had a competent housekeeper and friend who effectively unsettled the dust whenever the anticipated arrival of a guest was announced. Her name was Dorothy, and she regularly scheduled vacations whenever a long-staying visitor would arrive, giving her needed breaks from her duties without denying companionship to Grandmother Marsena. Dorothy barely knew "the vision," as Grandmother often called Sharene.

In less than twenty minutes after leaving Grandmother's room, Sharene had clothes and sundries placed to her liking. She turned down the top sheets.

Her room was on the second floor of the old house, directly above the room where her grandmother slept. For many years, Grandmother's room also had been on the second floor, two doors down from the guest quarters Sharene now occupied, but concessions had to be made for the stairs and her age, and Grandmother had moved her bedroom downstairs.

Sharene hadn't been around when the change of bedrooms had taken place, but subtle comments from Dorothy, as well as from Grandmother, had indicated that the switch hadn't come easily. Hadn't Grandmother spent most of her adult life sleeping in the second-story bedroom, most of those years with a loved mate who'd fathered their children? Then came a funeral, and her beloved had moved without adequate warning to another realm, hopefully a God-centered realm, without time to prepare Grandmother Marsena for the abrupt transition of living alone. For Grandmother Marsena, who'd aged quickly since that death, the move from the second floor to the first floor apparently had been almost as traumatic as Grandfather's funeral years before, when family had been present to help cushion the blow.

The young traveler from Alabama parted high-standing gold curtains, uncovering a long-neglected window, her window of the past. She looked at the maze-like back yard that was lit dimly by a less- than-full moon. She remembered many years, long before Grandmother and the gardener had given up maintaining that property, when she'd walked with her toddling brother, Peter, in the back yard of her grandparents. She remembered him being delightfully intrigued by every bush, flower, and butterfly. She thought again of Jordan Norton and thanked God for his willingness to understand, and for his patience.

Then she went to bed.

During the ensuing days, Sharene adapted a schedule that was easy to follow. She routinely stayed close to Grandmother and addressed her needs throughout the day. In the early evenings, she'd often slip away for a few hours of personal time, usually with Nora. The two young women had a competitive rivalry on the tennis court, begun the previous summer, which complemented their friendship. They regularly met under the lights on the far court of the city's small tennis complex, the court next to the woods, and would rather sit, wait, and talk, than take another surface to play on. The woods at their side added the element of privacy the teenaged girls relished as they ran through a running dialogue of Evons and Jordans and tennis.

Grandmother Marsena needed no assistance on occasions during the daytime when Sharene went to the grocery or drug store, and would have waved off any assistance at all, other than her granddaughter, had she been given the choice. Yet, a Mrs. Allison, a strong White woman with big Nordic bones, routinely relieved Sharene in the evenings, seven days a week. She was good help, quite jovial, and Grandmother Marsena had little room to complain. Mrs. Allison not only met the elderly lady's immediate needs, but performed a number of minor cleaning tasks that made Sharene's job much easier.

Late in the evenings, Sharene often sat by lamplight in her bedroom thinking about Jordan and her family. By that time, Grandmother almost always was peacefully asleep, and Sharene's thoughts ran rampant.

Would she and Jordan marry? What would college, after one more year of high school, hold for her? Was she in any way pleasing to God?

She wrote letters, too, and received responses from those she loved. Jordan was working for Mr. Adamson and thinking of her. Mr. Adamson jokingly had hinted that Jordan continue working at the store beyond the summer, he'd said in one letter, and Sharene's family was fine. Sales were good at Jake's grocery store, her mother was still making quilts, and Peter was playing Little League baseball.

Sharene had the luxury of a small lanai off her second-story bedroom, and went there often to watch the foliage below undulate in the moonlight whenever an unseen breeze would arise. She watched the changing shadows, while pondering what the future, her future, might hold.

What had been familiar and safe years before in the yard below the lanai now was dark and foreboding. The unkempt vines now strangled the hovel in which she'd once played and read by the hour. In those earlier days, she'd often isolated herself from the world until a familiar adult voice—be it Grandfather's, Grandmother's, her father's, or her mother's—had bridged her sensed separation with news of food or a visitor, and gently called her back to their reality.

Propelled by a South Carolina breeze, the night shadows often would dance and weave as Sharene's thoughts wandered to the past, sometimes spooking her imagination in creative, but unrealistic directions.

Evon Trask often was a third party to Sharene and Nora's evenings of tennis and revelry, and the visitor from Alabama had to admit that, on a personal level, she didn't like it. On more than one occasion she caught the older boy looking at her with penetrating eyes, possessive eyes, only to see the look quickly vanish without a trace, like an experienced hunter removing himself from sight while stalking his prey in the woods.

Evon was good to Nora, Sharene had to admit, at least when the three of them were together. He talked eloquently and treated her like a lady. Yet, the late-night intimacies between them that Nora sometimes alluded to when she and Sharene were alone didn't set harmoniously with Sharene's Christian morals.

They spoke once on the matter.

"Why do you make love to Evon? Surely you know it's not in God's plan for you," Sharene had stated bluntly to her close friend.

And Nora flared angrily for the only time during their friendship.

"What do you know about God's plan for me, Sharene Marsena?" exclaimed Nora Okatee. "God began that plan long ago when two of Major General's soldiers stripped me of my womanhood, beat me with rifle butts, and made me say 'please.' Life isn't pretty, Sharene, but at that moment pleading was better than dying on the spot.

"You American Christians have all the answers, yet know nothing of the other world.

"And do you want to know the irony of my situation, Sharene? To them I was just another weak female. Had they known so much as my name, I'd never have lived through their rape."

Evon, for obvious reasons, wasn't privy to that conversation, and Sharene had hugged Nora, apologized for her lack of understanding, and cried with her friend.

CHAPTER 5

It was well into the second month of her stay in South Carolina when Sharene made a serious venture into the back yard. With an adventurous midday plan, she kindly set out cookies and tea by Grandmother's recliner, turned on a favorite soap opera, and, without explanation, stepped out the seldom-used back door.

The mass of volunteer berries and vines towered above and across her path as she tried to navigate a route to the African hovel. Using ungloved hands, she gingerly grabbed prickly vines between her thumbs and forefingers, and placed them over her head and behind her. The going was slow, and the day both hot and humid. She soon found safer passage on her hands and knees and, beginning to perspire, stooped even lower toward the orange-red dirt.

Sharene detoured away from a large fire-ant colony that flourished there without competition, and a barbed berry vine, pulled high over her head, sprang back when she released it, scratching her temple. One isolated drop of Sharene's blood fell to the hard dirt and coagulated like mercury in sand.

The entire trek, or crawl, was hardly forty feet in length, yet the elapsed time it took to complete was long. There was something sacrificial about the beautiful maiden's voyage, hinting that more drops of blood from unclouded veins surely would follow before "the vision" reached her destiny.

When she did reach her immediate goal, the old, tired hovel, Sharene knew she couldn't stay long. Time had passed quickly, and the sun had moved in the sky.

She found the hovel as she'd remembered it; long and narrow like a baseball dugout, with a thick, thatched roof that so far had escaped penetration from the vines. Grandfather Marsena often had laughed about the difficulties of creating the hovel's roof without so much as a pattern; just memories from earlier structures built with slave labor and no written plans. He'd used the hovel to hang their personal tobacco and row crops. Not ideal, he'd told Sharene, but better than shipping such crops elsewhere to dry.

Like the cock crows at dawn and the donkey, with a solitary rider, parades into Jerusalem, did Sharene follow her instincts and give honor to a higher authority. Once within the wooden panels of the hovel, she walked directly to a weathered King James Bible she'd hidden beneath bricks four years earlier. The page ends had weathered from moisture, but the words, as always, hadn't changed. Then she prayed from what she thought was a safe, vine-covered refuge.

Sharene turned to the Bible's concordance and randomly picked a topic. SOUL. She looked to the entries in the book of Job about the topic, and began accessing information. She found comfort from Job 12:10, which stated, "In whose hand is the soul of every living thing, and the breath of all mankind."

Feeling a sense of peace, Sharene stayed far longer than she'd intended, perusing the Word of God and strolling up and down the narrow wood structure to view significant changes wrought by nature during those four years. The strongest vines had wanted to reach into the interior of what remained from its past, she mused, but had thought better of it. The vines instinctively seemed to know they required more sunshine and less of a shaded African hovel.

Sharene was happy, at peace, and fantasized about sharing her corner of the world with Jordan Norton. She romanticized about a white wedding in a briar-cleared, South Carolina back yard.

Then things changed.

The soul at rest in God's hand, a surrendered soul, knew fear in an instant as if she'd been a guest of luxury April 14, 1912, on the Titanic.

Without warning, a large rock crashed through the roof of the hovel and landed a few feet from where she sat. Sharene, in sudden panic, retreated to where she'd entered the small building and squeezed her body under a wooden table once used for sorting tobacco leaves. Her heart beat fast and she turned to prayer, a prayer for safety. A second rock fell to the floor of the hovel between her and where the original rock had landed, and, with no viable alternatives, she turned even more fervently to her provider.

The large size of the rocks suggested the assailant was within the perimeter of the vine patch, and Sharene knew in her soul that any attempts to run would be painful and fruitless.

Then the voice came, a guttural, unnatural voice saying, "I just wanted to get your attention, my sweets. We'll share more in the future."

Then he was gone.

The unknown attacker's clothing audibly zinged from the scraping of prickly vines as he moved away from her, leaving Sharene with the impression the assailant either was covered like a beekeeper or at this very moment had cruel blood dripping from his face and hands.

Sharene waited.

She knew he was gone, had heard his exit, yet waited several minutes more before grabbing one of the two rocks and stepping beyond the confines of the African hovel. She felt vulnerable, incredibly vulnerable, as she crawled back under the vines with the rock in her hand. Sharene's wary eyes, though low to the ground with limited vision, looked first for a male with a guttural voice and secondly for any male with imaginably wild eyes.

She saw that many of the vines recently had been cut, starting from the anthill out to the edge of the vine-covered maize. The vines looked as if they'd been cut haphazardly, and Sharene suspected a machete or a long knife had been used.

By the time Sharene returned to the main house, Grandmother was worried about her absence. The elderly lady wasn't upset, just wanted some companionship and a little more tea. She commented on Sharene's sweaty appearance and suggested that her granddaughter wear lighter clothing to play tennis in.

Sharene apologized, said she wouldn't do it again, then used the kitchen telephone, out of Grandmother's hearing, to call the police.

"I definitely don't want to alarm my grandmother, but ..."

The rural South Carolina police chief she spoke with said there was nothing they could do to help the situation without gaining access to the premises where the alleged incident had occurred.

Sharene called Nora, and the two of them went to the police station that evening to give details about the unusual rock-throwing incident, yet the police chief repeated what he'd said earlier. He said he would note the complaint in his daily logbook, but expressed skepticism that anything would come of it.

"Miss Marsena, searching for a man no one has seen for what at best is a marginal crime, without even going to the site because it might disturb your grandmother? ... Come on, at best, such a request is a stretch for any police agency."

Jordan happened to phone that night and was distressed when Sharene told him of her adventure in the back yard, about the rocks that had almost hit her. She assured him she was in no danger now, and reminded him that the middle of August was fast approaching. She said most likely she'd stay in South Carolina with Grandmother until her senior year began, so Jordan committed over the telephone that night to visit on his way to college.

They concluded their conversation with words of encouragement and an expressed eagerness for a special reunion.

Sharene and Nora continued their nightly tennis battles on the back court next to the woods.

Evon occasionally came to the semisecluded court to share small talk, watch two well-shaped young women swing racquets with nylon strings, and inwardly be aroused as they ran, sweated, and laughed. He added his enthusiastic, clear, articulate words to their carefree voices.

As the summer wore on, Jordan Norton, states away, began feeling the insecurity of his separation from Sharene Marsena. It wasn't a conscious thing, but even now, still in his teens, the lack of her daily presence in his life allowed Jordan to occasionally forget the priorities he professed to have.

A young lady from Pennsylvania named Chiska Sullivan arrived for the summer to stay with relatives and soon became infatuated with a recent graduate of Plateau High School whom, in her eyes, was available for female companionship. Almost an equal to Sharene's outward beauty, she used the Drive Inn crowd to champion her cause with Jordan Norton.

He balked at her overtures of kindness, but did recognize a clarity in Chiska's eyes, an aggressive boldness that again singled him out as important, reiterating a sensed prominence that only one other had ever conveyed to him.

But the temptation wasn't great when matched with his love in South Carolina. He continued to write letters to Sharene and, better yet, to receive them.

August 18, 1978, was the date set for Jordan's own bus voyage to rural South Carolina to reunite with the one he most wanted to be with. He could only stay in passing, college in the Northeast his eventual destination, but five days with Sharene sounded like heaven. Everything he would need for the next year, except what he carried with him on the Greyhound bus, would be flown ahead, then temporarily stored awaiting his arrival. The cost made Jordan wince.

The night before he was to leave, Jordan drove the streets of Plateau in his parents' car with John Riggs riding shotgun. They warily looked for police and held bottles of beer between their legs. Jordan wasn't crazy about John Riggs, or even beer for that matter, but he wanted to make a statement of independence as he left his hometown for the outer world.

Besides, his best male friend was busy romancing Chiska Sullivan.

The glass-slapping windshield wipers on Jordan's parents' car kept pace with the pouring rain as they pulled up to a preseason high school football workout. The lights around the field gave sparkle to the fast-falling droplets by highlighting what otherwise would have been an unseen descent.

The players looked wet and scrawny, their helmets partially shielding them from the elements. They wore no shoulder pads.

John was more experienced at drinking beer at a high school nonevent. He feared nothing. Jordan, on the other hand, tightly stored his cold bottle of beer between his thighs. Being "cool" on his final night in Plateau didn't need to include a brush with the law.

"They look like top-heavy chickens in the rain," laughed John Riggs.

Jordan didn't respond.

"You thinkin' about Sharene?" asked John Riggs, who'd graduated from high school with Jordan Norton, and now faced a lifetime of scrounging to make a living in Plateau, probably with a houseful of children and friends.

"You're doing the right thing, Jordan," he continued philosophically. "This hellhole ain't no place for anyone with a future."

"Then why don't you get out?" asked Jordan Norton, the illegal beer slowly warming between his legs as he maintained a constant vigil, watching for anyone who might approach the car.

"I got no future, Jordan. I got no interest in more education, and no skills," he said. "I'll just stay around here where I can help my friends to survive, and they can help me."

They parted that night, as close to being friends as they ever would be.

The morning of August 18, 1978, brought more rain, more shirt-soaking rain for those who had to be outside in it. Jordan read a Birmingham daily as he waited in the bus depot. He would have preferred a fatter New York Times, but that paper box was empty. The Times was on strike.

Inside the daily was a story about a young woman with obvious connections to America's world of high society. She'd been kidnapped mysteriously while on a tour of coffee plantations in rural Colombia, South America. A thumb-sized photo inset, on the upper left-hand corner of a larger shot of people from the tour talking with Colombian policemen, caught Jordan's attention immediately.

The woman looked remarkably like Sharene Marsena.

Peter Marsena, across town, noticed the same likeness later that afternoon. He watched televised news clips after school, or more accurately glanced at them, and yelled to his mother that Sharene was on TV. Had he stayed by the set a little longer, he would have seen a televised special about a strife-torn South American country where literally thousands of "security prisoners" were being held, many of them for ransom.

It wasn't until well into the future that Peter would grasp the significance of that day. Sure, what happened to Sharene August 18, 1978, was a crusher to everyone who knew her, and triggered much anger and regret. Still, the significance of another Sharene being kidnapped about that same time escaped his consciousness until he'd matured much and met a new friend with an unanticipated penchant for ladders and heights.

To flourish, seeds need water and soil. Peter had heard in his Sunday school classes that the tiniest of seeds, the mustard seed, could move mountains if converted into faith. Yet, the harmony of God's plan for Sharene Marsena didn't focus for her brother until the mid-1980s. He often looked at that August day in 1978, that damned day when perfection was soiled, and failed to understand the teachings Sharene shared from a portable stage that took her from Plateau to South Carolina to Georgia to South America and, ultimately, to her death.

"What was the purpose?" lamented Peter Marsena years into the future, and Dale Hemri knew.

Jordan would learn, too.

As the bus ride began, Jordan Norton's hopes were high. Apart for months, now he and Sharene would be together again. He'd been told that Grandmother's house was large, and that he would be allowed to stay in a room of his own on another floor from Sharene. His heart soared over the miles, sometimes making him giddy with anticipation. He tried to read a college catalogue and saw Sharene on every page. She popped up in a distant science class, behind an art exhibit, and among a crowd photo from a previous graduation at the college. He prayed for a wonderful, meaningful reunion with Sharene Marsena. He prayed for her health and the health of the country, and for everything good he could think of. His prayer was long by the bus window, so long in the plodding bus that his concentration eventually lapsed, and he pictured Chiska Sullivan in white before an amen concluded his devotion.

He looked at his wristwatch at the first bus change, noting a time of day that later would have relevance.

The second bus was crowded, and Jordan found a seat next to a child with curly hair and a baseball glove. The boy, about ten-years-old and heading home following a visit with his grandparents, was talkative and energetic, as if he'd just finished a big baseball game and was unwinding with jubilant peers. Jordan, also on an emotional high, became an enthusiastic audience, and talked freely too, as if the child could understand his interstate voyage to see a beautiful young woman. They were boisterous, animated, and laughed with no regard for others crowded into seats around them.

Even the inconvenience of a flat tire on the bus did nothing to dampen the twosome's eager chatter. It merely delayed Jordon's arrival in South Carolina.

"I bet your girlfriend's almost as pretty as my goldfish, Sylvia," the youngster said to his new friend, and Jordan tousled his curly blond hair, and laughed.

The boy's parents were waving and smiling as the bus arrived at the next stop. Jordan was introduced, said some complimentary things about their son, and, because his scheduled connection hadn't inconvenienced other travelers by waiting for his bus's late arrival, Jordan Norton sat for an hour waiting for the next bus to South Carolina.

It would be late before he tumbled into Sharene's arms.

The day unfolded differently for Sharene Marsena. She spent waking hours in an excited whir. Grandmother laughed at Sharene's absentmindedness as she turned to the wrong soap opera and started to walk away.

When alone in her room, Sharene knelt at the foot of her bed and prayed with fervor for her reunion with Jordan.

"I pray for these things," she said, glancing at the clock on the lamp stand by the head of her bed, an old lamp stand carved with wooden seraphs, "but what I really want, Lord, is that your will be done in me. I gladly will take whatever path is most beneficial to serve Your kingdom."

Mrs. Allison came at her usual time, and Sharene left to play tennis. Nora Okatee's skills were fast-improving on the court, and she was challenging Sharene nightly for her first-ever win in their rivalry. Nora refused to allow a postponement of the night's contest simply because some "handsome dude" was arriving for the express purpose of courting her opponent.

Sharene loved Nora more and more as the summer progressed. Her lively humor was infectious.

The lass from Alabama wore sweat pants to the courts that evening covering light yellow gym shorts. By age seventeen, she already knew what a temptation she was. Her mother had taught her much in regards to survival.

When they arrived, their favorite court by the woods was vacant. Sharene Marsena and Nora Okatee began warming up and laughing, each one's crumpled sweat pants placed on cool concrete adjacent the net on the side of the court nearest the woods. They paid no attention when the tennis players on court No. 2, the only other people around on a sultry, southern August night, popped their white balls into metal cans, sealed them with plastic lids, and walked away talking about cold sodas.

Sharene and Nora were well into the seventh game of the first set and didn't hear when the last automobile drove away. The night, other than the pounding of one solitary tennis ball, was relatively quiet. Insects did make some noise as well, buzzing the overhead lights and occasionally falling on what now was the only lighted tennis court, yet the comely maidens, oblivious to that segment of life's ongoing drama, continued to fight through long rallies. Each wanted the other to make the mistakes. Nora, who'd won sets, but never a match from her American friend, won the first set, and the two switched ends of the tennis court without the usual banter between them.

During the switch, Sharene rubbed sweat from her hands onto a small towel that had been hanging from the side of the net nearest the woods, then brushed remaining moisture from her hands on the backside of her light yellow shorts.

In deep concentration, neither noticed an additional soul walking toward them, silently crossing the three dark tennis courts nearest the street. Evon did nothing to hide his presence, yet was as invisible to the young girls as a hunter's bullet to a tiny bird. He had neither a need nor a desire to hide, because the girls' focus was elsewhere.

Sharene was preparing to serve and begin the second set when she caught sight of a shadow on the court next to them, and gasped in surprise.

"Sorry to startle you," said Evon Trask in his clear voice. "You were so into your game, and so I didn't hail you."

"Why are you here?" Nora asked curtly. She didn't want to be interrupted at this time.

"I have to talk to you," he said, and walked uninvited on to the playing surface of the tennis court by the woods, toward the young lady from Uganda holding a tennis racquet and displaying dark, shapely legs.

Sharene watched patiently as the boyfriend she disliked spoke in the ear of her friend. Evon blocked Nora's face from Sharene's view until the Ugandan lass bolted to her discarded sweats alongside the court, her competitiveness drained.

"I have to go," she said in haste. "You can continue playing with Evon."

And Nora Okatee, her friend, ran at a gallop through the three unlit courts, out a distant wire gate, and off into the night.

Sharene was in shock. Otherwise, she would have zipped the cover shut over her racquet and returned home herself.

But she didn't.

Instead, she and Evon, he in long pants, tennis shoes, and a baggy gray shirt, began hitting the tennis ball back and forth across the net. He was far from her equal on the court, and obviously there was no need to keep score.

After a few minutes of play, punctuated by numerous missed volleys by the male player, Evon left his feet to dive for a ball, something seasoned tennis players don't attempt lightly, and hit the white sphere over the surrounding fence and into the woods. Sharene instinctively jogged to the corner gate, opened the horseshoe clasp, and went into the woods after the ball.

The invisible hunter, who'd been waiting for such a moment, smiled, and exuded a puff of temptation that energized a man, a fallen human being with questionable morals.

Evon Trask made no noise as he followed Sharene through the open gate.

The woman of God felt her attacker's grasp before she saw or heard him. He drove her to the ground with a shoulder tackle and pinned her arms, her face slashed by low tree branches. Sharene's finely sculpted legs kicked wildly, and Evon, like a great shark in frenzy, ground close to his prey. He laughed excitedly as he brushed across her breasts and muscled himself into a dangerous neck hold that put the Alabama beauty's life in jeopardy.

He placed his left arm behind her neck and his right hand in a thrust position under her chin. She'd been loud in decrying his intended brutality, but went limp and quiet when his physical superiority became life threatening.

It suddenly seemed immaterial if anyone had or hadn't heard her initial cries for help. This demon-possessed man was about to have his way.

"Hold still, my sweets, and we will have some gentlemanly fun. Make a noise, and I will kill you."

He spoke in the same guttural, almost wheezing voice she'd heard from the African hovel.

Her exposed left thigh, below the yellow shorts, was pressed against a protruding rock that caused a bruise to form. The lights on the nearby, abandoned tennis court provided enough brightness for Sharene to see a shadowy face to hate. Seconds seemed like lifetimes.

She didn't think to pray.

His headlock was taut, absolute, and he smelled of cigarette smoke and sweat.

Sharene had no reason to doubt the validity of Evon's threat. Yet, ultimately, she was answerable to forces beyond her comprehension, and well beyond the comprehension of her Jewish father who'd rather have committed murder himself than allow the violation of his beloved daughter by such a beast.

And Sharene Marsena, her life and womanhood both at risk, suddenly experienced a peace no one lacking absolute faith ever will understand, and looked at her attacker for the first time with godly calmness. Then, for Evon Trask and the hunter to hear, she said,

"Please be with me, Holy Spirit," and screamed with urgency and volume.

Evon immediately abandoned the headlock and began punching her repeatedly, causing blood to flow from her mouth and across her white teeth. Sharene swooned into unconsciousness, her parting thoughts being of Jesus and Jordan Norton.

Evon looked around to make sure they were alone and, seeing no one, began to undress his unconscious victim.

A few feet away in the trees and the semidarkness stood the camouflaged hunter. He lusted after something greater than the fallen girl, yet approved of Evon Trask's clumsy efforts toward power and control, toward self-gratification. The hunter sensed his rival's love for the girl, and was both surprised and alarmed that no angels were sent to save her, to rewind time and give he, the hunter, more epochs to roam his domain.

The absence of angels made him dislike the girl even more. She'd now become even a greater threat to his fleeting existence in a universe ruled by the path of love carved into being by his rival.

Evon Trask left Sharene Marsena naked, violated, and unconscious. He ran across the still courts and into the South Carolina night as if pacing himself for a marathon or a lengthy jog into the abyss of hell. By the time he crossed the tennis court closest to the street, pleasure already had given way to stark fear.

CHAPTER 6

A fierce storm was breaking up in the late-afternoon sky, and radiant streaks of sunshine began to part the dark clouds. A short-lived thrust of the eternal, the sun's rays themselves, did their best to scatter the mostly spent clouds, but would have to return in the morning to finish the job.

It was September, and Sharene Marsena lay sleeping, both thunderclouds and heavenly rays dancing across her face. Neither shadows nor light were able to establish dominance over the other. Nature's display was visible on her closed eyelids like a tiny televised test pattern in a dimly lit room.

Jordan reluctantly had continued his trek to college at the stern insistence of Sharene's mother. He hurt deeply, and got no solace from the woman he loved. In hysteria, Sharene had vetoed his initial visit, shouting nonsense at him about whores and dirt and filth. He'd countered with kindness, understanding, and love, but Sharene had continued to scream incoherently. Responding to her emotional outburst, two hospital orderlies roughly had hauled him from Sharene's hospital room as if young Jordan Norton was the source of her pain.

After being removed from her presence, Jordan, alone, had buried his face and cried while sitting in a corner of the waiting room by a flowerless philodendron.

Days earlier, before daybreak on the 19th of August, an attending physician found Jordan and Nora Okatee in the same hospital waiting room, and suggested they go home. Sharene seemed strong enough to survive the physical abuse from the rape, he said, but was very confused and in shock. Time was what she needed most, he'd said.

"Everything is my fault," said Nora, as she led the grieving White male from the hospital and into the pre-dawn. "I had to have known."

Jordan felt naked and exposed. He slapped angrily at a metal street sign.

Nora talked rapidly during their walk to Grandmother's, talked as if Jordan might possess the power of exorcism to rid her of the ugliness she felt inside her soul. She had to explain everything quickly.

"The Major General's soldiers planted something ugly in me, worse than hate, and I stupidly gave it to Evon who inflicted it into someone as innocent as snow. Sharene is so innocent. Do you understand what I am saying?" she pleaded, seeking heartfelt communication with someone she'd just met.

"No," said Jordan as his footsteps numbly followed her through vacant streets as foreign to him as the emptiness he felt inside.

"There is something ugly loose in Africa, Jordan, and I blindly brought it to America first, and now to Sharene," said Nora. "God forgive me."

Exhausted from a long, bitter day that sorely had tested his spiritual and physical stamina, Jordan responded, with rote-like absolution, words he had little authority to grant. "I'm sure He will, Nora. I'm sure He will."

Jordan's first view of Grandmother Marsena's house was one of shadows and streetlights. He was tired, and had no knowledge of a King James Bible left open in the African hovel behind the house. Nor was he aware of a police logbook downtown that held useless information.

Mrs. Allison responded to Jordan's knock on the front door, let him in, and Nora Okatee, a Black woman in what appeared to her to be a black world, walked home alone.

Carol and Jake Marsena got into their huge, dependable 1969 Buick Wildcat and drove to South Carolina when they heard the news. Partially shielded from the purpose of their sudden trip, the child, Peter Marsena, was left behind to stay with friends. He felt confused and angry, and didn't understand why.

Carol was the first person other than Jordan and the medical staff to see Sharene after the damning violation, and she held and rocked her daughter for three hours. The bonding relieved much of Sharene's shock, and life began returning once more to an invaded body. Sharene shared fragments of her despair and anger, and the mother and daughter cried together.

Sharene refused to see Jordan Norton a second time.

Evon Trask continued to baffle the local South Carolina police department. Everyone knew what he looked like, yet no one had seen him.

After five days, at the gentle insistence of Carol Marsena, Sharene reluctantly agreed to a short visit with Jordan before he left for college. He was minutes away from returning to the same bus depot where his dreams had been shattered by Mrs. Allison's halting words that had pierced his heart like a well-placed rapier.

"What can I say to him?" Sharene had asked her mother before Jordan came into the room.

She sat in a cushioned chair, clothed in gray slacks and a nondescript blouse her mother had brought from Grandmother Marsena's. She was looking nervously around the hospital room when Jordan stepped through the door, closed it, and approached her silently, walking across the cold, but spotless floor.

Sharene prayed for boldness.

"You look better," he said. "How do you feel?"

"I can't see you anymore, Jordan," she began. "The love we had will never be the same. I can't live with pity, and you can never understand. Don't even try."

Jordan complemented her coolness with tenacity.

"Maybe I can't understand what you've been through, Sharene, for I am a man. But I do understand your anger better than you think. I trust, with the help of God, that you will adjust. But don't blame yourself, and don't blame God. There are forces on this planet we can neither control nor understand. All we can do is stick to the basics that have made us the people we are."

Jordan rightly sensed that his lover was getting angry, impatient.

"I have to go to college, Sharene, but I promise to write frequently. I'll see you at my first break, and we'll have a lot to talk about," he said.

"I don't want to see you anymore," she said, pleading for finality.

He started to leave, then stopped at the closed door. He turned full face in her direction.

"I'll see you in a couple of months, Sharene. Take care of yourself, and know that I love you very much."

She watched him go.

Sharene, who short days before had been the epitome of confidence and beauty, now was mired in confusion, distrust, and hate. Yet, she mumbled well out of Jordan's hearing, "I love you, too, Jordan," and fought back another wave of tears.

But that was in the days before now. Now, she was sleeping on a September afternoon with shadows of thunderclouds and heavenly rays alternately racing across her face. She was in Grandmother's house, in the same bed she'd slept in for nearly three months. Outside her window, below the lanai, was the same vine-laden African hovel where a Bible lay open to the elements.

On the side of her bed, facing toward the door, was a wooden stand, a delicately etched wooden table with cherubim and seraphim freely dancing on its sides and drawers. On the table were a night-light, a box of tissue, and another storm-tested Bible with a rough black cover and scars from heavy use. The edges of its pages were red-specked. On the Bible lay two hands, with the forefingers of each hand pointing upward.

Pastor Dale Hemri would have been more comfortable on his knees, but lacked conviction that doing so in front of others, even other Christians, was proper. Praying on his knees wasn't a public matter for Dale Hemri.

He prayed as she slept; prayers for physical and mental healing for Sharene, and prayers for personal wisdom and guidance for what he was about to say.

He opened his eyes and watched the shadows on her face, both the cold shadows and the warming light. He consciously took the side of light and was prepared to continue praying when Sharene Marsena opened her eyes.

She immediately smiled upon seeing him, as if her eyesight was quicker than memories. Then she closed her eyes tight and the smile was gone.

"Hello, Sharene. Is there anything I can get for you? Water? Food? A prayer?" Dale Hemri smiled at the latter.

She seemed to withdraw into the afternoon shadows, and the nonclerical side of Pastor Hemri felt slighted. Then, sensing her pain and anger, he proceeded to fulfill his purpose for being there.

"Sharene, just rest and listen," he said quietly, lovingly. "You don't need to respond unless you want to, but you need to listen. Are you with me?"

She opened her eyes then, eyes that lacked the trust that had always been between them. She said nothing.

"Good," he said. "I know you have been hurt deeply. I have no way of knowing the specifics of your pain and anger, but I would guess it is directed as much at God as it is at the young man who wronged you. My words may do little to stop your immediate pain, but they are intended to give you a better understanding of why things happen as they do."

Dale Hemri, the pastor and friend, stood up from his chair by the etched wooden table, carefully removed his suit jacket, and began pacing the bedroom. What seemed eons to the pastor were microseconds to God, and Sharene Marsena waited for some semblance of hope, a direction, or even a reason to once again lift up her head and continue with life. Her eyes were again closed, protected for the moment from both dark shadows and bright rays of light.

"No one ever said that being a Christian was easy," he said. "The majority of our rewards, through faith, only happen after we die. That's what makes us different, Sharene. To a Christian, eternity far outlives the present. The pain of this world is a mere interlude, a pause before the blissful, everlasting reality that is Jesus Christ.

"Without my faith, and your faith, Sharene, these words would mean nothing. But we neither can, nor would want to proceed without that faith. It gives us a meaning, a purpose that makes us the strongest people in the world.

"Let's go back to your current situation, Sharene. I cannot muster a guess as to why you've had to suffer like this."

He continued to pace the room, even taking the liberty to open the sliding glass door and walk onto the lanai from which the African hovel was visible below in fading light among thorny vines. He didn't know that a black King James Bible was in a secure location in the African hovel, nor that it had spoken to Sharene just days before. From its apparent isolation amongst thorns, it had told her, speaking of the Creator, "In whose hand is the soul of every living thing, and the breath of all mankind."

Possibly Pastor Hemri's purpose wasn't as precarious as he thought.

Junior padded in on the worn wooden floor and, ignoring the pastor, went to inspect the girl in the bed. He had no faculties to comprehend her plight, just wanted to share some comfort with one he loved. Without opening her eyes, Sharene reached a hand out to the dog, and he responded by nuzzling it, and sitting down for a visit.

Dale Hemri took hope in what he saw.

"Some people, and there is biblical support for it, feel that hard times are a special blessing from God. Hard times test us and make us stronger for what He would have us do."

The pastor then grabbed the Bible with the red-specked pages that so recently had supported his forehead, then his upturned hands. He turned to Psalms 94.

"Blessed is the man whom thou chastenest, O Lord, and teachest him out of thy law; That thou mayest give him rest from the days of adversity, until the pit be digged for the wicked," he read.

Pastor Hemri was close physically to Sherene when he placed the Bible back on the nightstand, and chanced to reach out and touch her forehead. He knew the coolness his fingers felt was misleading. Sharene Marsena was under attack, under siege.

"Some Christians, most notably Paul, have taken the attacks of the enemy as endorsements of their faith. That admittedly is a tough stance to take," Hemri said as he pulled away and, again, began to pace. "They figure that Satan, or the hunter, as I like to call him, would not wreak havoc upon their lives unless they were living in a God-pleasing way. It's a tough argument to refute.

"Some believers, the best example I now can think of being John the Baptist, worked to the bones for Christ and suffered immeasurably for their beliefs," he said. "John preached in poverty, baptized Jesus, then went to prison and was beheaded as if he'd been forgotten. Maybe God utilizes a few Christian martyrs to best circulate His Word. I don't know, Sharene."

The sun's rays were receding in the sky, and Sharene, covered from below her feet to her throat by a thin, flowered blanket, lie awake, her eyes closed, her face pointing upwards. Pastor Hemri switched on the night-light by her bed, and Sharene nestled further under the covers.

"I don't know why you had to undergo this torment, Sharene, but I do have to believe there is a purpose for it. You can forget all that I have said until now, but please hear and remember these final words.

"God wants you to rise up and trust Him," he said with conviction. "You have been His witness before, and you now have the opportunity to be His witness again. If you were praying for His will to be done, and He has much faith in you as a person and a believer, then maybe this happened to make you even more valuable to His kingdom.

"I promise you from the bottom of my heart, Sharene," and Pastor Hemri walked back to the nightstand and picked up the black-covered King James Bible, "on a stack of Bibles as high as this room, that your troubles weren't caused because you did anything wrong. He doesn't work like that. He loves you too much."

Pastor Dale Hemri walked away from her again, tugged on his sketchy beard, and, thinking about how to proceed beyond the moment, was oblivious to anything other than his own thoughts when Sharene opened her eyes and looked his way.

"Thank you," she said in a hushed whisper.

He whirled towards her and their eyes met in the artificial light. They looked at each other imploringly, and a spirit of trust was rekindled.

"I think," Sharene said bravely, "that you've helped me diffuse my anger. Now, you must leave for me to deal with the pain."

He paused at the door with renewed hope. He so wanted to help, to ease this child's suffering and turn on a brighter, more permanent light. But he knew he couldn't. How she would respond to this tragedy was in the hands of Sharene Marsena and the God they both trusted in, and submitted to.

Pastor Hemri exited without another word. The door he'd opened upon his arrival was open wider when he left. Light from Sharene's lamp curled its way into the dimly lit hallway that led to the strongly bastioned stairway that had stood for more than a century.

Sharene, wincing, moved to the side of the bed, purposefully planted her feet on the floor, and prepared to rise.

CHAPTER 7

It was almost one month before police located Evon Trask and manacled him for a return trip to South Carolina. He was found during a drug bust in Cleveland, Ohio—jittery and barely coherent from an unusual mix of black beauties and highly resinous Turkish hashish.

He carried his normal identification with him and the match with out-standing police warrants was routine.

Extradition proceedings met no obstacles, and Evon soon, with more fear in his heart than was evident to those around him, was deposited in the county jail where he'd once spent a night for drunken driving. This time they issued orange coveralls for him to wear.

Evon had left the tennis courts that night and hurried to a small apartment he'd rented from a local businessman; a small apartment where he'd entertained Nora Okatee on many occasions. He'd gathered what little cash he could find, changed clothes, grabbed a light jacket, and raced on foot to the nearby train-switching yard, where he'd hitched a ride in the first empty boxcar he could find.

The trip to an unknown destination had been cold and filled with worry. Evon had no regrets regarding the innocence he'd violated, but was engulfed with fear about being caught.

Those fears were realized in Cleveland.

The prosecution saw Evon's case mostly as circumstantial without the testimony of the only eye witness, meaning that Sharene Marsena, the victim, would be required to testify and face Evon Trask one more time.

For the protection of Evon's alleged victim, the suspected rapist was given a routine blood test.

Another victim of that August night, from a distance of many miles, was the collegiate freshman, Jordan Norton, who wrote faithfully to the woman he loved and received no reply. He had no gauge to assess Sharene's pain, and allowed his mind to cast blame for her silence on himself, for his inability to be present in her time of need. He counted the days until they could be together, and his academics plummeted.

Too, Jordan Norton sought solace in alcohol.

Few people in Plateau, Alabama, knew more than sketchy rumors about Sharene's plight, but almost everyone saw the change in her personality when she returned for her senior year in high school. Previously beautiful and outgoing, reaching out a friendly hand to everyone, she now was moody and distracted. The spark was gone. It wasn't that she didn't try to be friendly, to "rise up and trust," as Pastor Hemri had encouraged her to do, but some inner fear, or pain, had yet to be dealt with.

Jake and Carol tried what they could to be perfect parents and bring back the Sharene of old, but intuitively, even Jake Marsena knew that such healing, with time, must come from a higher source.

"I saw you on television that day. Why were you on television?" had asked Peter in innocence when Sharene first returned home.

She was quick to peruse the incoming mail and read Jordan's frequent letters voraciously, yet felt impotent to respond. On many occasions she began writing letters to Jordan, mentally struggled to make her thoughts coherent, then put her pen down without completing so much as a paragraph. She felt jumbled inside, and nothing she could think to say to Jordan Norton could make her feel deserving of the love he professed to have for her.

Sharene went through the motions of being a high school senior, and felt unworthy to be alive. She thought once of suicide, but quickly discarded the notion. She still had priorities.

Carol Marsena intercepted a phone call from Jordan shortly after Sharene's return to Plateau. Carol innocently had answered the ring, recognized the voice on the other end of the line, gathered in her iced tea, settled into a recliner, and talked at length with the student on the East Coast. Her message, blatantly straightforward, was for Jordan to give her daughter time to heal. A strong, loving mother, Carol firmly encouraged Jordan to wait and pray from a distance. She urged him never to mention the phone conversation they were having between mother and suitor, and Jordan Norton reluctantly agreed to comply.

Though not on any schedule, Sharene often found herself walking in the afternoons to the office of Dale Hemri, who almost always found time to share honest discussion and prayer.

The trial was to begin in the spring, and Pastor Hemri prayed daily for Sharene to experience a sense of closure.

He had no idea that their Maker had different plans.

Knuckles on a door often take on a personality. Many types of knocks, such as rhythmic repetitions, can be interpreted as being friendly, while firmer knocks can sometimes be cold and foreboding.

The knock on the door of the Marsena residence in early April of 1979, about two weeks before Carol and Sharene were scheduled to drive to rural South Carolina to visit Grandmother, and for Sharene to testify at a rape trial, was neither friendly nor foreboding. Instead, it seemed strangely sad and tentative, as if its author was hoping for a last-second reprieve from the visit.

Carol questioningly looked toward Sharene as the two of them heard the knock while sitting in the living room in the late afternoon. Peter was in his room listening to music, and Jake hadn't arrived home yet from work.

Sharene answered the door.

Two ladies, in their fifties with serious faces, stood on the porch. One was dressed in nurses' white.

"You must be Sharene," said the lady dressed in a light beige jacket. "You are just as beautiful as they said."

Sharene waited patiently.

"My name is Mrs. Morris, and this is Nurse Updike," said the lady in the beige jacket. "We have come from the county health department, or rather I have. Nurse Updike is here from Memorial

Hospital in the county seat. She's here to validate what I have come to tell you. Isn't that right, Jennifer?"

The woman in white, still with a grim face, nodded.

"This is very important. May we come in and talk to you?" asked the woman who had identified herself as Mrs. Morris.

Unaware of what was about to transpire, Sharene admitted the two women into the living room where Carol Marsena, who had heard every word until that point in time, was seated.

"This is my mother, Carol Marsena," Sharene said.

Carol immediately stood and pointed the women to two cushioned chairs. Then Carol and Sharene seated themselves on opposite ends of the sofa, facing the women to form an imperfect semicircle in the Marsena living room.

"You have a lovely home," said Mrs. Morris without conviction, her light-brown shoes covering large feet spaced unevenly, one ahead of the other, on the rug beneath her. She looked uncomfortable, and was almost dwarfed by Jake's favorite recliner. Nurse Updike, in contrast, took a more formal, professional pose, with her own back not even touching the upright back of the chair Carol had motioned for her to sit in.

A silence followed, one that could have lasted eons or microseconds, and all four women felt the tension the newcomers had introduced into the Marsena household. Peter's music invaded their silence with fast guitar licks and a rhythmic male voice. The music was not loud.

"I'll go get some tea," said Sharene nervously, rising to escape the discomfort.

"I think," said Nurse Updike, speaking for the first time, "that you are the one who should stay in the room." She gave Sharene a look of matronly nursing authority, and the apparent object of their visit, Sharene, regained her seat on the end of the couch away from her mother and below an unlit floor lamp.

Nurse Updike looked to Mrs. Morris for support, and the latter looked away and began playing with the metal snaps on her light windbreaker. Mrs. Morris looked in far more discomfort than Sharene, as if the words she needed to say would be better understood spoken through the lips of Rehoboam or Pilate.

"Is Mr. Marsena home?" asked Nurse Updike.

Carol said "no," adding that he was expected within the next hour. Then, the woman of the house sat straight upright in her seat and eyed the strange visitors with more than curiosity.

"My dear ladies," she said, "you have come into our living room, intimating your visit is of prime importance, made my daughter and myself extremely apprehensive, and told us nothing. Could you please be more forthright, even a little professional, and tell us why you are here?"

The visitors looked at each other briefly before Mrs. Morris broke eye contact and looked down to inspect and play with her wedding ring, which had represented family harmony for more than twenty-five years. She knew that her personal hardships over the course of those years, trying as they occasionally might have seemed, were minor in comparison with the pain and suffering she was seconds away from unloading on what seemed to be a loving, Christian family.

"I have been at this job for the state of Alabama for more than twenty years," began Mrs. Morris slowly, methodically, "and this visit is a totally new experience for me. Please, I ask for your patience.

"Miss Marsena," she said, turning from the mother to the daughter, "when your accused attacker was apprehended, we routinely gave him a blood test as prescribed by law. We always check, for the safety of the victim, to see if an accused rapist has a venereal disease, or a herpes infection that could have been transmitted in the act. If so, we are equipped to act quickly to best protect the woman," she said.

"Did he?" asked Carol Marsena, thinking they quickly could rush her daughter off for treatment.

"No," responded Mrs. Morris, "but we did detect an unusual virus. Without hesitation, we forwarded the young man's laboratory test results to the state health department which studied them, then forwarded their findings to the U.S. Department of Health."

She looked sadly at the mother and the daughter, took a deep breath, and unconsciously folded her arms, possibly to soften the blow she was about to administer.

Nurse Updike awaited her cue.

Carol and Sharene locked their respective visions on Mrs. Morris, and Peter's low rock 'n' roll filled the temporary void like distant African drums.

"If Evon Trask did indeed rape your daughter …"

"She has to say the word 'if' for legal purposes," interjected Nurse Updike in response to Carol and Sharene's negative physical reaction to Mrs. Morris's aborted sentence.

"If he indeed raped you, Sharene," continued Mrs. Morris, "we'll need a blood test from you as quickly as possible. We think you might have been exposed to a very new disease that can be quite deadly."

"How do we get the vaccine? Money is no problem. What are the chances of her catching it? Let's get the test taken right away, dear." Carol Marsena was reacting without facts, wanting to rid the situation before understanding it.

"How deadly is it?" asked Sharene quietly. Hadn't she already survived the violations of a stronger beast that had threatened to kill her?

"Our research is fairly young," said Nurse Updike, "but until now, we know of no one who has ever recovered once it evolves past the virus stage. The disease seems to have originated in Africa and is spread by sexual contact. We have given a blood test to an African exchange student who was Evon Trask's girlfriend. She has the virus, and we assume she infected him."

Until that very moment, Sharene had never considered Nora to be any kind of a negative influence on Evon Trask, let alone herself.

"Does this disease have a name?" asked the mother with a hint of hysteria in her voice. Now, her arms, too, were folded across her chest, and her face looked hard and cold. Was there no end to the pain her special daughter had to endure?

"It's too new," said Nurse Updike. "We know the disease comes from a virus, but there's no telling how long a person can live once a person becomes infected. It damages a person's immune system, and once the body loses the ability to repair itself, death, though not necessarily immediate, is often quite painful."

"Why have you taken so long to tell us?" barked Carol Marsena angrily.

Nurse Updike picked the words of her response carefully, like a politician trying to gain votes in a public debate lacking time restrictions. "I think the government's health officials went to great lengths not to make a mistake," she said.

Carol Marsena lost composure first and rushed to the other end of the sofa to embrace her daughter.

Nurse Updike was pained by the scene unfolding before her, yet instinctively knew that the hardest part for her was over. She now could shake the dust from her white shoes and, in evenings to come, immerse herself in televised talk shows and half-hour comedies which, at least for a matter of hours, could erase the pains of her job.

She chose not to look at Sharene.

Carol wiped her eyes.

"Can we take the test now?" Carol asked. "What are the chances of Sharene being infected?"

"We would like to take more than one test," said Nurse Updike, "so a drive to my hospital would be best. As for your second question, we don't know. We do know, however, that the chances of a male infecting a female in one encounter are far greater than if the woman is initially the infected party."

Sharene separated herself from her mother and leaned forward on the couch. She didn't speak. Her hands, almost alabaster in color, pointed slender fingers without rings to the tip of her nose, covering most of her cheeks and chin. The ugliness that had stalked her since South Carolina and was just beginning to recede suddenly returned in waves. The light that had always been Sharene's mark of individuality, the spark she hoped to rekindle one day and share with Jordan, was quashed again. These were the ugly realities of life that dulled her senses that afternoon in the Marsena living room, dulled them with the suddenness of a lunar eclipse.

"When can we take the tests?" asked Carol.

"As soon as you arrive at the hospital," said Nurse Updike.

"Please give us two hours and we'll be there," said the mother while looking at a daughter who deserved better.

Mrs. Morris and Nurse Updike left quietly. Each was saddened, yet confident they'd played their roles well, roles of necessity they hadn't created.

Carol Marsena walked to her slumping daughter, grasped hands, and gently pulled Sharene to her feet. They hugged tightly without saying a word.

When Jake Marsena returned home, the women he most loved were in his study praying on their knees. He called for Peter to close his bedroom door, and the African drumbeat was reduced to a mere throb.

CHAPTER 8

The trial of Evon Trask wasn't a big deal. The judge yawned as she came into chambers on a sunny spring day, and the court reporter told the bailiff about her husband's new job. A shorthaired, tan dog, with its ribs visible, lazily surveyed the entrance to the courtroom from a prone position, its chin supported by limp paws. Flies buzzed without purpose and, outside, occasional Chevy and Ford automobiles and pickups meandered from street to street.

The courthouse in the county seat had been a welcome landmark at some point in time, but now looked tired and worn. The white paint on the window frames was new, but the brick exterior was checked and faded like bad stucco in blistering heat. The courthouse roof was uncharacteristically steep, and the sun melancholy.

Officials who did talk about the Trask trial spoke of it as a done deal. Get a jury, parade a few witnesses through the courtroom, pronounce the expected "guilty, your Honor," and hang around long enough to hear what the judge would do with the bastard.

He was probably facing a harsh sentence, they predicted. After all, the victim was White, and it was the South in the 1970s.

Evon had been moved that day to a holding cell one floor below the courtroom. Unlike the Apostle Paul when he was in jail, Evon Trask spent no time in prayer. He knew nothing about prayer and intercession, only to nervously pace the tiny cubicle that included a white-sheeted bed that was hard and unforgiving.

He'd suggested offering a plea of temporary insanity, an oftentimes-successful ploy he'd heard of on television, but his court-appointed lawyer wasn't interested.

"You've got the softest judge in the entire circuit system," he'd told Evon, "and you are undeniably guilty. Our best course is to make a few points in your favor, fold early, and plea for leniency. No sense angering the judge with stalling tactics she's seen hundreds of times before."

The attacker of Sharene Marsena accepted the logic initially, but as his late-April court date drew nearer and nearer, Evon Trask began rattling his cage and demanding a new lawyer. No one of consequence heard his objections, however, and anger melted back into fear.

He felt no remorse for his calculated attack, had no concept of what negative consequences had been meted out to his victim, but was by-God ready to promise to never do it again. Evon said to the walls in his jail cell that he was more than willing to promise on a high stack of Bibles, or even on his mother's tombstone, that he would never rape again. Shoot, he'd promise never to jaywalk again if they'd just let him go free.

A health worker, with a solemn face and patience, had spoken to him through thick, steel bars about a new, lethal disease from Africa, and Evon Trask had erupted in a rage best contained in a cell of justice. He'd sworn violently at Nora Okatee, the source of all his problems.

"If there was a God above, he certainly wouldn't let this happen to me," he'd yelled at the health worker while pointing an accusing finger toward the man who'd relayed the unwelcome news. "Why all this hell on my shoulders?" he'd screamed.

Less than a mile away, Nora Okatee was preparing to go to the courtroom, all the time desperately wanting to return to Africa. It had been months since the Tanzanians had ousted Idi Amin from the leadership of her country, and things had to be getting more stable. Yet, Nora's father adamantly had urged her to get an education before returning to her homeland and family, and she'd deferred to his judgment. She wasn't just lonely, but hurting inside from the inadvertent pain she'd inflicted on her friends Sharene Marsena and Evon Trask.

She was angry with Evon, but her overall feelings about him were mixed and confused. For what purpose had Evon Trask violated her close friend?

Sharene, conclusively a carrier of the new virus, and her mother settled at Grandmother's house and waited for the trail.

"You'll do just fine," said Grandmother Marsena encouragingly, as if Sharene was preparing for her first prom.

Sharene, with no apparent options, soon would open yet another of life's doors and step into an unknown that no longer seemed bright.

"Give me a minute, please?" asked a young, young lady who was fighting the residue of rape and a terminal disease. She then ran to the lanai that overlooked the thorn-encompassed African hovel that held an open King James Bible that repeatedly spoke of perseverance and forgiveness, of pain and forgiveness.

She lifted her light blue spring dress with a thin, almost faded white-printed design, and dropped to her knees. She thought of Pastor Hemri's words of encouragement that she wasn't being repaid for past sins, and of Nora Okatee, who had suffered the same fate as herself years earlier, and still was in torment. Also, she thought of Evon Trask whom she soon would see for the first time since he'd muscled her to the ground, threatened her life, beat her unconscious, and taken away a young woman's biggest treasure. She thought these things and large tears of misunderstanding and vulnerability, of confusion, plunged down her soft face. She wiped none of the tears away, and several fell untouched from her ashen face, spotting the white-printed design and light-blue cloth of her chosen dress.

"I'm sorry," was all she could think to say to God before rising and returning to her mother.

Sharene felt a sense of inevitability as they drove to the courthouse that day, while Carol was engulfed in dread.

The younger Marsena, the one who metaphorically was being put on trial along with Evon Trask, gracefully knelt to pet an old tan dog at the door to the courthouse.

Once inside the courtroom, Sharene and Carol were spotted and whisked into a side room for final words of instruction from the prosecuting attorney. He wanted no part of the recently disclosed health issue, arguing that evidence without it was more than sufficient to convict Evon Trask and lock him up for many years to come.

"We would have to postpone the trial to study this new disease and then the newspapers would blow it all out of proportion. Do you want that?" he'd asked Sharene earlier. Overruling some minor concerns voiced by her mother, Sharene had agreed with the attorney, and the jury trial of Evon Trask had been kept on schedule.

On that April afternoon, the three of them—the prosecuting attorney, Sharene, and Carol—walked into the warm courtroom with sunshine streaking through dusty, partially drawn blinds. The attorney and Sharene took a seat at the front table, and Carol Marsena took a seat nearby in the front row.

Then they waited.

Flies buzzed, and slow overhead fans moved with little purpose. A few dozen White spectators trickled in hoping to witness a real life, good- versus-evil courtroom spectacle. They expected to be vicariously entertained like hundreds of times before while watching televised dramas and cop shows, when they'd dulled their senses with popcorn and beer.

Evon Trask finally entered from the left side of the judge's bench, and a security guard inserted a key to unlock his handcuffs for everyone in the room except the jury to see.

Carol, from the front row, stared with conviction toward this hated young man she'd never met. And Sharene, after acknowledging it was whom she knew it would be, stared down at her hands resting idly on the brown, wooden table before her. Without conscious thought, she moved her left thumb to caress the creased point at the base of her left ring finger where a ring would never be.

The bailiff spoke, and maybe as many as forty persons in the courtroom rose to their feet. The judge entered with robed authority, pounded her gavel much louder than seemed necessary, and the jury trial was on in earnest. The jury had been selected the day before without the attendance of Sharene and Carol, and, to the delight of the prosecuting attorney, five women were among the twelve jurors chosen.

"Women only have one sentiment when it comes to rape cases," he said to Sharene and Carol in the side room before the trial started.

Nora Okatee, who came in late and reluctantly, was an early witness. She said she'd left Sharene and Evon at the tennis court when Evon had relayed what he claimed to be an urgent message. He'd told her that her father had gotten through on the telephone and wouldn't hang up until she spoke with him.

Speaking to a diverse group of people, jury members as well as audience engrossed to hear every word she spoke, Nora said Evon had informed her that her host family had taken the call, gone to a neighbor's house to phone him, then asked that he find Nora. Hoping for news to come home to Uganda, Nora testified she'd quickly terminated her tennis match with Sharene and hurried to the home of her host family, where no one had heard of such a phone call.

Nora looked straight ahead without focusing on anyone as questions turned to her relationship with Evon Trask. She looked at the double-door exit at the rear of the courtroom and longed to be away on the other side of the world; nameless and free in a tranquil setting of dry spring dust and flies, of barefoot natives and tangible talk of food and babies and husbands.

She nodded in mute acquiescence when the physical nature of her relationship with Evon Trask was unveiled for all to see, and Nora, too, suddenly felt violated by his actions. The prosecutor pursued the questioning until her self-damning responses became redundant, irrefutably a part of the court record.

The defense asked Nora about the qualities of Evon Trask that had prompted the relationship, and she practically perjured herself by not using the word "lust." She eventually stepped down from the witness stand feeling both tired and hot, wanting more than ever to burst through the back exit of the courtroom and seek a simplistic existence her memories may never again allow.

A forensic expert was called to the stand to match evidence from the scene of the crime with Evon Trask's clothing. The paid specialist matched pieces of Sharene Marsena's hair and drops of her blood with clothing found in Evon's apartment.

Another witness subpoenaed from Ohio, a nervous man in his mid-20s who was slight of build and dangerously pale, repeated excerpts from a conversation he'd had with Evon Trask shortly before the accused rapist was apprehended. The man quoted Evon as bragging about a strong man's domination over "the prettiest virgin in the state of South Carolina."

Carol Marsena badly wanted to protect her daughter from this line of testimony; to cover her with a bright, protective cloak of innocence. She wanted the two of them to walk away forever from this ugly courtroom scene and find a blue, windless lake with small white sailboats idly waiting for divine direction. Once there, Carol Marsena, the mother, knowing they'd reached a safer haven, would remove the cloak and expose Sharene to a new, fresher world.

She also wanted God to intervene, to rewind time to where it was before an evil force had entered the life of her only daughter. She wanted God to replace the past with blue lakes, white sailboats, gentle winds, and love.

She wanted much.

Sharene, saddled with a disease that would kill millions, viewed the proceedings unfolding before her with peace and calm.

What did she have to fear?

In reality, there was no reason to send Sharene Marsena to the witness stand. Evon Trask, triggered by forces he might never understand in this world, was mired in his own guilt. Yet, wanting to leave no trace of doubt in the minds of the jurors, her attorney did call her to testify, and Sharene was forced to audibly relive the ugliest moments of her young life.

She did so bravely, confidently, and the admiring mother prayed that she could have some of her daughter's stamina.

Following her attorney's lead, Sharene told the jury and anyone else in the courtroom, including the hunter, about specific events on the night of August 18, 1978. She told of going to the tennis courts with Nora Okatee and playing some competitive rallies before being startled by her first sighting of Evon Trask. She spoke of Nora's sudden departure, and playing tennis with Evon until an extremely errant shot landed in the woods. She told of being knocked to the ground, then looking into Evon Trask's maniacal eyes as he threatened to kill her while fumbling with her clothing. She spoke of screaming, and fists being pounded into her face.

Sharene faltered when she was questioned about her subsequent waking and the ambulance ride to the hospital.

Then, at a moment that even caught the wary hunter off guard, Sharene Marsena looked directly at the young man who'd raped her, and, with divine inspiration, said, "I harbor no hatred toward you, Evon Trask. In fact, I forgive you."

The jury collectively looked skeptical and perplexed, yet missed nothing as Sharene concluded her thought. "Still, until you acknowledge your sin and seek repentance, you'll never know peace."

Evon Trask looked to his lawyer, to the back of the courtroom at Nora Okatee, and back to his own sweating palms. Something suddenly had jarred his consciousness, and he wasn't sure what it was. A trickle of fresh water had materialized in what had been a completely dry well.

He'd have plenty of time in the future to ponder that moment.

The hunter glared angrily at Sharene, then focused his energies toward the defense attorney who would further drag her beauty through the mud.

Evon's lawyer, feeling he had nothing to lose, wished to build a case of coquettish young beauty that intentionally had led Evon Trask toward false hopes of a lasting relationship, of physical intimacies. He had no witnesses to call, no substance to share, yet wanted to instill some element of doubt in anyone willing to listen.

Sharene's lawyer rebutted, but not before more damage had been done.

Carol's knuckles were white as she gripped the hard bench, and Sharene searched within herself for instances where she could be faulted for triggering Evon's lust.

Evon Trask never took the witness stand.

When the verdict was announced (the eight-year sentence added later by the judge,) Evon Trask was led away by officials with grim faces and badges. Evon's anger had been diffused.

CHAPTER 9

He knocked on the door lightly, almost apologetically, as if the time for a long-awaited reunion had arrived and he suddenly remembered his courage was back in the car, or back in Boston, or back in any number of brown beer bottles that had brought marginal solace for many months.

Standing at the doorstep of the woman he loved, Jordan Norton was shamed by the wantonness of his past year. He didn't blame Sharene for the pain he'd been through. After all, she was the victim, not him. Yet, as byproducts go, his poor grades and temporal lifestyle were related directly to Evon Trask's major sin behind a South Carolina tennis court.

Jordan's heart beat unnaturally, equally torn between love and guilt. His prayer life had strayed during his separation from Sharene, and he didn't think that night to seek spiritual support as he approached the door. He stood alone on the porch and waited for the unknown. Hadn't she requested never to see him again when they'd last been together in the hospital? Hadn't Mrs. Marsena intentionally kept him at a distance?

These thoughts flooded Jordan's consciousness in the seconds before Peter Marsena opened the door and howled with approval. Without a coherent word of greeting to the agitated suitor, Peter ran to tell his family who was paying them a visit.

Sharene was the final Marsena to greet Jordan, slipping quietly into the kitchen where Peter and Jake were pumping his hand and greeting him like a war hero. Carol's greeting, though cordial, was of a cooler nature.

Sharene said nothing as she approached Jordan from the rear, coming from the family sitting room where anyone could look through its window and see the steep-roofed church constructed years before with donated wood and human sweat. Still the tallest building in town, the church had been built thanks to the pure blood of ancestors striking forth in a faith that still burned, in vastly different degrees, in the souls of Sharene Marsena and Jordan Norton.

Carol herded the male members of her family away from the kitchen like sheep with a dog. One instant there were four Marsenas and one guest together, and the next instant Sharene and Jordan were alone.

They hugged tentatively, and Jordan felt cheated. He remembered the past when tight, feeling hugs were shared long before kisses. This hug was of a perfunctory nature, the kind a beautiful woman gives a handsome friend with her new husband watching. It lacked emotion, with bodies hardly touching.

Carol's counseling over the telephone had attempted to prepare him for this moment, but the realization of what had been lost between them put instant despair and emptiness in Jordan's heart.

"You look great," he said, and meant, as they pulled away from the hug. He looked into her eyes and saw no spark. The essence of who she was couldn't surface yet to greet her lover. She looked at him with little cognizance of whom it was she was looking at. Inside Sharene remained a fear of self, a fear of who she'd become with an unknown agent gnawing at her inner beauty, her strength; a disease that would destroy as readily as Satan's torch to straw.

She wanted Jordan to remember her in strength, not with the doubts she now was experiencing and the ugliness that surely would follow. She vowed to never share her plight with him, to force Jordan Norton away before dragging him down with her.

They went into the sitting room, into the dusk, and Sharene sat at a distance. Facial features were shadows in the fast-approaching night, her tears unseen by Jordan Norton.

"Things are different, Jordan," she said. "Do you understand?"
"No."

Sharene took a deep breath that was heard by a lover who expected the worst. Then, she proceeded to speak from a rehearsed, univentoried series of speeches she'd been preparing and rearranging for months. She didn't know which words would come out.

"Jordan, I still love you, but what happened to me in South Carolina hit deeper than you know. I'm not the same person you fell in love with. Something dark and ugly entered my body that night, and it won't ever go away."

"Yes it will," he said resolutely. "There is nothing wrong with you that God can't heal. If you keep the faith and we pray together, you will be healed and forget, Sharene. I promise."

The words were nobly eloquent for a young man whose college apartment smelled of beer and loneliness. Sharene, even in her weakness, especially in her weakness, brought forth something better in him, a new closeness to God beyond his comprehension.

"I was wrong to leave when I did," Jordan said, "even if that's what you said you wanted. I have rotted without you, withered like leaves separated from a tree. I didn't realize it before, but you are my link to all that's good.

"Remember the time I wrecked my car and you were there to heal my spirit and my body? We grew closer from that time of healing. Please, let me be with you as you recover from this. I love you like no other, Sharene."

"No," she said while sitting near an unlit lamp that, had its switch been flicked on, would have revealed a Sharene Marsena in tears and torment for the lie she felt the need to convey.

The room had become subtly darker, like an undisturbed tea bag in hot water, and the gabled church lights through the window, though now lit, were focused in another direction.

The distance between the lovers prevented any touches without a reach into that darkness, into the unknown. Jordan was willing, but was slowed by respect for her words.

She wiped tears from her cheek and, for the first time, he recognized the significance of the motion.

Clouds scudded in the sky, continuing to block any reflective light the night's partial moon had to share.

She tried again. "I'm trying to tell you, Jordan, nothing is like it was. Nothing. The Sharene you loved, the one you still love, is gone. There's ugliness in me now that I want you never to see."

Her tears ran rampant in the dark as she figuratively pushed away the one she loved. It was the right thing to do, she told herself. Without her, Jordan could one day have children and happiness. With her, he would know only barrenness and pain.

"If the love we once held means anything to you, Jordan, then please do as I ask," she said. "Will you do that?"

The crescent moon re-emerged from the clouds at that instant and projected a hue of light along the lines of her soft hair and right cheek. Jordan's heart swooned at the beauty he saw, and he fought for a reprieve.

"I know what you're going to say," Jordan began, "and it's what neither one of us wants. Don't send me away unless it's absolutely what you need to do, Sharene. We don't have to decide our futures in this room tonight. Don't shut me out because times are tough. That is the precise time when our love, with the help of God" (there he was again, speaking like she had taught him,) "can make the difference. Don't shut me in the cold, Sharene. Not at a time when we need each other the most."

He crossed the abyss with a gentle hand that wanted to quiet the unrest, to stay the rumblings of life and smooth the void that had come from nowhere to threaten the castle they'd once built. In the twilight, he delicately touched her on the face, and dragged his sensitive fingers along her cheek. Remnants of moisture communicated what he'd suspected and been unable to see.

Sharene froze at the touch. Inertia and desire, at odds with each other, tempered her will. Her heart pumped love, and she momentarily forgot her purpose, her plight.

She reached a hand to his, and it was not a hand of rejection. She felt the gentleness in his veins, the counterbalancing surges of love, and yearned to respond. She rubbed the back of his hand which still was on her face, and Jordan moved the rest of his body across the abyss, the restrictive danger zone, like an ally on Deliverance Day intuitively desiring to set her free from this evil that was blocking their relationship.

But he went too fast. Realistically, he couldn't have chosen any agreeable speed. In her eyes, speed itself was frightening, and its opposite, patience, a virtue that would erode the element of time she lacked most.

Jordan misread her signs, her conditional overture, and rose into a kiss which started soft and gentle. Sharene held her ground, though torn at the heart, and loved within like only he had ever made her love. She tentatively responded with a twist of the lips and he momentarily erased the last of the abyss, pushing a pounding body next to hers in a full embrace. Their lips pressed hard and he tasted her teeth, rubbed her back.

She wanted, and did not want.

Then, it was over as suddenly as if Carol Marsena had entered the room, flicked on the light switch, and stood, arms folded, in the doorway. It was over as suddenly as if the starter's pistol had been fired and the Boston Marathon had funneled through the sitting room, or if Sharene Marsena had opened her eyes and found the hunter in her arms instead of Jordan Norton.

She pulled away with a gasp, and repulsed his frightened attempts at reconciliation. In horror, he clearly saw for the first time the distance between them, the magnitude of the differences she'd been trying to define.

They rose to their feet, now an arm's length away from each other, and both shed tears unashamedly, without touching, without attempting to bridge the renewed abyss between them. Jordan, in less than a second, saw his future dreams waste away like hail on soft sandstone, and the hourglass of Sharene's life was turned upside down one more time.

Sand granules in her personal hourglass, responding to the powerful forces of nature, relentlessly renewed the process of squeezing themselves through a small opening of time that only would end at her physical death. At that point, only the Maker would have the power and authority to again right Sharene's spent hourglass.

Sharene regained composure first.

"We must pray," she said, "and then you must go, Jordan Norton. I don't expect to ever see you again. Know that I love you very much, and want the best for you."

He was shell-shocked. Seconds before embracing in the pinnacle of love, and now removed from her by the abyss of hell he had no monition to understand, no tools to combat. In his mind, two lovebirds had flown over a swimming pool in complete bliss, only to have one mercilessly shot from the sky by an unknown hunter. He wasn't clear whether he or Sharene had been the one targeted for the fall, but Jordan knew instinctively that he would swoop to save her if ever given the chance.

Fleeting thoughts, these, as her words, "I don't expect to ever see you again" settled within his soul.

She spoke again from the darkness inside a home whose sanctity she soon would leave. Sharene gained strength from his weakness.

"You must promise that you'll never seek me again," she said. "Do you promise?"

The strength of her conviction to spare Jordan from future pain temporarily blinded Sharene from the cruelty of her own words.

He looked blankly at the woman he loved, but his vision was clouded. He reached out and touched her.

"Don't," she cried from across the abyss. "Consider me dead, Jordan. As far as you are concerned, I died tonight."

She wanted to push him away from the twilight of her life, and move on. She wanted to push him away with finality so she could begin in earnest to shed tears of lamentation and penance for her decision to sever him from her brief, bleak future.

"I don't understand, Sharene, but what's new? You've often been a mystery to me, and usually gotten your way," he said.

Jordan paused, then, with brave conviction, and said words he didn't want to say. "I will leave, Sharene, and I will not look for you in the future. But, Ms. Marsena, if ever the time comes when you want anything from me, anything, ask it of me and I'll come as quickly and with as much love as I possibly can to help you in any way."

He made motions to leave, and Sharene turned on the light. They looked at each other imploringly with no more physical attempts to bridge the barriers they'd just erected.

The beautiful, mature young woman then smiled at him, and said, "Will you pray with me?"

Hurt, Jordan Norton broke with precedence, and, displaying a bit of the actor in him, said, "Go to hell."

Then he walked away from Sharene's light and into the darkness, to his parents' car, and drove to a nearby church parking lot where, with no one watching who didn't watch everything, he cried and prayed for more than an hour.

Sharene, with a shredded heart, watched the car's taillights pull away, then retreated to her bedroom to thank God for what had been and what was to come. Tears dotted her prayers like water spots on ancient parchment.

At some point in time, her bedroom door swung open and a shadowy figure entered the room. The mother knelt next to her penitent daughter and put a strong, caring arm around Sharene's shoulder.

"You did the right thing," said Carol Marsena softly, and the two women cried and prayed together on their knees.

CHAPTER 10

Jordan Norton received many letters from Chiska Sullivan during his freshman year in college. Not the bashful type, Chiska stated more than once that she was interested in establishing a relationship with Jordan on whatever level he deemed prudent.

But prudent wasn't the term Jordan had in mind when he began responding to Chiska's overtures during his sophomore year in Boston. It was more an outcropping of prurience that spurred his initial efforts to establish more than a passing relationship with an attractive woman other than Sharene Marsena.

In the final month of 1980, fifteen months after her predecessor had been raped behind a tennis court in South Carolina, Chiska Sullivan moved to winter-white Boston and began in earnest the relationship she had yearned for.

In direct contrast, the weather remained warm many miles to the south, in Alabama, where Sharene Marsena rose from her knees with renewed resolve to press ahead with her God-given talents. The past had been tended to, and the future, according to the most knowledgeable doctors her mother had been able to contact, likely would be short.

The decision about where to go after graduating from high school, something she had months to ponder following her rude introduction to a lethal disease, didn't come easily. Sharene wanted to make an impact for the Lord, but didn't know where to turn. Her prayers generated no discernable answers. Missionary work was considered, but only briefly because of the volume of maintenance drugs and monitoring that went along with the virus she admittedly had, but rarely felt.

Even her mother was silent on the matter for the most part. On one occasion, Carol hinted it would be desirable for her to be near her daughter during the tough times ahead, but quickly tempered that thought. She said Sharene now was an adult, and should decide for herself what roles she and Jake should play in the time Sharene had left … barring, of course, a miraculous cure or divine intervention.

Pastor Dale Hemri was a great ally, a comforter after Jordan went away, yet even he only could stand on the sidelines and pray as Sharene determined her future.

In the fall of 1980, Sharene Marsena, still beautiful and still committed to serving God no matter the cost, enrolled in classes at a small junior college in southern Georgia.

PART II

Sherm Purcell swilled water in his mouth, then spit it into the bathroom sink. He laughed. How many times had he asked the same question, and how many times, in his mind, had he willed another to do his bidding?

He smiled into the mirror and had no complaints about the reflection looking back at him. He was in his thirtys, clean-shaven, and handsome to a fault. The image in the mirror gave no hint about where he'd come from, or to where he'd return. Today, an English professor on a small campus in southern Georgia, tomorrow …?

The smile in the mirror furrowed as he gazed straight ahead and made a knot in his gold-flecked tie. Then he cinched it to his throat.

He pondered the forces in life that had triggered an unexpected detour and brought him to Georgia these past two weeks. Intrigue was substance, but damnit, he now was being gnarled between two opposing worlds. Both wanted the same prey, the prey he was twice contracted to deliver, but Sherm Purcell lacked the leverage of Solomon's sword.

He donned his corduroy sports jacket and looked toward the clock. Forty-five minutes until his only class would begin. He decided to leave now, and walk.

The warm sun further lightened his mood.

"God," he thought, "why is it so damned hard to vertically brush my lower front teeth?" Then he smiled, as he always did when he posed the same question, and wondered who in heaven would ask it for him.

But that was frivolity, he thought, unworthy of the magnitude of the day at hand. For this was the day the Venus's-flytrap of his plan officially would unfurl. Greenbacks were on the distant horizon, many of them, but now he must focus on the beautiful student whose appearance had been precisely what he'd hoped for, what he'd expected.

It was a wonderful, crazy world, he thought, with a wide, confident smile crossing his face. The smile was leveraged by a less- than-pure heart on a cool morning. He laughed at the opposing forces using him to get to that student.

"'Old Sherm will find a way," he muttered audibly, oblivious to the fact his words were heard and measured both by the hunter and the One who hears and understands all.

He'd purposefully made eye contact with the young lady several times in their two weeks of classes together, and thought he'd seen a shy spark of interest in return. He knew his strengths as a male, and could be both charming and ruthless when it came to achieving his desires.

She was in the second row today, and Sherm Purcell, the temporary professor, was enraptured by what he thought to be his own ability to meet this challenge life had presented to him.

"I would like to see you for a minute after class, Ms. Marsena," stated the teacher after walking up to Sharene before class began. He returned to his lectern and waited for the last of his students to file in for the morning lecture. Outside, it was a bright Georgia morning, and students entering the building on the way to Purcell's classroom had to adjust their eyes to the interior lighting.

Sherm had prepared well for his lecture on Kafka, and the time went quickly.

Sharene Marsena refused to catch his eye.

She came forward hesitatingly at class's end, and, without corporeal explanation, the two of them suddenly were alone beneath a slowly turning overhead fan. She wasn't afraid.

Sherm looked at his watch. He knew time was pressing.

"Look, Ms. Marsena," he said slowly.

"Sharene," said the beautiful freshman to the handsome, middle-aged professor.

"Sharene," he began again. "It's totally against the rules of this institution for a teacher to socialize with a student such as you. You understand that, I presume?"

She nodded.

"Would you meet me for dinner away from campus?" he asked, exhibiting a youthful exuberance he wanted her to see.

Sharene's response came in the form of an unanticipated blush, a fast coloring of her cheeks accompanied by a warming of her temples. "Give me some time," she said in confusion, and was gone as quickly as the others before her.

Roommate Kathy Grooven was Sharene's sounding board on the subject of Professor Sherm Purcell, and she wasn't the man's foremost advocate.

"What good can come from you meeting with him, Sharene?" she asked once Sharene had shared her dilemma. "He wants your body, like any other man would, and probably won't settle for anything less. And that's the one thing you simply can't share. Were you like me, with a normal body ..." Kathy Grooven, aghast at her own lack of propriety, reined in her words, but too late to avoid the awkward exposure of a sensitive topic between she and a woman she just was getting to know and love.

"I'm sorry," she said softly, yet felt compelled to continue her thought.

"Even if you had your God-given choice to share or not share what man most wants from women such as you and me, even then, I'd recommend you not meet with him. He's considerably older than you and more experienced. I've been wrong before, Sharene, but my advice is to stay away."

"What am I supposed to do?" responded Sharene with some emotion. "Am I to live the remainder of my life as a nun and withdraw from the opposite sex? I can live an open life, enjoy a few moments, maybe even sneak a kiss or two, and tell him if and when the time is right. As far as age, my dear, he just might be more understanding than a younger man."

Under her breath, Sharene added two more words, "Like Jordan."

The next evening, Sharene met off campus with the seemingly exciting professor and dinner was extremely pleasant for her, with subtle eye contact exchanged between them. They agreed to meet again, and again. Within a matter of short weeks, Sherm Purcell took her to movies and pizza parlors, to a nearby college basketball game, and to exclusive musical renditions of the works of Bach and Duke Ellington. He also took her to see live drama.

Sharene Marsena reveled in his wit, his stories of the stage and of teaching, and stories of his middle-class past. They shared glasses of red wine, and clanked their goblets in toasts to the whales, D. H. Lawrence, and to Sharene's younger brother, Peter, who'd written a short letter and innocently asked about Jordan.

Sharene's interest in living was rekindled by numerous meetings with a handsome, interesting man who refrained from physical advances.

Classes were going well, and grade aspirations routinely were met. She almost could forget what life had injected into her veins, but not quite. Not really. On Sunday mornings she would cry in the pews to the only one who truly understood. She prayed for understanding on the part of Sherm Purcell and for courage to tell him the truth. Too, she prayed for her family back home in Alabama, and for Jordan Norton.

Sharene didn't pray for a cure for her disease. Not that she didn't believe in His powers to provide such a cure, but because she felt unworthy to receive such healing in this lifetime. She felt lukewarm about her unsolicited sickness, and tried bravely to wait for the inevitable.

Against the expressed wishes of her pastor and friend, Dale Hemri, Sharene couldn't bring herself to become actively involved in a southern Georgia church. She attended, prayed, and smilingly exited each Sunday—one pretty face in what predominantly was a sea of collegiate faces whose addresses were penciled in printed church forms, and whose needs rarely were met.

Pastor Hemri's desire would have been to cry frenetically "Luke 17:6" to Sharene and other students in that cold church, thus encouraging them to achieve great things with any amount of faith they might have. But his segment of the flock, in Plateau, was keeping him occupied many miles away under a steep roof hammered in place many decades earlier by men of faith and not men of faith rewarded with hot coffee, and sometimes eternity.

Sharene was equally Christian and woman, and her capricious fling to test the spirit of Sherm Purcell, to titillate and move on, took on an ironic twist. He seemed the perfect gentleman, and she began to like him very much.

One evening, only a month into their whirlwind relationship, the two dined uncharacteristically close to campus, and Sherm Purcell lost his playfulness. He acted defeated for the first time since she'd known him, and Sharene reacted with concern.

"What's wrong?" she asked. Her emotions carefully were under control, yet she wanted the warm playfulness between them to return.

He cleared his throat and avoided her eyes.

"I haven't been totally truthful with you, Sharene. My intentions toward you haven't been totally honorable." He then looked suspiciously over his shoulder as if expecting Humphrey Bogart to walk into the uncrowded restaurant.

Sharene, concerned, missed the melodrama.

He paused in apparent thought, then looked directly into Sharene's eyes, the same type of look that earlier had kindled a spark and brought them together when he'd selected her from a literature class that didn't have a shortage of attractive southern women in it.

She was vulnerable now, and didn't know it.

"Let's walk," he said huskily, and she followed without a word, pausing and watching as he paid the tab and walked back to their table which was cluttered with half-eaten trout and untouched water glasses. He left a generous tip, they exited, and the outside air, though stuffy, was cooled by a gentle Georgian breeze.

Sherm looked extremely handsome in her eyes, and Sharene knew she would tell him soon, even if it ruined the electricity between them, the subtle lust that was so enticing, so wrong.

She'd never been to his residence, and had no idea even if he lived in the same city as the college. So Sharene was startled when, after walking only four blocks in the night air, he guided her down a short sidewalk leading to the porch of a small, clean, wooden cottage.

He withdrew a key ring from his pocket, and smiled. "Would you like to come in?" he asked quietly.

Having prepared herself long in advance for this moment, Sharene said, "I would be honored, but there's something I need to tell you first."

"Come in, and we'll talk," he said, again looking into her eyes, and Sharene Marsena reluctantly withdrew from what appeared to be an overture of friendship, and maybe much more.

She felt waves of frustration and confusion, and fought the urge to cry. Much of her self wanted to dive through that door and, once it closed behind her, touch lips with this seductive man. Yet, the turns of her life prohibited such a hasty, carefree response to temptation.

"I might be willing to come in, Sherm, but only after you hear what I have to say," she said.

She took a step away from him and toward the street as his key entered the lock and he opened the door into a dark interior. A tear fell, and Sharene felt a sense of panic, a strong desire to run away and scream "rape" as loud as she could before he could touch her, before he could hit and subdue and infuse her with more of the rottenness that had come to her through soldiers in Africa. Nora and Evon had been carriers of that rottenness, pawns in a cosmic battle to requite death for sin. It didn't seem to matter whose sin it was.

Then, an evil thought from a hunter in the night entered into Sharene's mind. Why not give Sherm Purcell what he desired?

But that thought was short-lived.

Sherm said, "I have something to confess to you, too, Sharene. Please forgive me. Give me a second to retrieve something from inside, and we'll both talk."

And he was gone without turning on a light.

Sharene, following another inaudible whisper from the hunter, had to fight off the strong temptation to turn and walk away, to negate what couldn't be without so much as a word of truthfulness. Didn't she know what he wanted? Wasn't she helpless to share, even if the trappings (as they seemed to be at this moment), of unwed Christianity could be shucked for a night? Was there no pleasure shy of heaven?

Streetlights illuminated her outer beauty, and God saw, understood, and lived the magnificent turmoil percolating within Sharene Marsena.

Sherm returned from the darkness to the evening shadows with something tucked behind him in his left hand. With his right hand, he erased the streetlight shadows by flicking on a yellow porch light that gave Sharene, as well as Sherm Purcell, an unflattering yellowish hue, a faded color much like aging parchment enclosed within the red-specked page ends of a weathered King James Bible.

They argued briefly, and lightly, about who would speak first, then Sherm Purcell settled the matter by pulling from behind him a framed eight- inch-by-10-inch photograph, and looked for her reaction as he gently pushed forth the picture for Sharene's inspection.

The yellow porch light dulled the picture's colors, yet she gasped, grabbed the photo encased under reflective glass, and studied it closely.

"It's not me, is it?" she asked in a hush without taking her eyes from a portrait of a beautiful young woman in a brown cashmere sweater. The young woman in the photo gracefully was touching a moss-covered, low-hanging tree limb, and smiling a soft, pleasant smile that exuded love and patient confidence. Deep green foliage from the tree completed the natural setting within the wooden frame that Sharene now held.

She looked long and hard at the photograph, while Sherm Purcell waited in silent anticipation.

"It's not me," she repeated with her voice trailing into a night whose darkness had been displaced on Purcell's small porch by artificial yellow light. "God, but it looks like me, as if I had a twin sister."

"Come in," he said. "I'll fix some coffee and tell you an incredible story."

She balked. Intuition told Sharene that her ugly narration had to be told now, before he told his story, and the photo gave her courage. It was as if the woman in the brown sweater offered her more hope at a human level. Maybe something of Sharene Marsena could still touch the souls of men like Sherm Purcell and Jordan Norton without dragging them into the muck of a disease that, in time, would steal her body. She knew her soul was in gentle hands, yet loathed the thought of dragging down those she loved as her strength waned.

Still standing outside his home, she continued staring at the photograph.

"I know that it's not me, but I never would have thought anyone else could look so much like me," Sharene said. "Even the eyes. Especially the eyes."

"Please think carefully before you answer this question," Sherm said.

Then, before asking the question, he quickly ducked back inside.

"Where are my manners?" he asked upon returning. "Since you refuse to come in, have a seat," he said, and produced two brown folding chairs. He set them down on the porch under the yellow light.

Sharene sat facing the doorway, with her back to the street and the relatively quiet Georgian night.

Sherm Purcell sat with legs straddling his folding chair, arms folded over its back which faced toward Sharene. He continued with his question.

"Please, Sharene, concentrate. What in the picture gives away the fact that this is not you?"

"Those are not my clothes," she said slowly. "And I don't remember posing for that picture."

"Other than that," he implored, "what about the appearance of the lady in the photograph would indicate that she is anyone other than Sharene Marsena?"

Sharene studied the photograph closely.

"This is minor," she said, "but she doesn't have the mole I have on the top of my left ear. Of course, that's something I easily could touch up with makeup, if I wanted."

"Great!" exclaimed Sherm Purcell, as if he were a child seeing the circus for the first time. "Now you have an inkling of what I want to talk to you about. Do you still have something you want to tell me?"

Then Sharene, sitting on Sherm's porch under unflattering yellow light, seized the moment like the woman Carol and Jake Marsena had raised her to be. She apologized profusely, then went straight to the point.

"Have you heard of a new, deadly disease that originated in Africa and the best of doctors know next to nothing about?" she asked.

He had, and Sharene sprang boldly into her tale of South Carolina and a friendship with a Black woman with a boyfriend who took more than a passing interest in her. She spoke about a competitive tennis match that was interrupted by an urgent message, and a subsequent tennis ball that was smacked over the wire-barrier fence into the woods. She spoke unflinchingly about threats, her scream, a beating that left her unconscious, and the violation of her womanhood. She told him about a trial in a rural, white courthouse that elicited testimony about rape, but not the new disease that now had infected her body. She talked about a verdict that settled the matter according to law. She spoke of her personal turmoil over the next year, talks with her pastor, and the huge gap that separated her cerebral Christian response of forgiveness from the somewhat tainted response deep inside her that still sought closure.

The temporary professor from a small southern Georgia junior college listened with ever-growing interest, and insects gathered above them to smack their bodies against the yellow light and die. Time wound yet another microsecond, and Sharene felt purged.

Talking fast, she was airing miscellaneous details about a King James Bible in an African hovel that was covered with thorny vines, about rocks and fear, when Sherm Purcell rose to turn his chair around, and sat down again with his knees practically touching hers. He leaned forward, elbows planted on his thighs, fingers from both his hands clenched only a fraction of an inch from Sharene's knees which were exposed below the hem of her cotton skirt.

Then he interrupted her monologue by asking, "Are you familiar with the term providential?"

She was relieved that he'd finally spoken, thus tempering the verbal deluge that had sprung from deep within her. She would have apologized for the burden she was unloading, but Sherm voiced no objection, and she did feel much better for having shared her story.

The insects buzzed the light and continued to sacrifice their lives, their frail bodies gathering without remorse in the glass fixture that held the yellow bulb.

"I think so," she responded to his question. "Doesn't that have something to do with God's will evidencing itself in human life, like explaining occurrences we couldn't otherwise explain?"

"Pretty close," he said.

During her unburdening, Sharene had returned the framed photograph to him, and Sherm had gently leaned it against exterior wooden siding to the right side of his front door. Now, he picked it up again, and looked at the Kodak reproduction with apparent tenderness. Sharene sensed that the kindness shown to her the past few weeks had been shared with another woman in mind.

"Where do I start?" he asked, not expecting an answer.

"How about telling me who the lady in the picture is?" Sharene asked.

A distant look came into Sherm Purcell's artificially highlighted eyes, eyes more accustomed to intrigue than Sharene could fathom, and he began a long dialogue orchestrated by flailing insects, passing motorists, and an easy breeze that audibly wound through nearby trees.

"Her name is Sandy Kroghan, and we are engaged to be married," he began. "At least we were engaged the last time I spoke to her, which was nearly one and a half years ago. Before our marriage date, Sandy, who's extremely independent, decided to take one last vacation without me, to South America. It was a package tour, so I didn't worry too much about it."

He leaned closer, and continued his story.

"To my knowledge, the first week went routinely, but during the second week a group from the tour, only about twenty people, split from the others to visit a coffee plantation near the town of Armenia, Colombia."

Sherm continued to deliver his soliloquy to a captive audience of one earthly being, plus others more aware of his intent.

"Apparently the twenty were easy prey for local bandits with automatic rifles. They stole everything of value from each of the terrified tourists. Then, according to those I've spoken with who returned from the ordeal, one thief held them at gunpoint while five others withdrew a short distance and heatedly talked for several moments.

"Evidently, Sandy's extreme beauty, something you know all about, Sharene, struck a cord, and the robbers added kidnapping to the offense of mere Colombian robbery.

"I'm told," said the man who patiently was setting bait like a skilled Northwest trapper of beavers, otters, or bear, "that they tied her wrists and hauled her away in a dusty green pickup."

Then he skipped ahead in his story.

"You can imagine how long it takes to inform next of kin and friends about anything happening as far away as rural South America," said Purcell. "I only heard the news late on the day following the kidnapping."

And Sharene, quiet, intent, her heart empathizing with one she'd never met, continued to listen without interruption.

"I apologized over the telephone to authorities of the school where I was teaching at the time, and packed lightly for a trip to Colombia to begin my search for Sandy," he said.

"Interestingly enough, a man, identifying himself as a CIA agent, caught me at the airport and urged me not to make the trip at that time. He said an international drug lord was involved in the kidnapping, that the U.S. government was monitoring the situation, and that I'd either waste my time and money trying to find her, or, more likely, get killed in the process.

"Anyway, Sharene, I went to Colombia, learned quite a bit about Sandy's situation there, and didn't get killed. I learned where they were keeping her, but had no chance of penetrating the drug lord's compound. I know for fact that she was still alive while I was there, but, feeling helpless on my own, I returned stateside to share my findings with the man from the CIA. He gave me no reason for hope, but I'm not giving up.

"I can do Sandy no good down there, but you can, Sharene.

"Would you like to come in for some coffee?" he asked. Sherm smiled then, and Sharene hesitated.

"Are you a Christian?" she asked for the first time in their one-month relationship.

And the sinister, invisible hunter—nearby, as he so often is—leaned forward to catch Sherm's response.

"I'm not very good at it," said Sherm Purcell.

The hunter laughed.

"Would you like to come in for some coffee?" he repeated.

"No," she said slowly. "Maybe that should wait until another day."

The breeze carried the scent of sweet magnolia blossoms, and the unusual pair continued to talk for long minutes on the porch.

"Will you help me?" concluded Sherm Purcell.

"God will be my witness," she responded intriguingly, and met his gaze under the yellow light with a warm smile he couldn't interpret.

Still lacking an answer to his question, Sherm Purcell walked her home, the two of them lightly speaking of unfinished trout dinners, friendships, and Kafka.

"Remember to pray," said Sharene Marsena from her and Kathy Grooven's doorstep.

And Sherm Purcell walked away.

CHAPTER 2

Until this very moment, Sharene Marsena always had the option to pick up her marbles, close the barn door, and live the remainder of her life with Sandy Kroghan only existing as a photograph, and not a real person. But that option was seconds away from being erased permanently as propellers on the airplane in which she now sat audibly began turning in the Washington, D.C., night.

She looked through the window porthole. It was about 3 a.m., and no one could be seen along the paved airport apron or inside the airplane hangar directly outside her window. One door of the hangar was open, and, from night lighting generated from its interior, Sharene could see the silhouette of another small, black plane that looked similar to the one she was sitting in. The light from the hangar created a rainbow-like hue on the double-windowed porthole by her seat, a hue accented by water droplets from a driving rain.

It had been five- and-a-half weeks since Sherm Purcell, or an individual using the name Sherm Purcell, figuratively had introduced her to a look-alike in trouble, a woman held against her will in a rural fortress in the drug-rich country of Colombia.

Now, Sharene Marsena was seconds away from embarking on an arduous, life-threatening mission to offer her self as a decoy, to possibly offer her life to save another. And even now, as the props began to whir, she had her doubts about Sherm Purcell. Was he who he said he was? Did he have a stake in this rescue mission? Did he even know a person named Sandy Kroghan? Did he really defy the CIA and travel to Colombia to look for his kidnapped fiancee?

Her thoughts tumbled like clothes in a dryer with a large glass window, visible to anyone taking the time to look inside.

Sharene watched the ground slowly slide beneath her as the pilot walked the plane to the runway prescribed for takeoff. She could see no one inside the airplane from her window seat, but knew the pilot and copilot were studying gauges in front of her behind a pleated maroon curtain. They revved the engines to a high pitch, then proceeded slowly, then faster through the early morning hours. The rubber wheels bounced as if they had too much air in them, and soon the airplane went airborne, giving Sharene a sensual rush of blood inside her stomach.

The plane circled in its preordained route while gaining altitude over an illuminated city that experienced intrigue daily. Then, the airplane headed south.

CHAPTER 3

Sharene returned from the cold church in southern Georgia and found Kathy Grooven entertaining a guest Kathy never had liked.

"Mr. Purcell seems most anxious to see you," said Kathy, after meeting Sharene at the door. "I served him some coffee. If you would like to play some tennis later today, let me know." Then Kathy Grooven retired to her room.

"Let's walk," said Sharene following a prolonged silence far less cordial than what the previous night would have suggested. "You can tell me what you want me to do."

She had prayed for tortuous hours the night before, reaching out from the depths of her soul to the loving God she sought direction from. Across town, Sherm Purcell had tossed lightly before falling into a restful, dreamless sleep.

They walked, and words for Sharene didn't come easily.

She now understood that this man, who had wooed and tantalized her heart, had been acting out of selfish motives. All the time, he'd been seeking her assistance to help free his captive lover. Sharene knew he'd been totally deceptive, yet it didn't seem to matter. She hadn't been up-front and honest either. She'd used him, also with selfish motives, to bring a spark of meaning back into a confusing world.

Their relationship was murky at best as they walked in the wind.

They walked toward the heart of the city, away from her and Kathy Grooven's rented apartment, and away from the small campus. Everyone they encountered, walking with or against their chosen pathway, seemed on a Sunday pace of haste and patience, of rest and frenzy. The older ones walked slower with canes and halting steps, seemingly with a patient vision for an improved tomorrow. Some knew the shape of that tomorrow, while others tapped blindly onward with dull memories of past loves, past pleasures.

The young looked to extend their years, to speed the clock to maturity by laughing hard and pushing toward an undefined limit. They collided while chasing Frisbees in a small park, and forced laughter to cover the pain.

"You are the focal point of the best plan we can devise to save Sandy," said Sherm Purcell, as they walked on a windy, but pleasant, sunny day. "We want a switch. We can train you to get out from the inside, but not her. The CIA has a contact person inside the drug lord's compound who will help you."

The middle-aged people were the ones in the cars with air conditioning and small children strapped down in back seats. Proportionally, they wore more sunglasses and were dressed in nicer clothes than the others, as if they'd just been released from cold, southern churches. They obeyed speed laws, and weren't cognizant of slow-moving elderly pedestrians or high-energy youth until their paths happened to cross at an intersection, or an errant Frisbee scudded out of control in the street in front of them. The small children, strapped in seats behind their parents, peered from car windows and eagerly pointed at dogs being walked by their masters. Yet, the childrens' collective excitement and visions were overridden by the preceding generation, their parents, who sought temporary reunions with grandparents. Those reunions, when they'd leave behind their offspring for longer stays, would free those parents for quiet hours and televised sports, for peace and a beer.

The wind picked up. Papers stirred in an abandoned lot passed by Sherm Purcell and Sharene Marsena.

"I've known for some time that you were the only realistic hope for Sandy, but didn't know if I could muster the courage to ask for it," said Purcell. "Then, you said you were dying from that mysterious disease, and suddenly everything seemed so providential."

The wind rippled needles on a pine tree that towered above the post office. Flowers danced effortlessly, gracefully, at the tree's base next to tightly pruned bushes whose squat forms were anchored in the hard, southern dirt.

"How did I become involved?" Sharene asked.

A green-trimmed taxi with a bearded, Black driver hoping to pick up a fare cruised slowly beside them until Sherm waved him away with a curt, backhand gesture that Sharene didn't see.

The two of them, seemingly on a casual, Sunday stroll, passed a bank and a bakery, and neither of them thought about stopping. Their direction was established, yet neither knew what path to take.

Sherm continued to unravel a believable tale of intrigue and coincidence.

"You know how young boys will sometimes say "I'm in love," with no thought to accuracy? A fellow I know said that about you. He said he intentionally brushed against you one night while leaving a basketball game between his school and yours, and never will forget the scent of your hair. He claims to have known some of your classmates from Plateau and occasionally would visit them, asking for school annuals to look at your pictures. Anyway, he says he never met you, but has a living memory of your appearance. I trust that memory, especially since I was in the room the first time he saw Sandy.

"He made me want to know you, to discover if your beauty runs as deep as hers."

Sherm Purcell and Sharene Marsena crossed the street and found the breeze suddenly dormant until they'd again come to an alley or open space between downtown buildings. Only then would the stirring of molecular-driven heat ripple their hair and clothing with omnipresent persistence.

Young adults in their autos passed them a second time, this time without their children, heading in the same direction Sherm and Sharene were walking. Many had sunglasses draped across their noses and their sights pointed toward low-energy pleasure.

"He knew through a friend that you were coming to this school and, fortunately, I qualified for a late opening in the English department. I had no idea you would be in my class. Providential," he repeated, displaying a smile she always had liked. "And when you first walked in, I thought Sandy had escaped from her captors in South America."

The business district was big enough for a hearty walk, but not much more. They passed a little drive-inn restaurant that advertised lime freezes, and Cupid pierced Sharene's heart with a painful thrust all the way from Plateau, Alabama, or maybe Boston.

She briefly wondered if Jordan was experiencing the same painful memories.

They passed a squat real estate building, then a side street that marked the end of the business district. They continued to walk through rows of mortgaged houses where middle-aged, middle-class parents were mowing lawns, trimming hedges, or sipping beer on back patios or in front of television sets. Across town, their children were entertaining grandparents.

The sun spent more time free from widely scattered clouds than behind them, and Kathy Grooven looked for someone else to play tennis with.

"Why did you take so long to approach me?" asked Sharene. "I'd think you would want to rescue Sandy as soon as possible."

Sherm Purcell looked carefully around him as if searching for a Maltese falcon or a camouflaged hunter seeking to dash his efforts with the flick of a lighter or wave of an ancient desert broom.

Sharene suddenly felt chilled, and didn't understand why.

Grandfathered into the residential district was a small car lot with used Dusters and Chevys and two white Cadillacs for sale. Sherm and Sharene walked in front of the lot, and the sidewalk gave way to a well-traveled dirt path.

He stopped then, and looked around at the panorama of a quiet Georgia neighborhood on a Sunday afternoon. His eyes were quick and experienced, and Sharene sensed the subtle urgency of the man who had wooed her to gain an ally for his loved one.

He saw no one close, and said, "The CIA hasn't approved my plan yet, and I don't have the resources to proceed without them. I had to get close enough to you on my own to find out if you could carry this out. And, since I view you as Sandy's absolute final hope, I had to do it cautiously. Now, after discovering the type of person you are, I believe you can do it."

He grabbed her arm almost roughly then, as they stood on a dirt path in the public right of way in front of a row of middle-class southern Georgia homes, and asked, "Are you interested?"

The Marine band began to play in Sharene's mind. Was this her one opportunity to be of use to her God? She blocked from conscious thought the fact that Sherm Purcell was the only person in her world who knew, for fact, that a person named Sandy Kroghan even existed.

She did remember her God.

"At what point will I have to decide?" she asked, and watched as Sherm Purcell peered back and forth warily like British or American soldiers nearing the beaches of Normandy at 12:15 a.m.

They crossed the two-lane street and turned back toward the business district.

A miniature twister, lifting dust and small fragments of paper above a vacant lot, stole their attentions. Hardly four feet above ground at its highest point, the baby tornado lived the duration of its life while Sherm and Sharene watched. First a wisp of power, a circling wind triggered by the elements, and then the twister quickly succumbed to nature's course. Like locusts after a woe, it died without fanfare, returning to the dust it had been made from.

"Listen," said Sherm Purcell, as they watched nature's tiny whirl of wind forever die, "I might not have much opportunity to speak with you in the days ahead, but in this package of chocolates is a time, date, and location where a CIA operative will be available to talk with you. You won't be asked to make a decision until after that meeting, yet I'd advise you not even to go there if you're merely curious."

He handed her a tiny, wrapped package, no bigger than an index card with depth, and urged her to put it away from view.

"Do you have children?" she asked on impulse, and he looked around again without responding to the question.

They approached a spot below the awning of a chain department store cater-cornered from the bank, and pedestrians seemed to come from nowhere. The chain store was the biggest business open on a southern Sunday, attracting patrons to its spacious aisles that separated display tables laden with colorful summer clothing, lamps, and books about Buddha and Jesus Christ. Customers of all ages and body shapes had responded to an old SALE sign at eye height on a large plate-glass window facing the street that tastefully had been altered with bright yellow paint. What had been a SALE sign for many months now was a SALE sign bordered in yellow with quotation marks and exclamation points. Middle-aged women without their children hurried into the store to look around, socialize, and maybe buy a plastic spatula or a roasting pan.

Sharene intended to pursue her question about children, but lost the thought when two men, merged among the arriving shoppers, stepped away from the crowd and into Sherm Purcell's path. She saw them first, as Sherm was focused on her reaction to his vague plan to save a beautiful woman.

Sharene hadn't expected trouble when she'd innocently run after an errant tennis ball one and a half years earlier, and she didn't suspect trouble now.

She would in the future.

The shorter of the two men, wearing a gaudy silver belt buckle inlaid with turquoise stones, a buckle anchoring the leather belt that circled his plump waist, halted Sherm Purcell's progress by placing hands on both of his shoulders. He smiled with malicious insincerity; and the second stranger, by the physical placement of his body, made many shoppers heading into the store walk around him. The taller man held his right hand beneath the light-blue windbreaker he was wearing, and the bulge beneath the windbreaker indicated he held a gun.

"Is it Dr. Purcell?" asked the smaller man, smiling with uneven teeth. "You must come with us."

The short assailant removed his hands from Sherm's shoulders, and the confrontation next to the newly doctored SALE sign, at least to those passing by, appeared to be cordial in nature. Still, the two men were neither Black nor White, and looked strangely out of place in a southern American town—like steel balls among marbles on a Chinese checkerboard.

Sherm showed no indication of surprise, nor hinted he had thoughts of attempting a heroic escape. He seemed almost unconcerned about the safety of himself and Sharene Marsena.

"An important person wants to see you right away, Mr. Purcell," said the man with the gaudy turquoise belt buckle. "You must come now. We have a long trip ahead of us."

"May I first have a word with my student?" asked Purcell.

"You may speak briefly while I listen," said the short, smiling antagonist. His comrade remained silent, pointing the protrusion beneath his jacket at the man they soon would be taking with them.

"Don't say anything, Clara, just listen," said Sherm Purcell, as he turned to Sharene. "I have to go away for a while. In fact, you may never see me again. So I won't be around to help with the major decision you have to make. Follow your heart, and don't let me be a major factor in what you decide to do.

"Now, I want you to remember two things. Don't call the police, and I love you very much."

And, still under the department-store awning, they embraced in complete candor; their windblown lips from different worlds meeting momentarily for the first time until the short, smiling stranger pulled them apart.

"We have to go," the man said, and quickly ushered the confusing professor into an everyday Duster or Chevy or white Cadillac, and, with the taller man at the wheel, drove away.

Sharene got no license plate number. In fact, she stood shell-shocked for several moments in the middle of the sidewalk while middle-aged parents passed by her seeking bargains, maybe even treasures, in the recesses of the chain store.

She blindly walked halfway down the block to the nearest bench, sat down, and tried to cry in fear and frustration.

What had happened to her life? Why couldn't she simply go to college and die? Why was life so hard and confusing? Did God really love her, or was she simply a pack mule increasingly burdened with strife until a time when she would stumble and fall in the mud, then expire?

She looked around with soulful eyes, seeking a friend to confide in. None appeared, and Sharene lowered her head into her lap and began to cry the public tears of someone wanting, no needing, solace. No one came. Then, as her body involuntarily rocked back and forth in public loneliness and despair, words, then phrases began to align themselves in her mind; words programmed in her heart and soul a decade earlier to serve during times of crisis.

"Amazing grace, how sweet the sound, that saved a wretch like me ..."

Then, Sharene Marsena remembered the friend she'd been seeking, opened her eyes to bright sunlight, stood once more on her feet, and continued her walk with neither the presence of Sherm Purcell nor any thought of opening the small package he'd given her. She occasionally looked around her with wariness, wondering what invisible evil was stalking her now, then prayed once more for protection, and that His will be done.

The hunter, across the street, shook his head in disdain.

It was late afternoon when Sharene Marsena returned to her and Kathy Grooven's apartment without the man she'd left with. Shadows were advancing among the trees, and Sharene's heart jumped when a stray black dog loped around the corner of their rental apartment, was equally startled by her presence, then ran away.

She unlocked the door, stepped inside, and flicked on the light switch. Blocking her path on the linoleum-floored entryway that led to the living room was a large cockroach. To her right was a bookcase, and Sharene grabbed a hardback book from it, maybe a Steinbeck, and threw it at the insect with tentacles. She missed, and the cockroach scurried from view into a small coat closet built off of the entryway.

Sharene, her back against the wallpapered entryway wall, slid into a sitting position on the cool floor and began to laugh.

What began as the seed of a smile went through a complete metamorphosis in a matter of seconds. She quickly was engulfed in uncontrollable, almost delirious laughter that grew loud, then louder, until she broke into a fit of coughing that wouldn't stop until she'd raced to the bathroom and her energies were drained from her body by the vomit and blood that spewed from her beautiful mouth. She hung over the toilet bowel for several minutes until the episode passed.

Sharene Marsena, knowing in her heart that she wasn't alone, rose, retrieved the small box of chocolates she'd left sitting on the bookcase, walked to the living room, sat down, and opened the small package.

After taking mental note of an approaching time, date, and location, she grabbed the telephone and placed a long-distance call to Pastor Dale Hemri.

CHAPTER 4

Classes weren't the same with Sherm gone. She hadn't realized what a vital niche he'd filled in her life until his dramatic exit. Too, she worried. Not enough, though, to contact local or state police. His voice had been firm on that matter.

Sherm's literature class now was taught by a stiff-lipped young lady who seemed more concerned with her authority in the classroom than the sharing of meaningful works of language.

Not a word of explanation was given about the change of instructors.

Always a conscientious student, Sharene skipped class one day and took a walk to a nearby stream where she threw rocks in the water and sat cross-legged beneath a thick-limbed tree with many pointed needles and rough, gray bark. She thought about an upcoming meeting, and an important decision only she could make. She sat quietly and prayed for wisdom while her smooth young legs, temporarily uncloaked from beneath her sweat pants, sprouted wind-chilled goose bumps and were creased by the rough, brown grass.

The next morning Sharene Marsena woke with a fever.

It wasn't the tie- you-to-the-bed-and-throw-away-the-key kind of fever meted out by the strains of Asian flu crisscrossing America that year, but it did keep her uncomfortably bedridden for many days with no indication of letting up. She struggled to see the Georgia doctor in charge of her medications, and got more counseling than relief. He offered an option of hospitalization, which she declined. Her body ached like that of a running back after a grueling football game, yet all she got from the visit to the doctor were Anacin and more prescription drugs to supplement a weakening immune system. She returned to her apartment and felt deserted, bereft of friends, and longed for the past with Jordan Norton. Sharene shivered under the covers on warm Georgia days, and wondered if her end would come in such a mundane, practically meaningless setting.

Pastor Dale Hemri had bolstered her mood days before when she'd utilized the confidentiality of a pastor to tell him about Sherm Purcell and Sandy Kroghan. He'd given no specific insights as to how Sharene should answer the challenge, yet had spoken to her about God and His priorities for her life. Pastor Hemri had suggested that the Lord Almighty likely had etched His preferred, ordained response somewhere in her heart. She told him in response that she didn't feel etched upon, but would continue to seek God's will.

Pastor Hemri, well into the conversation, gently had offered his opinion that maybe her time for action was far shorter now that she was ill, and possibly she'd have to step out in faith before the actual etching was discovered.

Sharene sweated while shivering with cold chills, and had her basic needs tended to by Kathy Grooven who believed she had no reason to fear Sharene's deadly virus.

College, which had little meaning for her now, slipped away from Sharene's consciousness as her bedridden status went into a second week. Yet, Sharene remained keenly aware of a tiny piece of paper, a piece of paper secured from a small box of chocolates. That typewritten message sat on the stand beside her bed, and she picked it up periodically to study its message, as if the words on it somehow might change.

Then, after a lengthy talk with The Almighty, she made a gutsy, conscious decision for health.

Within three more days, with ample drugs and water, Sharene Marsena was back on her feet and feeling alive. She dressed for the out-of-doors, the first time she'd done so since becoming bedridden, and thanked Kathy Grooven for her invaluable kindness.

She called her mother, apologized for not phoning at the usual time the previous two Sundays, and politely listened as Carol Marsena explained how sick Peter had been, but now was much better. Most of what Sharene had intended to share over the telephone with her mother suddenly lost its timeliness, and Sharene elected to wait until the family was together to outline the bulk of the opportunity being presented to her.

But she did share enough to pique her mother's interest.

"I don't want to be specific at this time," she said to her mother miles away in northern Alabama, "but an exciting opportunity to do something really positive could very well arise in my immediate future. It would involve travel and a touch of drama. I can't tell you more right now, but please pray for me to both recognize and act upon God's will for me."

The mother, Carol Marsena, who subconsciously knew that her grandfather had taken great pleasure in helping roof the steepest part of Plateau's big church, was both excited and apprehensive at the same time.

"What about college?" she asked.

"Mother, please don't be an obstacle," said Sharene. "I know my time left on earth is short. What I'll do, if things work out, will do more good for others than selfishly sitting in classrooms until my time has come. I love you very much, but you can't alter my decision. That decision now must be made between the Lord and me. Please pray for His guidance."

Always a mother who trusted her children, possibly on occasions more than reason might warrant, Carol Marsena unequivocally gave Sharene her blessing at that moment, and asked to be kept informed of any future developments.

"Always remember that your father, your brother, and I love you very much," she said.

"I love you, too, Mommy," said Sharene, and hung up her telephone.

Carol Marsena felt a swoon of uneasiness in her stomach as she cradled the telephone receiver at her end of the connection. Sharene hadn't called her "Mommy" for more than five years.

CHAPTER 5

When a friend dropped her off at night at an inexpensive motel in a nearby town, Sharene was filled with so much apprehension that her emotions would have been unbearable had her life not been teetering already over the edge of a high precipice. She walked toward room number eighteen with the purposeful resolve of a teenaged Olympian approaching the ten-meter board for that first historic dive. She had absolute faith that she would knock on the door, but didn't know when the burst of courage to do so would come.

The curtains, in what appeared from the outside to be a small room facing the street, were drawn shut across a window to the left of the only door. A subtle, secondary light offered minimal illumination from the interior of number eighteen, and Sharene had no idea who, or what, awaited her inside.

Unarmed, she knew she was no match for any male wanting to overpower her. A flash of fear arose, residue from South Carolina, and she paused for the umpteenth time to pray for protection. This time, standing on the sidewalk immediately in front of the motel room the box of chocolates had directed her to, she smartly prayed for protection covered with the blood of Jesus.

Encouraged, she took final steps to the door and knocked lightly.

The dim inside light was extinguished, and Sharene Marsena boldly held her ground.

A shadowy face peered through the window curtain to the left of the door, and Sharene, courtesy of exterior illumination from low-powered light poles placed around the motel's parking lot, briefly glimpsed the round face of a man before he closed the curtains and withdrew into the room's interior.

A dead bolt snapped loudly, and the door opened from darkness into the slightly lighted night where a brave young woman stood on the doorstep of room number eighteen of a nondescript Georgian motel. A sleeveless arm, without a visible body, motioned her into the darkness.

Sharene didn't move.

"Turn on a light," she said with more conviction than she felt.

Steps receded into the darkness, and the man turned on a low-powered light that allowed Sharene to see the light's source, a small lamp sitting on a wooden stand placed on the left side of a narrow, tidy bed. Although the fluorescence was dull, she clearly saw the foot of the bed and, to her right, a narrow hallway that led at its end to what appeared to be a closet with full-length doors. She crossed the threshold, and now had a better view of the wooden headboard of the small bed and a slick, brown vinyl chair to the left of the door near the window with the drawn curtain. Also in the room, to the right of the hallway, were a small, gas-burning cook stove and an ice box.

The man, still standing, waited patiently on the far side of the bed to Sharene's left. He was slight of build and smooth-shaven. The light bulb under the shaded lamp highlighted the left side of his face, but planted a partial shadow on the right side.

Sharene stood only steps into the room, with the door open behind her.

"Come in, Sharene," he said in a voice that sounded surprisingly kind. "What we have to discuss won't take long."

He remained perfectly still, much like a cat poised over a hereditary foe of small stature, or maybe like a patient friend not wanting to cast alarm. Sharene was unable to discern between the two.

Then a wave of calmness swept through the maiden from Alabama, a peace she couldn't comprehend, and she walked to the vinyl chair to the left of the doorway and sat down. She watched closely as the man crossed her path, closed the only exterior door, and snapped shut the loud, ringing dead bolt.

"My name is Welch," he said as he paced to the far side of the bed away from where she sat. He grabbed an old wooden folding chair propped against the wall, righted its legs, and sat down himself. He leaned forward with his chest touching the bed between them.

In spite of the dim lighting, she saw both sides of his face now and had little intuitive reaction to what he represented in her life.

"Purcell has convinced us that you are the one and only person who can tackle this mission, save the girl, and come back alive. I've only met Miss Kroghan through photographs myself, but you certainly do look like an exact duplicate.

"Maybe, for starters, you can edify me by explaining what it is you have to gain from all this," said the man who called himself Welch.

Sharene responded calmly.

"I don't know if you'll understand this, Mr. Welch, but I'm a Christian, and my time on this planet is short. Good deeds won't secure a place in heaven for me, yet I must live my faith with actions that are in harmony with who He wants me to be. What I have to gain, Mr. Welch, is an eternal peace that will continue well beyond my earthly death."

Welch rubbed his chin as if searching for stubble or pock marks, then massaged the temples above his face with open palms. His hands continued in an upward motion, catching medium-length hair between his index fingers and middle fingers like a barber preparing to apply scissors.

She sensed he was tired, and probably had come through multiple time zones for this meeting.

"Where is Sherm?" she asked.

Welch picked his words carefully.

"I don't know for sure, but I'm confident that he is safe. The people who kidnapped him aren't likely to harm Mr. Purcell. My guess is he's probably in a certain South American country where money and drugs rule. Mr. Purcell will be all right. He's what we call a survivor.

"Ms. Marsena," he added, with his inflection denoting a topical change of conversation, "I must ask at this point that the contents of this conversation be held in strictest confidence. Lives are in the balance, including my own, where the eternal peace you speak of may not be everyone's final destination. Errant words from you possibly could limit the ability of this mission to 'harmonize,' as you put it."

Sharene's concentration was distracted as she spotted a light-brown object heading down the recently painted, beige wall facing the head of the bed. A large-bodied, long-legged spider, maybe two inches long from leg tip to leg tip, moved diagonally along the wall in spurts of subterranean-generated life. Her focus turned to the intruder that had the appearance of a cane spider Pastor Hemri once had described to her. She wasn't afraid, but momentarily was distracted.

Welch followed her eyes when she turned her head to look at the wall by the headboard, and, seeing the spider, grabbed and rolled up a newspaper he'd earlier placed on the nightstand on his side of the bed. In one continuous motion, he lunged across the bed and smashed the arachnid with the rolled newspaper before it could gain amnesty behind the bed.

The spider fell out of sight behind the headboard, leaving a small stain on the wall that represented the end of a short life.

Welch regained his seat on the wooden folding chair, returned the newspaper to the second nightstand, and continued his discourse as if nothing had happened. Sharene, on the other hand, though unmoved by the loss of the spider, was unsettled by the man's decisive quickness in implementing its death.

"Before I specifically tell you what we'd like you to do, I'll tell you how it will be accomplished," said Welch.

The man in the tank-topped T-shirt with unruly hair visible along his neckline leaned toward her across the bed once more, as if trying to make certain no one else would hear his words.

"We will, if you are willing, fly you from a private airport in Washington, D.C., to a mountainous training camp in a South American country where you will be given a rigorous two-week course to prepare you for your mission. Once the training is complete and your instructors are confident in your ability to carry out the mission and survive, you and at least one trainer will be relocated by airplane to the South American country where Sandy Kroghan is being held. A switch then will be made, where you will become Sandy Kroghan in the eyes of her captors. You must remain in their compound for several hours and perform some tasks we'll teach you to do. Once that's done, you will escape from the compound according to a plan we've taught you. A helicopter will be waiting for you in a nearby field, and you will be flown out of the country, your work completed."

The man who called himself Welch leaned back in his folding chair and stuck his left foot, covered by a worn, leather moccasin, on the bed between them.

Sharene started to speak, to insert a question about time into the discussion, but was interrupted as Welch retracted his left foot and bent toward her yet a third time. He said, "I must warn you, Ms. Marsena, that the people who hold your look-alike captive won't hesitate to kill. Don't accept this assignment lightly, or for romantic reasons. The two weeks of training will be hot and strenuous, and your hours at that compound could be hell."

Sharene's infected blood cried out to do the right thing, regardless of cost. Too, an energized flow of adrenaline was rejuvenating her veins.

The hunter listened from inside the room without interfering with the human interchange being made in his presence. His stake in Sharene's future was graver than he cared to admit.

She prayed under her breath, then, for direction, and the hunter evaporated from her presence like Dracula in sunshine.

"How will we (Welch smiled at her pronoun selection) accomplish the switch?" she asked, once again maintaining the posture of feminine correctness she'd held before the spider crossed the wall.

"We have an informant within the fortress who knows much about the Cablos' operation. He tells us that in about one month Ms. Kroghan and two of Cablos' soldiers, maybe even three, will travel to Meino Cablos' house by the sea for a week of respite from the stresses of living in the middle of an international drug-trafficking operation. We are confident that we can subdue her captors and rescue Ms. Kroghan at that time."

Sharene interjected quickly, "Then what's the purpose of a switch at all? You don't need me at all!"

Again, the man called Welch chose his words carefully, stroking his chin as if testing to see how his morning shave was holding up.

"Now, Ms. Marsena," he began slowly, "I certainly don't know what exact words Mr. Purcell used to bring you here tonight, but let me guess. Would it be accurate to say that Mr. Purcell-l-l," and he intentionally slurred the final consonant of Sherm Purcell's last name, "shall we say, 'intimated' that your value would be in the saving of Sandy Kroghan's life?"

Sharene glanced at the spider stain on the wall, and then back to the federal agent who carefully was studying her reaction to his words.

She refused to respond verbally.

"Am I accurate in assuming that Mr. Purcell simplified the story he told you?" asked Welch. "I'm not surprised. I know Mr. Purcell far better than you do. The truth of the matter, Ms. Marsena, is that I wouldn't be here to meet you in an attempt to save one civilian life. My time is too valuable. No, Ms. Marsena, I'm asking you to help destroy a family-owned drug empire that's already killed dozens of people who got in its way, and ruined the lives of countless others through the international distribution of illegal drugs."

"And how am I to accomplish that?" asked Sharene, who tentatively was becoming excited by the conversation.

"To our knowledge, the entire operation runs on a pyramid-type structure with no guidelines in place to transfer power peacefully," said Welch. "The top figure in that pyramid is Ms. Kroghan's boyfriend, Meino Cablos. You are being asked to help us kill Mr. Cablos, then get safely out of the country while we undermine a pyramid lacking its dictatorial leader."

Sharene rose abruptly from the brown, vinyl chair, and Welch feared for the success of the plan.

"I have to be alone to think and pray," she said. "Maybe you understand my concerns, and maybe you don't, Mr. Welch."

He stood up as well, walked around the foot of the bed to the door, and unlocked the dead bolt. Yet, before opening the wooden door into the night, he returned to the side of the bed nearest the window and flicked off the dim lamp. Residual light generated by outside streetlights sifted through the closed curtain, keeping the room from becoming completely dark. Welch's eyes adjusted to the dim lighting quicker than Sharene's, and he walked past her and peered through the curtain. Seeing nothing unusual, he returned to the far side of the bed and turned the light back on.

He returned to the doorway.

Sharene stepped within touching distance of the undercover agent as she prepared to leave, then tried to speak. She was silenced when he gently placed his right forefinger to her lips. Then, the man who called himself Welch gave the holy sign of the Catholic cross, and, without another word, walked into a nearby room down the hallway, into what she assumed was the bathroom. He returned with a small package of chocolates. It was a duplicate of the one Sherm Purcell had handed her when last they'd been together, the package with the note inside that had brought her to this room at this time.

She still lacked an emotional response about this man called Welch.

He smiled big, and she suddenly sensed that he would respect her decision regarding his proposal, whatever that decision would be.

"If this isn't what the Lord wants you to do, then I wish you well in whatever you choose to do with your life. But if it is, be on time, and be prepared to leave that night."

He handed her the box of chocolates, opened the wooden motel door, and watched in silence as Sharene walked away. She left with many more questions than answers about what life had in store for her, about where her willingness to serve would lead.

From the rear of a car parked in front of motel room number eighteen, she was hailed by a new voice. It said, "Clara, I think Ecclesiastes might have the answer you seek."

Sharene walked away quickly without ever seeing a face to accompany the voice. Under no circumstances was she going to respond to that strange name Sherm Purcell had given to her.

CHAPTER 6

Carol Marsena lifted the lid of a large, yellow kettle, and steam rose from it in vaporizing wisps that quickly disappeared as if Elijah himself was offering brief sacrifices in the Marsena kitchen.

It was a special occasion for Carol and Jake. Their only daughter was home, and the family again was together. They didn't want to let their thoughts wander beyond this one evening.

Peter, on the other hand, looked toward tomorrow with a smile of anticipation. He had no way of knowing how much his sister was suffering.

Carol smiled as she ladled the hot clam chowder Sharene had always loved into four deep soup bowls. She walked into the dining room and handed one bowl to her daughter and a second to Peter, then fought back tears as she retraced her steps into the kitchen. Regaining her composure, she returned with bowls of chowder for herself and Jake.

The father of the house said grace.

Sharene, extending delicate fingers with no rings on them, reached for corn bread and homemade strawberry jam, while Peter jabbered about roughhousing Bobby's little sister in the Tagwell pool, and about loud birds that had interrupted their play temporarily.

Jake spoke of work and the need for new tires on the family car.

Sharene smiled like her mother, only prettier, and gave no indication of the tumult raging within her body and soul. Her hair was longer than when she'd graduated from high school, and, fluffed with curls, touched fully on her shoulders. She pleased her mother by walking into the kitchen and ladling more clam chowder into her bowl.

"Remember when I told you that you were on TV?" asked Peter of Sharene when she returned to the table with more chowder. "Well, you probably already know this, but it wasn't really you. Last night they showed her again, and she looks just like you. She got kidnapped a long time ago and they think she's still alive," he continued importantly. "In fact, they are offering a humongous reward to get her back.

"And that's the only reason I knew it wasn't you," he continued, while giggling chunks of corn bread out of his mouth and into his left hand. "No one ever would pay that much to get you back."

Sharene scooted her chair away from the table as if to give chase, and Jake Marsena, with prompting from his spouse, assumed the task of counseling young Peter on his choice of humor.

After dinner, Carol and Sharene removed dishes from the dining-room table and replaced them with more bowls from the same Tuscan set, bowls filled with ice cream smothered with fresh peaches.

"I'm sorry," said Peter after receiving words of instruction from his father, but both he and Sharene knew he didn't mean it.

"Sharene, did you hear about Jordan?" Peter asked eagerly, excitedly, as if this impending transfer of information was the sole purpose of the meal.

The elder Marsenas exchanged glances of concern.

"No, I haven't," responded Sharene, displaying her own eagerness. "What's new with Jordan Norton?"

"He's getting married!" exclaimed the youngest at the table, oblivious to the new wound he'd inflicted upon his sister.

Sharene gasped. She reflexively looked to her parents who both nodded in silence, fully aware that nothing they could say to their daughter would diminish this new and, to her, unexpected source of pain. Sharene tried to smile, and found she was lightheaded, dizzy, as if she'd been bending at the waist to pick up bright lilies sprouting from the earth on a sunny day, stooped too long, then stood up too fast. Her blood and oxygen suddenly were out of sync.

It was several moments before she caught her breath enough to ask, "Whom is he going to marry?"

"Chiska Sullivan," said the mother.

"That will make Chiska very happy, I'm sure," Sharene said quickly, with little inflection in her voice.

The ice cream was melting and the Marsena family ate dessert in silence. Sharene dabbled in her bowl with a spoon, but ate no more.

Long after the dishes were washed and after Sharene had time to retreat for solitude, the beautiful maiden with imminent death tainting her immune system returned and asked her parents to turn off the television because she had an announcement to make.

Waiting for Peter, who'd been listening to records in his room, Sharene silently prayed for the Holy Spirit to speak through her. A separation with their blessings was her goal, and hopefully some trusting acceptance for a mission she hardly could speak about. She knew, too, that this might be the last time shy of heaven that she and her earthly family would be together. Sharene, in that prayer, asked to shake the role of daughter and sister, and speak with the authority and conviction of a saint.

She asked for much.

"How long is this gonna take?" asked Peter impatiently.

"I'll only take a few minutes of your time," she said softly.

Jake wanted to claim his monthly cigar to assuage an undefined anxiety, but only in passing. The cigar had to be smoked out-of-doors, and his daughter's announcement would unfold in front of his favorite recliner. Carol and Peter sat across the modest living room from Jake, at opposite ends of the powder-blue sofa. Sharene stepped past a roll-top desk made of oak decades before by Jake's father. On it was a bright lamp that provided most of the lighting in a living room whose overhead light had been earlier turned off to avoid planting a glare on the television screen. Sharene walked between the sofa and Jake's recliner and sat to her mother's right in a stiff wicker chair with gray cushions that Carol recently had purchased at a church auction. It wasn't comfortable, but Sharene didn't notice.

"What I want to tell you, I can't say for fear of jeopardizing others. What I ask is for your faith and your prayers.

"I'll soon be heading out of the country on a mission I feel is for God," Sharene said. "I've prayed unceasingly on this matter and am convinced this is what He wants me to do."

Even young Peter gave Sharene his rapt attention.

"I don't know when I will be back."

Fornice Street, like the Marsena living room, immediately went silent like the recesses of Calypso's Cave long after Odysseus's daring escape. Angels atop the high gables of the nearby church were awed by the sudden stillness of the night.

It was impatient Peter who broke the stillness that could have lasted anywhere from an eon to a microsecond.

Like his namesake wielding a sword in the Garden of Gethsemane, Peter totally misunderstood the implications of the moment, and asked, "But where are you going?"

Carol Marsena noticed a resolve about her daughter at that moment that she'd admired often, a resolve of faith not easily shaken.

"You cannot go where I go, Peter, but there will come a day when you will understand what this is all about. It's best at this time that you know nothing about my journey," she said kindly.

Then the quiet father, who rarely raised his voice, rarely so much as voiced a strong personal opinion, rose to champion the cause of fatherhood.

"You will do no such thing unless I hear much more about this whole affair," stated Jake Marsena sternly while rising to his feet. His voice bordered on anger as he stomped across the room and towered over Sharene. He spoke to her firmly about family and family values, about how Sharene couldn't ignore their love for her and cast lots into the unknown.

"But it's not the unknown to me," rallied the daughter.

Jake stilled what he interpreted as impudence with a stare that temporarily unnerved Sharene. She looked away from his challenge and tried to regroup her thoughts.

The man of Jewish roots who'd publicly affirmed, yet never fully accepted Jesus Christ as the Son of God, stared across a chasm at his beloved daughter whose faith was firm. He sensed something was missing, some key to the enigma Sharene was proposing to live, yet bulled dead ahead with what to him was the conviction of right.

"I'm not saying you can't do whatever it is you are proposing, Sharene, but you must at least share a purpose for your actions. We who love and have devoted our lives to your growth and happiness deserve to know more," he said.

Carol Marsena spoke from her end of the powder-blue sofa. "Jake, she is nineteen years old, and I don't think ..."

Jake cut her off abruptly like neither Sharene nor Peter had ever heard him do. "I don't care if she's fifty-two, Carol. She still has a responsibility, a duty, to respect and uplift her family."

Still standing, Jake's heated looks went from Sharene to Carol and back to Sharene.

Sharene, sitting in the uncomfortable wicker chair, looked up at her father and felt deep love for him. She wanted to say the right thing, but the words that materialized in her mind were all wrong, too easily misinterpreted by her father's tenseness and too easily misstated by her own.

She forgot to pray.

Jake momentarily paced away from her, then turned and asked, "What can be so mysterious about a mission for God? His missions have been going on for thousands of years and there have never been any great secrets."

Sharene didn't want to cross her father ever, especially in his current state of anger, but needed to express herself and, from some hidden source, found a sudden peace and sense of power she'd never known before. It was as if her lack of prayer made no difference. She now was receiving the benefits of an earlier prayer that had invoked the blood of Jesus.

Sharene arose, then stepped forward to touch her father's arm and plead with her eyes. Jake Marsena's uncustomary anger was melted by her gentleness, and he allowed his only daughter to lead him back to his chair. He was worried, subdued, and almost apologetic.

Still blessed with her inner calm, Sharene walked to the sofa and sat down on the end by her mother. From her mouth came words she barely understood.

"I'm not going to tell the three of you who I'm not," she said. "You know. You know who I am and who I'm not better than anyone else. Yet, if there is any weakness in your understanding of me, it's in my spiritual life. You raised me to believe and trust with all my heart in the Living God, and I do. But since my encounter in South Carolina, ..." and she paused to look directly at Peter, who barely understood the word 'rape' and had no knowledge of a new disease that had polluted the blood of his sister, "since then," she continued, "the immediacy of my personal timetable has changed. You, Father and Mother, and especially you, Peter, can coast for a few years assuming the Second Coming is years, decades, or even eons into the future. I have to realize and live my personal spirituality now."

"But why can't you share how you're going to do that?" persisted her earthly father.

"My options are not your options," said Sharene. "My options to realize my potential are severely limited by time. Those options are based solely on faith and wouldn't stand up to your scrutiny."

Since sitting beside her mother, Sharene had delivered all of her words quietly and lovingly, yet with firm conviction.

"I'm hurt by your lack of faith in your family," said Jake. "You are violating a sacred trust that you've been taught since the day you were born."

He rose again, then paused while towering over both women in his household. He looked taller than Sharene could ever remember.

"Come on, Peter. Let's go for a walk," said Jake. "We have important things to talk about." And the father and the son walked out of the Marsena living room and into the night, shutting the outside door behind them.

Peter left the room with a look of fear, as if he were going to be punished for something he neither did nor understood.

After leaving the house, Jake Marsena and his only son proceeded into a world of artificial streetlights, flailing insects, and an occasional automobile driven by others fighting comparable battles initiated by a common, silent enemy dressed in camouflage.

Inside, Sharene turned to her mother with calmness, and asked, "How will we ever explain this so he can understand?"

Without addressing Sharene's situation, Carol Marsena responded with her own brand of resolve. She said her husband understood far more than Sharene was aware of, that the blueprints already had been etched, and that one day soon a true Inner Light would illuminate the soul of her father. When that day came, she said, Jake Marsena would cast aside all worries and doubts, and become aware of the perfect unity of God's world.

"I don't know what the catalyst will be, or even if one will be necessary, but one day soon your father will understand all that you have tried to tell him about your trust and faith in God," said the mother.

Sharene hugged her mother at length, then went to her room to read and sit quietly. She opened a book called Ecclesiastes and turned to the third chapter. She hummed as she read, hummed a popular rock 'n' roll tune she'd played many times on her turntable, and the incongruence of the two—scripture and rock 'n' roll—somehow merged in perfect harmony. "Everything ... purpose ... time ... heaven."

The reunion with her father later that night in front of the television set commandeered by Peter was courteous and warm. Jake loved his daughter dearly, but lacked understanding about life's purpose for her. They spoke quietly, sporadically, and tenderly, yet Sharene, intuitive in many ways, was unaware of the new pain that had settled in the heart of Jake Marsena.

For, somewhere on his long walk with Peter, even Jake didn't know where or how, a falling sensation of sadness had penetrated his soul. On one step of his walk through life Jake Marsena was a loving, yet angry, protective father trying to spare his beautiful daughter from additional suffering. But, by the time that seemingly inconsequential next step reached the pavement, a light of recognition blinked on in his soul. He realized in that very instant that his daughter, Sharene Marsena, no longer was his. The sudden recognition brought tears to his eyes, and a man who loved his family deeply began weeping in the sight of his son.

"What's wrong, Father?" asked Peter with genuine concern.

And the father of two only could shake his head and look away into the troubled Alabama night. Had he known what to say or understood the magnitude of change within himself (neither being the case,) even then, words wouldn't have been spoken to his son at that time.

He neither understood the insight nor where it came from, but in that instant Jake Marsena knew without doubt that Sharene now belonged to another, more competent being. He felt sad, yet at the same time a small measure of gladness because Sharene's priority could offer renewed hope and joy for her, in stark contrast to the frustration and anger he'd internalized daily since the violation of her womanhood so many months before. He felt stained, yet for the first time since that damned event in South Carolina, cautiously hopeful.

The tears, like the anger before them, were rare experiences for the father, indicative of emotional peaks he still didn't understand.

It was too soon.

What made that night's reunion in front of the television set especially difficult for Jake was the knowledge that he wouldn't see his daughter again. Lights were creeping in like the dawn of a new day, the lights within his soul, and Sharene's special corner of the picture was either empty or too bright for him to see.

Peter continued to watch TV. No one expected him to understand.

Sharene felt nauseous, and was the first one to say good night and leave the living room. In the bathroom down the hallway, she turned up the volume on the bright-faced clock radio to muffle any sound she would make, and placed her beautiful face over the cold, porcelain toilet bowl. Then, she heaved and shuddered painfully until almost all of the chowder and corn bread was gone from her body. She continued to convulse until her stomach was empty, then heaved some more. Her blood splashed the sides of the white toilet bowl until her exhausted body quit convulsing. Then, she flushed it all from view.

Sharene, gulping in new air, shut off the radio with thoughts of annoyed determination crossing her mind. She failed to hear the Christian radio station's final offering, "All is right with my soul."

To no one's surprise, Sharene boarded a bus back to Georgia the following morning.

127

CHAPTER 7

Life was easy for Sandy Kroghan. She was beautiful; she was smart; she could converse with anyone; and, of primary importance, her parents were rich.

Her mother and father had started a patenting business long before her birth and, with hard work, became eminent parts designers for a major airline. Sandy took yachts, large swimming pools, and servants to be her birthright, things that never could be lost. She exhibited the confidence of a youthful Esau in the matter.

Although her parents always were too busy to be Christ-focused in their own lives, they sent Sandy to a private Catholic school grades one through twelve. The fact that God legally had been banned from public schools about the time of Sandy's birth didn't play into her parents' decision to send her to a private school. Instead, it supposedly was a documented fact at the time that private schools gave students a richer education, and Sandy's parents wanted nothing but the best for their daughter.

Sandy got just enough religious instruction at the school to introduce her to guilt and confusion.

In her junior year of high school, the lovely Sandy Kroghan had an affair with a young student teacher from an affiliated private school and became pregnant. Wanting to do the right thing, Sandy's parents insisted upon, and paid for, a top-quality abortion. The would-be father escaped the wrath of the Kroghans and the retribution of the two Catholic schools by moving voluntarily to another state to peddle his educational expertise.

As expected from birth, Sandy enrolled at a small New York college after graduating from high school, but soon expressed disdain for what she was being taught. She felt smart enough to mingle at the adult parties of her parents, and certainly couldn't justify time spent earning a college degree on the grounds of what it could do for her financially. She attended at the insistence of her parents, and participated minimally.

Cocaine had been an occasional recreation in high school, in fact had provided a social bond with a certain student teacher from another school who'd impacted her life, but in college the expensive drug became routine. She liked people, and people she liked, liked her cocaine. Readily available at the time, the white powder from South America consistently usurped time that could have been spent on homework. Close to flunking out of college in her sophomore year, Sandy was saved that social embarrassment one night by a thundering knock on her door. The toilet couldn't flush fast enough to swallow all of the evidence, but it probably did reduce the magnitude of charges against Ms. Kroghan and five others who were in her apartment at the time.

It undoubtedly angered the arresting officers to learn that the six students were back on the streets within a matter of hours. Sandy's parents posted stiff bail and provided high-quality legal services for all six of them.

No one went to trial, but in the plea bargaining that deterred such an unwelcome event, Sandy Kroghan, facing graver charges than her peers, agreed to do community-service work at a Salvation Army shelter in Queens.

And, ironically, it was the time she spent working at the Salvation Army that proved to be a turning point in Sandy's young life. She always had been recognized for her physical beauty, but the street people, the homeless she worked with at the Salvation Army, saw even more in her. They saw someone extending compassion beyond her birthright, and responded to her as an equal. They joked with the beautiful "volunteer" through broken or wide-gapped teeth, and took her to meetings where brass horns blared loudly and bright uniforms were worn.

Some of the homeless even talked to her about hope.

Sandy Kroghan, for the first time in her life, glimpsed something of true value at Salvation Army meals and meetings. The plastic façade of being rich in a world of cocaine and self-generated arrogance was being stripped from her reality as she began grasping the seemingly incongruent concept that Christ's atonement-for-soul offering was identical for rich and poor alike. Distant Catholic teachings about a camel and the eye of a needle subtly resurfaced, adding some insight into her muddled, protected past.

Sandy's involvement with the poor made her feel good inside, and it showed in her beautiful smile that always had melted the hearts of the rich and student teachers, yet was merely one of many beautiful smiles at the Salvation Army.

When her hours of public service were completed, Sally Ann workers urged her to stay on as an employee and work for limited wages. They didn't really expect a rich, beautiful, young woman to return to share permanently with the homeless and downtrodden, but asked for the sake of their clients.

Sandy smiled again, and her eyes glowed. "I'll come back some day, if only for a visit," she said.

She returned to her parents and shared her desire to return to college and study social work.

Mr. and Mrs. Kroghan not only opposed the idea, but booked Sandy on a tour of South American countries to give her time to better evaluate her future options.

And so, at age nineteen, and trying to turn an important corner in her life, Sandy Kroghan boarded an airplane for a tour of several South American nations. She knew much for a nineteen-year-old, had had an abortion, and had experienced the worlds of drugs and the homeless. Still, Sandy Kroghan knew there was much more to be learned. Of prime importance to her, she'd never even known love, and longed for that experience.

Christ Almighty, she'd never so much as ever been engaged.

CHAPTER 8

It was late afternoon when she arrived, and the streets were crowded. At first Sharene compared the scene to Hollywood representations of India, but only briefly. The gross numbers probably were comparable, but the colors and people were radically different. This unnamed city, somewhere in Paraguay, had the tattered colors of ancient Baghdad. People meandered about as if on a mission to shop in open markets, feed the family, and get everyone to the big stadium in the heart of the city in time to view a preliminary match leading to the World Cup soccer championships.

Sharene was tired. She'd slept some on the small plane, even when it had stopped to refuel, but was a far cry from being rested. When she merged with the rambling crowd after deplaning, she wondered if she'd ever gain a speed comparable to the thousands of others grinding through the streets around her. Although they weren't moving quickly, all were moving faster than Sharene Marsena, and suddenly being beautiful and from Plateau, Alabama was inconsequential.

Perspiration rolled down her face because of the humid, afternoon heat that reflected off the pavement. She held several bills of Paraguayan currency given to her when she'd left the airplane, and fought through a mass of natives in tank tops and colorful pants. The natives, though not in haste, seemed focused on traveling in the direction from which Sharene had come, making her steps that much more difficult. She repeatedly bumped into men, women, and children, and said, "I'm sorry," as if anyone could understand her, or even cared.

On the first major thoroughfare she came to, Sharene Marsena spotted, then corralled a taxi driver who repeatedly nodded and smiled, was most interested in the currency she waved, but was unable to determine where she wanted to go. After several major attempts to communicate both verbally and with gestures, the taxi driver smiled one last time, pointed to his wristwatch as if he had a pending soccer match to attend, and drove away, leaving the young traveler exasperated and too tired to think straight. She was alone in the heat of a foreign country; alone in a large, undulating crowd of people.

Sharene had exerted volumes of energy trying to communicate with the taxi driver, and then, after crossing the wide sidewalk, wilted to the hard surface below her, her back against a building. She rested in a sitting position. As she sat there, exhausted, Sharene found herself reciting a rote rendition of The Lord's Prayer. Still, the mob of people seemed content to pass her by like the priest and the Levite had another needy person many centuries before, only this time with even less interest in her presence.

"May I help you?"

The words, in perfect English, seemed to come from nowhere.

Sharene looked up and smiled weakly at a sturdy woman in army fatigues with short-cropped hair.

The answer to her prayer had come quickly, as if the Lord was listening intently and eager to help.

"Oh yes, if you will," responded Sharene hopefully, while trying to shake loose from the wave of fatigue engulfing her body. "Could you help me up?"

The welcome, European-looking woman in a short-sleeve khaki T-shirt reached down like a man, grabbed Sharene's hand, and hoisted the one in discomfort to her feet. The woman's application of muscle to technique made the ascent effortless, and she held Sharene's hand longer than necessary. She broke physical contact an instant before alarms would have sounded in Sharene's mind.

"I'm looking for the Napoleon Mark," Sharene said. "I believe it's close, but haven't the slightest clue in which direction I should go from here."

Many Paraguayans, without comment or apparent concern, detoured around the two White women now standing on the sidewalk by the building. Seemingly as many in number as the sands by the sea, passersby paid minimal attention to Sharene and her new friend, only taking an extra step or two to move around them and move on with their lives. Contrary to the streets of New York City, where Sandy Kroghan and countless others regularly checked their watches and raced to the next appointment or deadline, the element of time in this Paraguayan city, other than to attend a soccer event, seemed to be of far less consequence.

The crowd flowed like a slow-moving river, which, no matter the directions of its many tributaries, eventually would have its waters reach its destination in an ocean. The individuals in the crowd, like water in the river, inevitably would return to their source. Once there a second time, each would learn if their fate was to be wafted to the heavens, given another chance to right past wrongs, or be tossed into a bottomless pit.

The strong woman in battle fatigues said, "Follow me," and began strolling through the crowd like Francis Marion, craftily, without drawing notice to who she was or where she was going. Sharene followed instinctively, fighting off exhaustion with adrenaline. She lost what bearings she might have had within the first four steps, if not before, and banked her hopes on the woman artfully gliding through the crowd before her. She must maintain contact, Sharene thought to herself over and over, yet on two occasions the woman slipped from view, leaving Sharene sweating, panting, and near panic in a hot, foreign world she didn't understand. She was too tired to think, maybe even to pray. Then, within no more than two minutes of the last sighting, the unusual woman would reappear, slouching in a shaded corner of a crowded bazaar, or standing boldly, arms folded, in the direct flow of foot traffic in front of Sharene.

The woman's focus always was on Sharene Marsena, and Sharene, without a solitary thought to do otherwise, continued to follow.

When she did enter the Napoleon Mark, Sharene thought the open entrance of the hotel's wide front doorway was a wrong turn. She pivoted to return to the bright sunshine when, with one extra glance, she noticed the same Napoleon Mark insignia on the wall behind the clerk's counter that was on the envelope she'd been waving along with the Paraguayan currency. The envelope was sweaty in her hand, but the insignia on it was identical to the one on the wall.

The woman in army fatigues again disappeared from view.

Sharene Marsena, lacking energy, shared her name with the squat woman behind the counter and was handed the key to a room. Without an additional word, the woman led Sharene to her quarters like a mother would a toddling child—slowly, patiently, almost with reverence. She took the key back from Sharene's grasp, opened the door for her, handed it back, and left smiling.

The tired American traveler closed the door, leaving the world behind, and, without so much as a splash of water on her soiled face or arms, dropped upon the hard bed and fell asleep.

After seeing "the beautiful American" to her room, the clerk returned to her station and talked in the local language with the short-haired woman in army fatigues who'd reappeared in the hotel foyer. The two were most amiable, and, after minutes of quiet dialogue, the woman who'd led Sharene to the Napoleon Mark wrote a brief note and handed it to the clerk. The clerk placed it in a small, wooden cubicle behind the counter and went about her business.

Sharene thought it was early the following morning when she opened one blurry eye, saw streams of what she didn't recognize to be night lighting, and closed it again. She imagined a new place, a cheery place, and Jordan Norton sleeping on the bed beside her. Sharene wanted to reach to this loved friend, to delicately finger the features of his young face, to watch him awaken and know she was inches away waiting for the day's first kiss. But, strangely, she was anchored to the bed, unable to reach toward her lover.

Then, Sharene remembered his engagement to Chiska Sullivan, and broke away from her fantasy by turning her body toward the water-stained wall next to her bed. Coming to her senses, Sharene acknowledged that Jordan probably would never again be beside her, and that this wasn't such a cheery place after all. She, one who'd never previously been any further from home than Washington, D.C., now was in a moderate hotel in an unnamed city in Paraguay with a small amount of local currency. And all she had to look forward to was encapsulated in her faith that someone would come for her and somehow arrange a trade of her diseased body for that of another.

Sharene sat upright, then clutched the leather purse tied securely to her waist by a black thong. She recognized it was dark outside and switched on a soft light emitted by a lamp placed on the stand by her bed. From the purse, she pulled out her wallet with an unstamped passport and a miniature, complete Bible with minuscule print. Her eyes were strong, and she turned the small pages to the third chapter of Ecclesiastes to justify her insanity. Then, she purposely turned to the final chapter of Galatians and read a verse from the middle of that chapter that said, "And let us not be weary in well doing: for in due season we shall reap, if we faint not."

She returned the wallet and the Bible to the leather pouch, drew water into a mid-sized porcelain bathtub, secured a towel, undressed, and bathed. The cool water cleansed her body like a dip with soap in an Alabama lake, and, with additional therapy generated by several hours of sleep, renewed her sense of purpose.

Sharene found no one in the foyer of the Napoleon Mark when she ventured forth with the key to her room dangling loosely between her thumb and forefinger. The hands on a wall clock near the insignia behind the clerk's counter informed her it was well past midnight. She ventured through the open-air doorway of the hotel and saw that the crowd so evident upon her arrival practically was gone. Occasional drunks and stragglers pierced the otherwise quiet night with grunts and echoing cobblestone shuffles, but the lass from rural Alabama was unafraid. She discovered the night air to be soothing as she walked toward a nearby hooded street light. Yet, as she stopped to gaze around her, she found the air, if she remained immobile, almost too cool on her sensitive skin.

While absent-mindedly window-shopping a short distance from the Napoleon Mark, courtesy of the night's artificial light, Sharene sensed someone close at hand. Then she heard gruff breathing and smelled the scent of cheap tobacco and alcohol she'd always associated with Jordan's high school drinking buddy, Riggsy.

She turned toward the aroma and saw, at close range, an obviously drunken, middle-aged local man watching her with penetrating interest in his red eyes as if she were a dream and he were Sigmund Freud. Then, as she watched in growing dread, his curiosity metamorphosed to another level, from appreciation to desire, and he reached to touch the apparent apparition standing before him.

Sharene backed away, step by step, until she was pinned against a big glass window separating an array of sweets and candies from the outside world.

The stench alone was stifling to the young woman, and she reacted by bolting away from the man's obvious desire. She ran hastily, foolishly, directly away from the Napoleon Mark with terror in her heart. She heard the man running behind her, coming closer, and was surprised when his steps went silent. Sharene ran a little further, less than twenty yards further, then stopped and turned in the direction from which she'd come. In the distance, she saw the Napoleon Mark and the safety it represented for her life, but she saw little else. Thinking of the Mark as a safe harbor, a refuge, Sharene slowly and cautiously retraced her steps, constantly searching the night shadows for her would-be attacker.

As she approached the area where noise from his pursuing footsteps had ceased, Sharene heard a low moan. A few more steps and she saw her pursuer writhing on the cobblestone at the end of the square about fifty yards from the hotel. Cautiously, she came closer and became reacquainted with the man's offensive smell. She quickly assessed the situation and found she was safe from harm with her potential assailant inexplicably disabled on the cobblestone. No one else could be seen, and Sharene had no explanation for what had just transpired.

She returned to the Napoleon Mark while the woman in khaki, unseen by Sharene, watched her from the shadows. Sharene proceeded to her room, read two passages from Ezekiel, and confined herself to her bed for the rest of the night.

She was awake and thinking of Sherm Purcell the next morning when the artificial lights outside her one window were replaced by nature's early radiance. Another day had arrived.

She swung her bare feet onto the cool tile floor and dressed in the same clothes she'd worn the previous day, the only clothes she had with her.

Sharene had arrived at the airport for the second CIA meeting with spare clothing, enough to fill a medium-sized suitcase, but had been discouraged from taking that suitcase, or anything in it, with her.

"You are entering a new world," she'd been told, "a world where mobility equates to life."

Hence, she dressed quietly this morning in the same clothes she'd arrived in.

The inflow of early morning air that came through the window she opened was fresh and clean. Sharene looked at red and beige and gray roofs outside her window, most of them small and flat, and on them saw many short, heavily clothed women draping laundry over clotheslines. It already was a clear, blue day, and the women's laundry moved gently in a warm, sun-driven wind.

Lacking direction for the hours ahead, Sharene left her room and entered the hotel lobby where a different female clerk handed her a note. All it said in scribbled penmanship was "ten a.m." It hardly was past nine, so she entered a small restaurant in the hotel, ate a filling breakfast of potatoes and eggs, and returned to wait in the open-air lobby. She sat in a stuffed red chair that matched the décor, and noticed for the first time the heavy accordion-like bastioned door, made of metal, which obviously provided protection for those inside whenever it was closed and locked.

An elderly local man wearing striped wool pants and sporting a full, Amish-looking beard sat in a full-armed wicker chair across the lobby from Sharene. He looked above the American girl at large reproductions of French nobility captured in gold-painted frames of etched wood. He stroked the black-and-white house cat sitting on his lap. The cat looked completely at ease, as if it and the elderly gentleman met there daily at 10 a.m.

The cat shed both black and white hairs on the man's worn, striped pants.

The man occasionally stole glances at the pretty White woman sitting before him, wondering to himself why life had planted her in the Napoleon Mark.

Sharene, aware of his looks, returned no smiles or nods of recognition. The previous night's frightening experience had better prepared her for her mission.

At ten minutes past the hour, the cat withdrew from the elderly man's affections and walked across the stone floor to make an acquaintance with Sharene Marsena, but Sharene wasn't interested. She was contemplating her plight if no one came to offer direction, plus didn't want cat hairs on her only clothes. She leaned over and explained quietly, but audibly, to the cat that she had too many pressing concerns for her to strike up a relationship.

The old man, listening to her words in the quiet room, said, "I speak American."

Before she could respond, the tall woman with smooth, muscled arms extending from a sleeveless khaki undershirt, the same woman who'd escorted her to the Napoleon Mark, stepped from the out-of-doors and into the lobby. In one curt, succinct wave of her arm, she motioned Sharene to step out of the hotel. Then she walked to the old man and quietly spoke in his ear.

The old man rose with a chuckle, and took the hard coins she offered him.

Sharene didn't see the coin exchange between the strong woman and the old man because, with the morning's sunshine penetrating the doorway, she was busy double-checking the safety of her Bible and passport.

Without a word, the woman motioned Sharene into a camouflage-decorated Jeep that looked as inconspicuous on a busy pedestrian-dominated square in this downtown Paraguayan city as hot tea on a hot Alabama afternoon. The vehicle's color didn't detract from the surroundings, but foot traffic was all that Sharene previously had seen on the rough cobblestone in front of the hotel. People ebbed and flowed around the slowly progressing Jeep like membranes around an amoeba, and Jake Marsena's daughter soon was lost once more.

The woman skillfully manned the vehicle through the human masses, and the Jeep gained some speed as they reached the outskirts of the city. She eventually eased the vehicle from the cobblestone onto smooth pavement, a regular two-lane road where the Jeep darted around and through a collage of very old trucks and pickups. They also met a new Ferrari heading into the city, some rustic English automobiles—snub-nosed, with high rooflines—and a mixture of animal-drawn carts and wagons both taking goods into the city, and returning empty; the latters' missions accomplished.

Sharene and the tall woman spoke little on the trip. Both were intent on how the Jeep was being driven. Jerkily, but always under control, the woman, who called herself Nadia, wove the two-passenger vehicle with an open top and roll bar through a mix of slow and fast-moving traffic. She drove between donkey-driven carts carrying bags of rice to market and occasional sports cars driven by youths whose fathers made big money in the meatpacking business.

After passing one such donkey cart heading away from the large city, Nadia cranked the steering wheel to the left and turned off of the pavement onto a summer-dusty road with no signs to indicate where it might lead. The dust immediately enveloped the open, slow-moving Jeep and the women it carried, curling upward from what soon no longer could be called a country road. Nadia seemingly drove by memory over storm creek beds and parched terrain that virtually became trackless as dust gave way to rocks and hard-baked earth as they reached higher elevations.

When midsize green tents, partially hidden by gnarled hardwood trees, were spotted on flat terrain, Sharene was again tired and dirty. They'd only been gone from the hotel two hours.

Nadia applied brakes to the camouflage-decorated Jeep, coming to a halt a few feet in front of one of the three tents. By now, the sun was high overhead and the temperature well into the nineties.

The dust, absent during much of the steep, rocky ascent, was again present on the small plateau the tents sat on, and swirled around Nadia and Sharene upon their arrival. Waiting for the dust to settle, Sharene was slow to dismount from the Jeep to the soft earth below. Nadia got out from the driver's seat, circled around the vehicle, then extended her right hand toward Sharene like the most gallant of gentlemen. Nadia smiled, a pretty, but strong smile, and looked directly into the American girl's trusting eyes. Sharene accepted the offer like a reputable Southern lady, and, once Nadia had control of Sharene's right hand, Sharene Marsena inhospitably was twirled and dumped on to the dirt like an insolent student of Bruce Lee. Sharene gasped for air and rolled into a protective fetal position as the woman walked close to her, close enough to inflict more harms if she wanted to.

"That's better," the tall, strong woman in khaki said. "This is a new world where you trust no one but yourself, Sandy. Get used to that name. From now on, it's the only one you have."

And the woman left Sharene quivering, from both fear and confusion, in the Paraguayan dirt.

She didn't stay down long. In less than a minute, Sharene warily rose to her feet to survey the small camp dominated by three green tents. One, the one Nadia had withdrawn into, was partially supported by a small, windblown tree, while the other two were wholly supported by stakes and ropes. The one to Sharene's immediate right was twice the size of the others, with one solid rope, doubling as a ridgepole, protruding from each end of the tent's ceiling, then angling down to big metal stakes where the rope was looped and tied in two places. Smaller ropes branched from the larger one and were threaded through strategically placed stakes anchored in the ground.

Sharene thought she heard water flowing beyond the large tent, and cautiously headed toward that sound to explore its source, and possibly get a drink, when a man's head popped from the big tent's flapped door.

He said affably, "Sandy, come join me. I have much to share with you," then quickly withdrew from view.

"This place is weird," mumbled Sharene Marsena while rubbing her backside and looking back toward Nadia's tent. Then, without further hesitation, she walked, Bible and passport strapped to her side, to the tent entrance from which the strange little man had appeared and disappeared.

He greeted her warmly, opening the tent flap before she could reach it.

"Welcome, Ms. Sandy. My name is Cameron, and I want to teach you some fine elements of survival," he said.

And the man with double-thick glasses, who couldn't have weighed 135 pounds in his olive fatigues and plastic green visor, unrolled an Afghan rug teeming with handguns and rifles and crossbows and grenades and incinerating devices she'd never seen before, even while watching television.

"You don't expect me to kill anyone?" she asked incredulously, and the man named Cameron laughed heartily.

"Absolutely not," he said. "I just want to train you so you can kill someone if that becomes your choice. Our goal is to get you prepared for anything once you get inside Meino Cablos' domain. We definitely want you to get out alive. If you kill the bastard while you're there, so much the better."

And that was the overriding theme during her two weeks of intensive training in the heat and dirt of Paraguay.

Lessons began immediately after a lunch served by Cameron; a meal of corn bread, rice pudding, and oranges.

Sharene had mixed emotions when she picked up a firearm for the first time, and, while squinting down its barrel, pulled the trigger. Was this something she wanted to learn, or did she even have a choice in the matter? She had some serious questions to ask of Ecclesiastes third chapter, about "… a time for every purpose …"

Most of that first afternoon was spent with the man called Cameron. Sharene quickly sensed that the unusual little man was a trained teacher, a more than competent one who possibly had been without a student for some time. It didn't seem to matter to him that Sharene had no background in the field of armaments. Cameron knew both the basics and how to communicate them. In short hours, Sharene learned much inside and outside of the large tent, both chalkboard technique and in-the-field application.

Time went by quickly, and not long before dark she was given thirty minutes of free time to prepare for dinner. She walked out of Cameron's tent in a daze.

What was life preparing her for? The conflict between what she was being trained to do and what she'd always been taught would have been stronger, should have been stronger, except for the casual inevitability of her surroundings. She'd agreed to accomplish a mission, "a mission for God" she'd told her parents, and now Sharene

Marsena was on the training grounds, readying to do battle against a powerful, unseen enemy.

Life had taken her many turbulent miles since she'd been fifteen years old and dating Jordan Norton.

Attracted by the distinct sound of gurgling water, Sharene found a small creek flowing behind the tent. It only was about three feet wide, a few inches deep, and rolled at a brisk pace over and around small boulders. She knelt on two knees and splashed water on her sweaty face. It was the best moment of her day, and she stooped even lower, cupping her hands to shovel clear water into her mouth. Not satisfied, she bent the rest of the way until her lips touched the surface of the gurgling water.

"You'll never make Gideon's army," said yet another strange male voice from alarmingly close range.

Startled, Sharene scrambled to the other side of the creek.

Standing across the creek about five yards away from her, in his mid forties, was a handsome Caucasian man who hadn't shaved for two or three days, making his facial features darker from the neglect. He was taller than Cameron and Nadia, with a muscular neck and what looked to be a hard, seasoned body.

And he was laughing.

Sharene crossed her arms in a weak display of self-defense.

"Do you always scare women when they drink from streams?" she asked, her voice reflecting the heat and alkalinity she'd experienced most of the day.

"Only when they are women I need to train not to drink with their heads down," he said. "You'll soon learn, when drinking this way, to face in the direction an enemy might come from, Sandy."

His words were matter-of-fact, yet authoritative, in the same instructive mode she'd heard much of the afternoon while working with Cameron.

Sharene walked a few steps above a bend in the small creek and crossed it a second time, at a narrower point where she didn't have to get wet. Then, she turned her back to the man and started walking away from him toward the tents.

"I'm supposed to have a few minutes to myself before dinner," she tossed over her shoulder without her usual intonations of kindness and love. Sharene was embarrassed that he might see her wet right shoe and wet pant leg caused by her instinctive scramble across the creek to get away from him. The dust damply clung to her shoe and pants as she walked away.

The man watched her leave, sat down on a large boulder, and lit a cigarette.

Sharene hurried away from the second man and the narrow stream, but didn't know where to go. She hadn't seen Nadia since she'd been dumped unceremoniously in the dirt, and wasn't eager for a reunion with her. Yet, Nadia's tent, where Sharene expected her bedding would be, seemed the only logical place for her to go.

When she reached that tent, Sharene, only pausing for a two-second prayer, parted its flap and found the strong woman inside. Nadia was reading in semidarkness while lying on a folding cot. Her head and shoulders were propped up by a rolled up, dull-green sleeping bag. Sharene found the tent's interior to be surprisingly warm and comfortable.

Sharene's cot, the maximum ten to fifteen feet it could be distanced from Nadia's cot and still remain inside the tent, was covered by a rolled out sleeping bag with an issue of GI clothing on top of the flat green bag.

"I think they'll fit," said Nadia in a friendly tone while rolling her body away from the magazine she was reading. "If not, we'll find some that will."

Sharene faced Nadia with her back against the tent wall. She still might make Gideon's army.

The fresh clothing, unappealing as a soldier's uniform may have seemed days earlier, was too tempting, and Sharene, still facing Nadia, changed her outer garments. The tall Germanic woman resumed reading her magazine and paid little attention as Sharene undressed a few feet away.

A small number of black flies commuted the distance from one woman to the other, making their resonant noises and drawing occasional arm swipes of a disinterested nature.

The hunter stepped through the zipped tent entrance and took a seat at the foot of Sharene's cot. Neither woman had the ability to see him, as their senses weren't wired for demon detection.

Sharene, now more comfortable in clean, dry clothes, hugged her pillow and stared across the space between them.

"Why did you throw me in the dirt?" she asked testily.

The other woman placed her magazine on the canvas tent floor.

"I thought you understood," said Nadia. "This isn't a normal place. You have arrived in a camp with three experts who have two weeks to make you into the type of woman who not only can penetrate the well-defended barriers of a sadistic enemy, but also accomplish some necessary tasks and come out alive. Everything we do and say to you in these two weeks will be aimed toward those objectives, Sandy."

"Words work," said Sharene.

"Words with demonstrations work better," responded Nadia.

The hunter listened without turning his head one direction or the other, as if looking straight ahead through the closed end of the tent were all that was necessary to fulfill his vision. He seemed to absorb their words through an invisible, ephemeral body that could change shape at any instant.

"I think it was a cheap shot, Nadia," said Sharene Marsena, with a fire of righteousness ebbing forth in her veins.

And the hunter, for the first time, looked in Sharene's direction.

Nadia chuckled silently, picked the magazine up from the tent floor, and went back to reading.

Sharene was irritated by what she took to be a snub, yet refrained from making another verbal response. Without conscious thought, she fumbled among her sum of personal possessions, not much, and pulled out her small Bible.

The hunter didn't wait for Sharene to open it, but left in search of an unprotected soul.

Cameron immediately stuck his head into the women's tent without a knock or word of salutation, as if fired by a desire to catch the attractive newcomer in a compromising position.

"Time to eat," he said, then shut the tent flap behind him without even looking toward the other woman, the strong other woman whose weaknesses wouldn't surface in this camp.

"Bastard," said Nadia without emotion, with the same matter-of-factness that seemed to permeate the tiny encampment. It was as if Cameron's unannounced entrance into their tent was on the same plane as Sharene being dumped on the Paraguayan dust, the ongoing vigil of persistent black flies, and the training of a naïve woman from Alabama possibly to take the life of another.

Sharene opened her Bible to one of David's Psalms of praise and was safer than she knew.

"What are you reading?" asked Nadia of her new tent mate.

Sharene instinctively wondered if she should hide her Bible. Would this powerful woman take away her only remaining link to reality? The thought came to her out of thin air, without forethought, yet only lasted for an instant. Thanks to the teachings of Pastor Hemri, an evangelist named Paul, and even the Apostle Peter, her response to Nadia's query was quick, honest, and direct.

"It's a Bible," she said, "the Holy Word of God, and if you take it away from me I won't have the courage to proceed on this mission."

Nadia softened.

"I attended church at an early age and it probably did me a lot of good," she said. "Yet, I haven't known anyone who's followed through on those teachings for many years. I haven't had much use for them myself, this line of work and all."

"I'm sure the need always has been there," Sharene retorted, blocking the other's view of the small Bible with an elbow and a pillow. In self-protective mode in a strange environment, she didn't feel like sharing.

A mountainous silence, only broken by the sound of a distant macaw seeking its mate, followed, and Nadia peered toward Sharene, who was becoming less and less visible as daylight began to give way to darkness.

Sharene rose, found matches at the base of a nearby kerosene lamp, lit both the match and the lamp, lay back down, and resumed reading her Bible.

The lamplight brought everything back into focus for Nadia, and, without making a sound, she got up and cautiously walked toward Sharene's light. "Which book are you reading?" she asked tentatively, displaying an air of femininity, of curiosity.

Sharene looked over her right shoulder at Nadia, and no longer was afraid of the powerful woman. Nadia smiled almost shyly, showing a beauty Sharene previously hadn't been privy to, and at that moment the two of them became bonded at a higher level that only one of them understood.

"Ecclesiastes," said the newcomer with the small black book. "Come on, let's go eat."

For days, with no contact with the outside world, Sharene rigorously was tossed back and forth between Mike (the man by the stream,) Cameron, and Nadia, and back again. In roughly two-hour sessions, the three would share their specialties with a woman who steadily evolved from the naïve to the trained. Mike primarily taught psychology and tactics, Cameron weapons, and Nadia basic hand-to-hand combat.

The latter was the most trying.

The mental aspects taught by Mike were easy, though fast-paced and intricately detailed. Cameron's mechanical teachings, bolstered by the strange man's exuberance for the topic, were doable in spite of the fact he insisted Sharene learn the science of munitions as well as their applications.

Yet, the teachings from woman to woman were slowed by a competitive rivalry that fed from the streams of a common past. Sharene learned to love Nadia as a revered sister, and Nadia reciprocated with feelings that made the strong woman in khaki apprehensive.

Hadn't she loved before and found a sort of peace by withdrawing from her own gender? Men were easy, predictable even, and she had no doubts as to where she stood in their presence. But women?

Sharene was free in her love, as if the work of establishing boundaries between them had been accomplished many centuries before. Her edginess from the first night waned, and she focused on a mission authorized by the third chapter of Ecclesiastes. Her current life situation demanded no less.

Nadia threw Sharene in the dirt. Then she did it again and again, always trying to communicate subtle shifts of weight, twists of the torso, and hand placements that would make Sharene more of a weapon and less a beautiful woman. Nadia taught kicks to ankles and thighs and groins that could fell an attacker. And the student went through the motions in weakness, kicking predictably slow without the intensity of one whose life soon would be in the balance.

"Don't you care what happens to you in that fortress?" screamed Nadia in frustration on the third day of training. Sharene was sweaty, dirty, and tired, and thought she was doing her best. She returned Nadia's glare, looking at her with clear, light-blue eyes, and patience. The teacher, now in olive fatigues and a sweat-lined baseball cap, stood inches away from her student under the hot sun, her feet an inch deep in Paraguayan dust. Nadia grabbed Sharene's brown T-shirt like an angry drill sergeant and shook her violently, looking for a flicker of fear, anger, or even distrust.

"Don't you care that you are going to die for a woman you don't even know? You don't have to die, you know!"

Their eyes remained locked, neither of the women backing away from the moment's intensity.

"Doesn't your God allow you to pick up a parachute if you step out of an airplane?" Nadia screamed. "Do you think you can walk on water?"

Nadia's dirt-brown fingers clung tightly to the front of Sharene's sweat-laden shirt, and her outburst poured forth in animated torrents. Their noses practically touched, and the men, listening from inside their tents, knew better than to intercede.

Then the teacher, not getting the reaction she demanded, took her lesson to another level, and struck Sharene hard on the mouth with a fist that could have come from an irate man, even a demanding sexual attacker.

And Sharene Marsena, far away from home, comfort, and friends, fell again in the dust that clung wetly to her perspiring arms and face. Again, she regained her feet, this time with the tainted blood of one whom easily could have been a virgin, but wasn't, flowing from her mouth and battered white teeth.

Hadn't she, with the patient help of God, picked herself up from more trying circumstances than this? On her feet, Sharene leveled another wordless challenge toward her attacker, a look of plucky persistence that didn't know how to surrender, a persistence in spirit that reached beyond the immediate to the ends of Revelation, well beyond the scope of human dreams. Samson, though blind, had such a challenging demeanor when he'd prayed for renewed strength, parted the two middle pillars, and died with the Philistines.

Sharene's kicks came harder, more precise, as the two women continued to spar in the midday heat, and the mouth of Sharene Marsena continued to bleed. Red, sacrificial blood marred the beauty of her soft chin, stained her brown T-shirt, and fell with shapeless finality on the thirsty South American dirt.

Nadia was mesmerized by the change in her student—excited by it. She circled and fought and cajoled and taunted, all the time extending her gifts as a teacher to impart maximum knowledge to a woman who suddenly seemed ready to learn from her arsenal of trade secrets.

And Sharene did learn. Within the next hour, she exhibited a much better, more purposeful comprehension of the teacher's exemplary instructions than nearly three grueling days of repetitive two-hour lessons in the hot sun had taught her. Maybe the basic groundwork had been laid previously, but the desire, the heart, and will to survive purposefully was fueled by Nadia's blow to Sharene's mouth.

Jake Marsena's sensitive daughter now circled and kicked smartly, yet with no animosity in her bones. Like a packhorse returning from weeks in the wilderness, Sharene smelled the pastures of home.

After that hour had elapsed, including one fall of her own when Sharene kicked her legs out from under her, Nadia halted the lesson. Nadia's short hair and khaki clothing were drenched in an exhilarating kind of sweat. She looked for the first time at her own sleeveless T-shirt covering her gasping bosom, and saw there the blood of a beautiful woman. She looked upon that blood pumped by a strong heart, and, for the moment, thought she saw the wars of Christendom with a new fighter.

"That's enough for now," said Nadia, offering another rare smile that hinted of honest femininity. "You'd best take care of that bleeding."

They walked to their nearby tent with arms draped around each other's necks, conversing and laughing like drunks headed to the night's final pub. At the tent flap, Nadia halted their walk with a muscular arm command.

Shaking her head sadly, Nadia told the misplaced Alabaman in a loving, soft voice, "There's just one more lesson I must give today, and it's undoubtedly the most important." Then, with unexpected suddenness, she grabbed Sharene's arm and tossed her into the dust one more time, adding insult to what had been a flicker of pride.

For the only time during the day, Sharene didn't get back on her feet quickly. Instead, she looked up questioningly at the face looking back at her from a higher vantage. Sharene looked at her female instructor with patient sadness, communicating, with a look, her feelings of wanton betrayal.

She never knew, nor asked for Nadia's inner emotions at that point in time.

"Be vigilant, Sandy. Never get comfortable while you remain in the danger zone."

Nadia, without another word, held the tent flap open for more than a minute to allow Sharene to get up from the ground and step inside. Then, getting no response to her gallant gesture of peace, Nadia entered the tent and dropped the flap behind her. Sharene remained alone in the dirt for several moments, oblivious to anything other than her and Nadia's strange relationship.

She eventually arose, went inside, and, without acknowledging Nadia's presence, went directly to her tiny Bible.

It was Mike who first noticed the change.

The women had bathed as best they could in the small, cool stream, and now were talking quietly in the kerosene-induced lamplight and shadows within their tent. They had no cognizance of the weather outside.

But, only two tents away, the male leader of the group squatted at the entrance of his tent with a short, brown cigarette without a filter held alternately between his fingers and his lips. The tip of the hand-rolled cigarette glowed whenever he inhaled, yet no smoke was visible in the night.

With neither words nor movement, Mike intently watched as the night steadily grew darker. Celestial bodies from the world above, so recently illuminated after the close of another day, were being snuffed from view by a fast-moving bank of clouds propelled by a strong wind well above the earth. The wind's lowest remnants touched Mike's cheeks and flared the tip of his cigarette. Beginning at the same time, the evening's temperature dipped rapidly like perked coffee poured into a bowl of ice cubes.

Cameron opened his tent flap, possibly thirty feet away, and saw the glowing tip of Mike's cigarette. He looked above him and couldn't see the moon or any stars because of the fast-arriving blanket of dark clouds that blocked their light. Both Mike and Cameron knew from experience that a storm was imminent.

The weapons expert left a dusty trail no one from this world would see, padding in silence in the direction of the cigarette. Once there, he posed a question to Mike and listened in silence to the answer. Then, both men walked through the dust and the darkness to once again check and test every anchoring stake and rope on each of the three tents. They worked quietly and efficiently, as if the lack of light was no obstacle to them.

The women had no inkling that clouds had obscured all vision of the celestial skies above. Activities in their tent, without that level of cognizance, were far different than those of the two men.

Once purification was restored to her soul by the gurgling stream's waters, Sharene again went directly to her small-print Bible to find some semblance of justification, direction, or even hope for her situation. The new power in her kicks and jabs had to be in accordance with God's purpose for one Sharene Marsena, she thought. Laying down one's life for another was noble and acceptable, but was becoming a calculated force to take another's life also in His will for her?

Suddenly Ecclesiastes 3 and " … a time for every purpose under the heaven …" needed support.

Blood occasionally dropped upon Sharene's pillow, and the gums supporting her white teeth hurt. Turning away from Nadia's unassuming gaze of concern, she reached to the bottom of her small purse, below the sewn side pouch where her Bible normally was stored, and fished out a small vial of pills prescribed months earlier by a South Carolina doctor. That they were placebos had been her first thought when she'd picked up the prescription, but now, for the first time, Sharene felt the need to learn if they had any healing power. She swallowed two pills, then propped herself up with an elbow, her back still turned toward Nadia.

Without a concordance, she again picked up her Bible and turned hungrily to Isaiah.

Nadia rose from her cot and walked deliberately toward Sharene, effectively reducing the physical and emotional gap between them.

"I have some words that need to be shared," said Nadia. "Keep reading if you want, but I know you'll hear me.

"I'm an actor, Sandy, and sometimes a very good one. It goes hand in hand with my job. It's often necessary that you dislike, or even hate me if you are to learn what I have to teach. And what I have to teach you, Sandy, is very important because your life, and the lives of others, very well could depend on it.

"The growth in your skills today was phenomenal," Nadia said. "I've never had a student, man or woman, advance so rapidly. And I know that, realistically, it wasn't me who triggered the change in you."

With bleeding from her nose and mouth stopped, and no exterior marks left by the smashing blow to her face, Sharene again was a vision of beauty. She listened to Nadia's words, at the same time perusing Isaiah 35, the flourishing of Christ's Kingdom. She picked that moment to roll toward Nadia for the first time since being approached, gave the Germanic woman a perfunctory glance, then returned without words to her Bible.

Nadia continued.

"Although you responded without parallel, I sense you weren't responding to me. You never came close to hating me for all I could say and do."

Then Nadia's voice changed slightly, subtly, in a manner blatantly obvious to the hunter and his rival, yet to a degree rarely comprehended by human beings.

"That you are a beautiful woman is obvious, Sandy, and in a selfish way I resent you for it," she said. "Men, even the two in this camp, always will give you more interest, more compassion, than they'll give me. And, though they probably don't realize it, it's more than physical appearance. You aren't like any of us. Inside you exists a touch of eternity, a peace generated from the past and most likely a peace generated well into the future. I've read some of your Bible and never found what it is you've found there. I'm not saying this very well, but what I'm asking is for you to teach your teacher, Sharene."

Sharene responded promptly to her own name, her blood already dry on the pillow. She swung her feet to the tent floor, and Nadia instinctively backed away in a defensive posture.

"Are you going to knock me down again if I become vulnerable and share what it is I have to teach?" asked Sharene with a touch of meekness in her voice.

Nadia smiled for the second time in the past few hours.

"I deserve that," she said, then sat cross-legged on the bumpy canvas tent floor like a fourth grader waiting for a puppet show. Sharene saw a new grace in Nadia's enthusiasm, her demeanor, and a complete metamorphosis from the combat instructor who so recently had smashed her in the mouth and goaded her to fight harder.

Sharene sat in comfort on the edge of her cot. She physically was positioned higher than one who so recently had been teaching her survival techniques for a violent world governed by greed, drugs, and, beyond Nadia's comprehension, a roaring lion actively stalking the earth seeking whom he might devour.

Sharene leaned down toward Nadia and spoke to her in an imploring, yet gentle tone that transcended their existence in the Paraguayan outback.

The powerful, proud hunter sitting next to Nadia on the floor, sensed a loss of control, but vowed, as he'd done so often in the past, that the loss would be temporary.

"What you see or like in me, be it physical or spiritual, is either a gift from God or a reflection of His presence in me," said Sharene. "The Son, Jesus Christ, gave his life so that the Father would not only overlook, but forgive the ugliness and sin that's part of my nature. I am renewed, forgiven in Christ, and as long as I focus on Him, all things are possible."

Nadia, now alone on the tent floor, wrapped her strong hands around her ankles, squeezed them, and said nothing. She knew from reports she'd studied that the woman now sharing her Christian beliefs soon would die from an incurable disease, if not before then in the stronghold of Meino Cablos. Where did her God fit into that equation, she thought?

"What you see and like in me, Nadia, is available to every man, woman, and child on the planet," said Sharene. "God loves mankind that much. All you have to do, from what I'm taught, is simply confess Jesus Christ as your Lord and Savior, and be baptized."

The pain and sweat from a grueling day suddenly was erased, and Sharene's eyes glowed with unmistakable love. She turned to her Bible, sharing and explaining scripture that had special meaning in her life—and Nadia, the former teacher who would resume that role in the morning, listened with tempered enthusiasm.

Didn't this beautiful, idealistic child know what lie immediately ahead of her, pondered Nadia?

The rain started slow, like drumbeats for a dirge, wetting the canvas tent roofs sporadically like Sharene's blood had done hours before to the soft, alkaline dirt. But within minutes, the elements came harder, much harder, and the preliminary offerings became torrential.

The women acknowledged what to them was an unanticipated downpour by speaking louder than nature's clamor. The men, meeting one tent away, spoke of a rising stream and of their wisdom for planting tents on higher ground.

Wind and rain thrashed the sides of the three tents as if they were vertical lakes on a Dali painting.

"What was your family like when you were growing up?" asked Nadia above the storm, hungry to bridge a world full of differences in the short time available to them. "Did they hug you and read you to sleep?"

The trained soldier no longer fought the impulse to love the vision sitting on the cot above her, who was smiling and sharing freely. She knew Sharene would die soon, was saddened by that knowledge, yet selfishly wanted to learn and grow as much as possible from the other's gifts, the other's smile. The frequent references to Jesus and God obviously had their place for Sharene Marsena, but Nadia, the soldier, wanted practical lessons that could one day help her face her own death with the same lack of apprehension.

While the harsh storm bashed the three tents and Nadia's spirit continued to thaw, their conversation evolved to men and women, to love; and Jordan Norton's name arose like a phoenix. Nadia, who professed to know men far better than women, was fascinated by the personage of Jordan Norton and pried for details. What did he look like? Was he a good student? What did his parents do for a living? Where is he now? Why did the wreck draw the two of you closer together?

Sharene talked openly, without reservation, as if speaking to a high school girlfriend late at night over a bowl of popcorn. She was lonely and, being human, felt the need to purge her imperfections and disappointments. She understood the limitations and trials of her earthbound future far better than Nadia suspected.

Nadia listened ravenously, as if the life of this other woman was far more significant than her own, and pounced like a jaguar when Sharene referred in passing to a special written code between Jordan and herself.

"I've never shared it with anyone," Sharene said softly, pausing to flash a sheepish smile of remembrance incapable of traversing the many miles between rural Paraguay and Boston, Massachusetts.

"It was just kid stuff, fun stuff. Tell me before you forget." And Nadia pursued the subject relentlessly, with an intensity that stopped the flow of a purging conversation.

Then, with no more talk of God and Jesus between them, Nadia got her way, and the women parted company for the night. Sharene, exhausted, soon fell into a deep, dreamless sleep, while Nadia's eyes remained open peering into the darkness. Much of what she'd heard made sense, but relinquishing her marginal control over life to someone who'd died thousands of years ago was insanity.

Outside, where replenished starlight from the heavens occasionally was visible between retreating clouds, a solitary figure crossed the muddy landscape without leaving a track. He'd paused long by the women's tent and, overall, was pleased with the time he'd spent fanning one woman's doubts. Subtle nudges to the one without the Christ had convinced her to place self above the good-will offerings of both the one called Sharene and the one Sharene believed in. This pleased the hunter. It was an important step, he thought. Halting what could be a noble, self-denying plunge to benefit the cause of his chosen enemy, at least reducing this woman's potential impact on others while doing so, could lengthen his time to prowl destructively on earth, even delay or halt his personal torture foretold in Revelation. Beyond reason as even he knew it, the hunter stubbornly clung to the belief that the inevitable wasn't inevitable at all.

One of the hunter's biggest strengths, as witnessed moments before with Nadia, was his uncanny ability to fan the lie that giving up self to his hated enemy, the one Sharene Marsena was willing to die for, was in any way restrictive. The hunter's powers in the earthly domain, where he now ruled, irreparably would be damaged if it became common knowledge that submitting oneself to Jesus Christ only enhanced one's abilities, powers, and potential to find meaning and truth about God's yearning desire to shower them with gifts.

Like Nadia with men, the hunter had no doubts about where he stood with nonbelievers. If only he had more sway with God's true children, he lamented.

The storm left as quickly as it had come, and the residue of its waters sparkled in the brightness of the ensuing morning. The native grasses, occasional flowers, and stubborn trees that lived for such cloudbursts glutted themselves on the life-giving rain before it ran away in the enlarged, now-brown stream, or evaporated. The morning's light, both bright and beautiful, emitted messages of hope and survival.

Mike looked outside his tent without stepping from its entrance. The mud would be a problem. He donned heavy boots, wading forth first to Cameron's tent, then to the tent of the women. He informed all three of them that he would spend the full day working with Sharene. It was time she became acquainted with more of the specifics of her mission, he said.

The mud was deep as Mike and Sharene took a direct path from the women's tent to Mike's tent.

They took towels and wiped mud from their boots at the entrance of the tent, but didn't remove their footwear.

"What does this look like to you?" asked the intelligence expert, pointing to a detailed blueprint draped on an easel positioned next to a stout wooden desk that looked as natural in a remote corner of Paraguay as a live pelican would in a football locker room. Sharene was unaware that the desk, like an assault rifle, broke down into parts and easily could be boxed and shipped almost anywhere with minimal inconvenience. Mike previously had set the desk up in many tents, in many countries. It was a luxury, but Mike was no ordinary operative. The blueprints changed from country to country, but neither the overall goal of the mission nor the desk.

"I would presume it's a replication of the property where Sandy Kroghan is being held," said Sharene. "It's big."

"You are entering a crucial stage of your education, Sandy."

Mike momentarily paused to look directly into Sharene's eyes, and smiled somberly, fully aware of the sacrifice that lie ahead of her. "In the days to come, you must learn every room, every hallway, and every door. You must learn what you can of every window and cranny. I won't let you rest until you know the exact layout of Cablos' entire complex in your sleep.

"Now, I'll step outside for a cigarette and leave you alone for five minutes to study what you think are the most important aspects of the layout," Mike said. "Then, I'll return, quiz you on your observations, and we'll have established a starting point for your studies."

Mike walked to the tent flap, then paused, turning to see the Sandy Kroghan look-alike scooting closer to the blueprint and easel.

"And Sandy," he added, making one step back toward her, "we've no way of knowing which pieces of the puzzle in front of you will be important and which ones won't be important. So, damnit lady, learn them all. We want you to walk out of there alive."

Then he retreated, smoked his cigarette outside in the crisp, morning air and the sunshine, and returned.

The day became one big memory lesson for Sharene, and she did well to a point. She soon could picture the layout of the overall fortress as it was presented on the blueprint, but couldn't assimilate quickly the required information whenever Mike figuratively would try to walk her from room to room. She proved to be much like an adequate student of the French language who does well as long as time is available to first translate visuals into English, and then into French.

But that wasn't enough for the mission ahead of her.

Mike wanted, even demanded a familiarity of the layout that was at least comparable to that of Sandy Kroghan, a woman who, once injected with a fear of her captor and his soldiers, had been allowed unrestricted movement around the camp.

As the cloudless, sun-drenched day evolved, causing mud on the landscape to dry, then crack, Mike began drawing sketches on paper draped over the easel. He wanted Sharene to visualize every room in every building behind Cablos' locked gates from an eye-level perspective. He made drawings complete with doorways and windows for each room, and Sharene's mental obstacles suddenly were removed with the rapidity of a child learning to ride a bicycle— one attempt among many a discouraging crash, the next attempt launching a lifetime of success.

At one point, Mike pointed to a representation of a door near the rear of the complex, saying drugs came and went through it at all times of the day and night.

"It's rarely locked, Sandy, and it will be your primary escape route," he said.

Pleased with her progress, Mike proceeded to take the lessons to yet another level by playing an audiotape of Sandy Kroghan's voice. He said the tape had been supplied by their inside contact.

"Is all of this information accurate?" asked Sharene.

"We are very fortunate, Ms. Sandy. Our source, whom you will contact when you are there, is very thorough," said Mike.

A fragment from a distant conversation with Sherm Purcell flickered in Sharene's mind at that moment, but only for a second.

Sweat was streaking down both of their foreheads in the middle of the afternoon when Cameron interrupted them with a tray of food.

"The humidity is crazy," was all he said.

In the far tent, alone much of the day, Nadia, like the professional she was, searched Sharene's scant belongings, taking time to peruse Sharene's small Bible. Of particular interest to her was an address in the front of the Bible. With no thought of impropriety, Nadia took out a pen and jotted down the address in her own notebook, writing PLATEAU, ALABAMA, in large block letters. Then, she put the Bible back, returned the rest of Sharene's belongings to their original state, and spent the rest of the day playfully writing a letter she didn't intend to send.

It began, "Dear Jordan ..."

Its second paragraph was a myriad of notes and partial notes, of erasures and lines and arrows and asterisks. Nadia didn't know what she wanted to say, or even if she wished to speak as Sharene or as a friend of Sharene's, but was totally cognizant of the power she could wield over a young man from Alabama whom she envisioned to be handsome and articulate.

Yet, as Nadia reveled in her ongoing fantasies of power and desire, life during the final week-plus of Sharene's stay in Paraguay evolved into a boot camp for Sharene Marsena; a boot camp with three instructors and only one soldier.

She learned fast.

Cameron trained her to disarm locks and construct incinerating devices and smoke diversions from ordinary supplies. Mike taught her how to walk, how to wear her hair, and how to kill Meino Cablos from close range if the need arose. And Nadia continued to throw

Sharene in the dirt, training her to outfight any man in any situation, continually emphasizing, over and over again, the constant need to be aware of her surroundings.

At the end of a week, Nadia went into a small village about fifteen miles away for supplies. Before leaving, she interrupted a lesson between Cameron and Sharene to ask the latter if she had postage for a letter. Sharene was confused by the request, and Nadia laughed.

It wasn't meanness that prompted Nadia to mail the typed letter to Jordan Norton, having scribbled the words 'please forward' on the outside of the envelope. Neither was it a conscious desire to undermine the female student's faith. In fact, Nadia's motives, at least in her own mind, were professional and true.

Combating Sharene daily in artificial life-and-death situations had convinced the stronger woman that Sharene Marsena, even with her fast-improving skills, lacked the survival instincts of a Francis Marion or John Wayne to fight the good battle and return for duty the next day. She feared Sharene simply had taken on the mission to die nobly—to save Sandy Kroghan, maybe damage Meino Cablos' drug operation, then return to the dust her God said she'd come from.

To avoid additional pain from the sickness within her was one possible explanation, thought Nadia, and to become a human sacrifice for her God another, but the female combat instructor would have none of it. This woman from rural Alabama, a special being with an infectious inner beauty, must live and touch others far beyond the immediate days ahead.

Maybe Jordan Norton could kindle in Sharene a renewed desire for life.

Nadia drove to the village, paid Paraguayan currency for supplies, posted the letter, and, on the return drive to camp, brought a hitchhiker along with her.

Sitting alternately in the passenger seat beside her and on top of the tightly strung radio antennae was a powerful, crafty being, the hunter, who fanned Nadia's benevolent justifications for an action that primarily was motivated by greed.

For, in reality, Nadia was on fire to meet and flex her own power over the man of Sharene's heart. The instructor never would become the compassionate, beautiful person Nadia both loved and failed to understand, but Nadia knew without doubt that she could wield power and control over Sharene's lover. Wasn't he of that gender she knew so well?

The final days in the training camp went by quickly, with the three instructors alternately waiting through the days and into the evening hours to tutor their solitary student. Sharene didn't complain once about her long hours of training. Instead, she steadfastly added to her knowledge and skills like a monk caught in a vision.

On the final Thursday in Paraguay, Sharene began vomiting violently, and Mike, Cameron, and Nadia, fearing for both their pupil and the plan itself, nursed her as best they could.

Cameron calmed her more than the others. He talked and laughed through her pain until, late in the evening, her convulsions subsided, and Sharene, physically exhausted, went to sleep on her cot in the end tent. She awoke in the night, weak and alone, got up, lit her lamp, and dug for a small vial of pills, hoping that a few of them would stay in her system long enough to provide some relief. She dropped one of the pills and watched, under the lamp's light, as the errant capsule rolled from view beneath her cot. She consumed two others, turned her face into the pillow, prayed, and went back to sleep.

By morning, Sharene was able to walk to Cameron's tent for breakfast, eat lightly, and continue her studies. Without apparent explanation, her crippled immune system had been bolstered in the night.

The same small airplane that had ushered Sharene to Paraguay two weeks earlier was scheduled to pick them up Sunday morning at the airport in which she'd arrived. After picking up the military-looking foursome, the plane would fly to an innocuous, routine fuel stop in Peru, then continue over the Andes Mountains to a late-night abandoned landing strip in rural Colombia.

Sharene Marsena entered her final hours in Paraguay with a major sense of uneasiness, not much different than her emotions when she'd left the small airplane and first set foot in South America.

The unknown loomed larger to her than any assumed scenarios. Since arriving in this landlocked country two weeks earlier, she'd been trained for survival, possibly even to kill another human being, and the ontological implications of that violent possibility were an emotional blur. Within her was a collage of emotions. She felt disdain for Meino Cablos and his drug operations, empathy for an abused woman who well could have been her, doubts about the future of her own mortality, and still maintained a focused faith in one passage of scripture.

Sharene fed from Ecclesiastes 3 like Martin Luther had feasted on Romans 5 centuries before.

She was a far better soldier thanks to her stay in Paraguay. Like grunts from World War II, and possibly some allied combatants in Korea, Sharene's life purpose now was to offer herself, if need be, as a living sacrifice for God, country, and humanity.

"To every thing there is a season, and a time to every purpose under the heaven: A time to be born, and a time to die ..."

Mike's plan for the operation, as announced shortly before leaving that final Sunday morning, seemed unbelievably simple after all of the tortuous training Sharene had been through. Yet, it could work.

On the following day, Sandy Kroghan, plus at least two well-armed bodyguards and a driver, were scheduled to leave Cablos' stronghold for a long road trip to the drug lord's fortified sea cottage southwest of Cartagena, on the Caribbean coastline near Panama. Traveling in one of Cablos' limousines, they likely would drive over sometimes-rugged roads on a route taking them across the Magdalena River, through the streets of Medellin, and on to the sea. Such a trip by airplane would have been more convenient, but an enemy of Cablos's drug operations, the current Colombian government, controlled most domestic airports. Plus, a sizeable reward had been offered for a beautiful Caucasian woman not easily camouflaged in a landscape renowned for hunger, greed, and drugs.

Mike knew, but wouldn't yet reveal, the location where he, Cameron, and Nadia would ambush the limousine. He foresaw little difficulty in their operation as long as the guards hadn't been instructed to kill the American woman rather than allow her to be captured. If they had been given such instructions, something Mike said he wouldn't put past the violent drug lord, both they and their ally in the limousine would have to act quickly, and with precision.

Once the limousine was under their control, the switch would be made and the real Sandy Kroghan would go with Nadia where she'd be placed on an airplane and flown out of Colombia. Mike, Cameron, and the driver then would return to where Sharene would be waiting, and she and the driver would make the trip to Cablos' fortress. Sharene would feign an illness then, and their plan, with the possibility of many variables and contingencies, would unfold.

"You must gather the information and possibly kill Cablos that night," said Mike. "The helicopter will be waiting for you at five a.m."

Mike met Sharene's eyes purposefully, and said, "Your mission is far more important than you know, Sandy. We haven't been totally candid with you.

"Meino Cablos is an evil man who spreads darkness over thousands upon thousands of people. You know about his drugs, but you don't know what he does with the millions of dollars he receives from selling those drugs," said Mike.

"Have you heard about the munitions cartel that exploits international tensions by selling high-technology weapons to nearly anyone with money who's hungry for power?" he asked. "Many can get their hands on such damned killing weapons, Sandy, but few have the connections and talent to routinely put them in the hands of those who support their own political ideologies.

"Cablos not only can, but buys and sells such armaments on a regular basis, earning him even more money to invest in drugs and further a business cycle orchestrated in hell," Mike said emphatically.

He continued. "No, Sandy, we haven't told you everything, and time prohibits us from doing so now. The decision about whether you even attempt this mission remains one hundred percent in your hands. You still have the option of walking away and washing your hands of this whole affair. No one ever will hold anything against you if you choose to do so. Yet, I urge you to do what is right and consistent with your beliefs," said Mike. "May the peace of God be with you as you make your decision."

And a slim parcel of time was inserted into the equation …
… a time for every purpose under heaven.

"The decision is yours to make, Sandy …"

"Quit badgering her," snapped Nadia with anger in her voice. "Give her some room. You have no right!"

"Get behind me," Mike retorted in a strained voice of his own, and Cameron and Sharene felt the tension in the air.

No one moved.

An inexplicable wind fanned the flame in the lantern immediately to Mike's right, and Sharene slowly, intently, moved off of the cot she was sitting on and positioned herself cross-legged on the hard tent floor.

"Are you all right?" asked Nadia, and Mike motioned her back with an abrupt arm command.

Three instructors looked on, anxious for the next words to come from a woman sitting cross-legged on a tent floor in the outback of Paraguay. Sharene's slender fingers, without any rings, stretched from her chin to a focused temple.

"Yes," she said slowly to no one in particular. "I really am all right." And she rose yet one more time to her feet.

Sharene looked directly toward Mike, the leader of the group and said, while nodding her head in affirmation, "You're right, of course. I can't deny my beliefs now. I'm in."

CHAPTER 9

It had been more than a year since he'd heard from or even about Sharene Marsena, and he'd forgotten much.

Chiska was a beautiful woman who loved him dearly, like a territorial wolverine, and he'd had little time for melancholy. Chiska always was there to cook spaghetti and laugh, to massage his back and laugh, to listen to his daily tales and laugh, and to do his laundry regularly as if he, Jordan Norton, were doing her the favor. She was pure to their relationship and wanted the world for the man she loved.

Chiska's only battle with Jordan came early in their relationship when she wanted him to curtail his bouts with alcohol. As happened so frequently between them, she'd remained patient and persistent, laughed, and finally won the battle. Not long after that victory they discovered how nicely their physical bodies fit together.

The subject of Sharene Marsena never was discussed between them. Occasionally, a conversation would halt abruptly at the spoken name of Jordan's former lover, and both of them would feel discomfort, but only for a little while. Chiska's laughs, her soft, loving interjections to thwart such awkward moments, routinely would lead them away from danger.

Jordan thought he was in love with the caring Miss Sullivan and proposed marriage. She had the same thought for some time, and accepted. The marriage was scheduled for the following fall.

After many months of happiness in Boston, Chiska, against her better instincts, acquiesced to a request made by her lover to return alone to Plateau to visit family and friends during his collegiate spring break. Jordan was content with his current relationship with Chiska and had no ulterior motives for returning to Plateau without her. Chiska said nothing, but prayed to God that Sharene Marsena was millions and millions of miles away. She still feared her rival.

That, roughly, was the status of Jordan and Chiska's relationship in regards to Sharene Marsena when Nadia's letter arrived on the second day of Jordan's visit to Plateau, Alabama.

His heart tumbled when he read her name on the envelope, tumbled like a year-old haystack after the cornerstone bale has been removed, or like a young fighter-pilot's stomach the first time a vertical dive is engineered. He gasped, and a virile young man suddenly felt faint. Perspiration graced his brow.

In contrast to the spiritual gaffe that had lasted many months and been fueled by corporeal desires pleasing to the hunter, Jordan Norton now felt an urgency, before opening the letter, to pray to the God of Sharene Marsena, and to Jesus Christ.

His parents weren't home, and Jordan dropped to his knees in front of the family sofa with the unopened envelope dangling from his right hand. Jordan closed his eyes and touched his forehead to the front quarter of the davenport's velvet cushion.

"Heavenly Father," he began, like the believer he still was, "I'm a mess right now. You alone know how I've loved Sharene. I told her I'd go anywhere to be with her. But for some reason that you understand far better than me, life took her away like sunshine in April; present, beautiful, and radiant one minute, then gone in a long, pouring rain.

"I tried to love her, Lord, tried my best to follow, but that didn't seem to be what You or anyone else wanted. Now, Chiska is here, and I think she's what I want and need. But this letter I hold unopened in my hand rekindles a damp fire. Please, don't let it mess up what Chiska and I have. I still love Sharene, Lord, but the wounds are deep.

"I guess, Heavenly Father, I'm asking that this message from Sharene does no more damage to my life. I'll do whatever Sharene asks, I've promised no less, but please spare any additional pain, especially for Chiska. I promise on a stack of Bibles that Chiska and I will live our lives for you if you do this one thing.

"Thank you for your presence, and I apologize for being away so long. In the name of Christ I pray, amen."

Jordan's first sight upon opening his eyes was a small pot teeming with the tight-budded daisies he'd bought that morning for his mother. He couldn't explain why they were his favorite type of flower.

Then he rose from his knees, sat on the sofa with the day's Alabama sunshine streaming over his right shoulder, and opened the letter.

He read slowly, introspectively, and perused the typewritten epistle three times before he retrieved a pencil and paper to dissect its second paragraph.

The code was fresh in his mind, as fresh as the memorable taste of litchi fruit Pastor Hemri had once imported from Hawaii, then shared with he and Sharene. Hadn't he spent much of his adult life idly dissecting second paragraphs and found, without fail, that only Sharene's offerings brought a higher meaning to him? He pieced the code carefully together to avoid error, assembling his findings one letter at a time.

HELP. DANGER. COME. Nine p.m. FLIGHT. The next entry was a numerical date three days advanced from the checkmark his mother had put that morning on her kitchen calendar.

Jordan Norton only pondered momentarily before going to visit Mr. Adamson to ask him about a loan. The letter, though postmarked in Paraguay, said in code to meet Sharene in Cartagena, Colombia.

Chapter 10

Dressed in military fatigues and carrying dark duffel bags, Mike, Cameron, Nadia, and Sharene filed from the small airplane late at night. The runway had been rougher than any other aspect of the long, two-legged flight from Paraguay. They piled their bags into the trunk of a waiting automobile and watched as the airplane taxied back down the bumpy runway, audibly regrouped its engines, then sped down the dirt track for liftoff and an exit from strife-torn Colombia.

Darkness was combated by a half moon.

The hunter's nighttime vision was impeccable. He knew the child at the wheel of the automobile even before she illuminated her face while lighting a cigarette. He'd watched her kick men in the groin and laugh at their vulnerability. He liked her spirit.

Sharene saw her, too, when the match was lit, but gave her little thought.

The transient from Alabama wondered within her mind about her own physical appearance. She felt the ramifications of an aging process accelerated by a debilitating illness, and, lacking a mirror, sought any gauge to determine how much she'd hardened physically, as well as mentally, over the past two weeks. She found none, only an overall feeling of fatigue. She felt as if most of her natural defenses were collapsing within and around her.

The young driver closed the trunk as the departing airplane stole the attentions of the new arrivals. Mike sat in front, while the others piled into the back seat with Sharene positioned in the middle.

"She looks just like her," said the girl, and Mike nodded.

"Want a cigarette?"

They drove only with parking lights until they'd separated themselves from the airstrip, proceeding at a modest rate of speed over rutted terrain. A road materialized in the partial moonlight, and the girl stepped down on the accelerator.

All four passengers, as well as the driver, focused intently on the dark course laid before them. No one spoke.

After nearly a mile, the young girl turned the headlights on full force, and Sharene breathed easier. More rocks and vines than trees were visible to the car's occupants as they traveled along one side of the rutted road. The girl hit forty miles per hour on the speedometer and slid, under control, around a blind turn.

Sharene smelled the dust.

Then, as if riding on a roller coaster sliding on to another loop, the vehicle jumped up on to black pavement and the sound of the car changed immediately from tire-jarring bumps to a quiet whir.

The pace of the vehicle quickened.

"Where are they?" asked Mike.

"They were crossing the Lorry Bridge about an hour ago. Just about where you thought they'd be," said the girl.

She slowed the speed of the car considerably as the first set of headlights approaching from the opposite direction came into view around a corner. All five watched closely as an old farm truck with high wooden racks rambled past in the semimoonlit night.

"I can't talk you into letting me go along?" asked the girl, almost playfully.

"Not an option," responded Mike quickly. "I need you to make Sandy's arrival in Colombia as restful as possible. She has some intense hours ahead of her."

"Sandy," he said, while turning to look into the back seat, "meet your hostess, Mikki. She'll do whatever is necessary to make you comfortable until we return in the morning with your guide to Cablos' hideout. Get as much rest as you can."

Cameron and Nadia, likely thinking of a road heist in their immediate futures, said nothing.

Sharene began to cough nervously, then harder, as if her lungs lacked a God-given suppressant for tickling, pneumonia, or anything else lungs need suppressants for.

She was coughing hard against the roof of her mouth when Mikki turned down a narrow lane lined with barbed wire that was highly visible in the headlights. A slight bend in the roadway, and Mikki pulled the car into a wide, dirt driveway in front of a flat-roofed, two-story house.

"Take care of her," said Mike, as he slid from the passenger's side and into the driver's seat. "We'll be back in the morning."

Cameron helped Sharene, still coughing, out of the door on his side of the back seat and passed her along to Mikki, who, with one arm supporting the Sandy Kroghan look-alike, walked to the house and unlocked the front door. Once inside, Mikki turned on the electric overhead light and helped the weakened beauty into a kitchen with yellow cupboards and a small stack of dirty dishes.

The auto had been turned around, driven back down the dirt lane, and was climbing back onto the pavement when Nadia spoke for the first time since returning to Colombia.

"You didn't have to make her that sick!"

Mike said, "The first thing Cablos will do with her is take her to his personal doctor. We need real symptoms and no blood test. A blood test and we're dead," he said definitively without looking away from the road.

"What you mean, my leader, is that one Sharene Marsena will be dead," retorted Nadia sarcastically.

Mike looked toward the back seat for far longer than he should have while driving at night, and said, "I don't ever want to hear that name again. Do you hear me? Never."

Back at the house, Mikki quieted Sharene's coughing by boiling water, adding to it lemon juice and a shot of bourbon, then making certain she drank it. After consuming most of a second hot drink, Sharene's attack subsided.

"Thank you," said Sharene weakly.

"You owe me one, Sandy," said a female almost as young as Sharene, but not nearly as pretty. "And I'd like to even the score right now. Tell me, how do you plan to take out Meino Cablos?" she asked eagerly, like a ten-year-old child on Christmas morning.

The question had been foremost in Sharene's thoughts for the past week. Wasn't Cablos a major enemy to mankind? Didn't Ecclesiastes 3 say, 'To everything there is a season, ...' and short verses later say '...a time to kill? ...' Was there ever a better time to kill than now? Wasn't she dying and he an evil threat to thousands of people?

"I don't know if I am," she responded to Mikki's prodding, while putting down the mug that held the last swallows of her second hot bourbon drink. "His death isn't my prime objective."

Already, the Christian lass from rural Alabama was speaking like her unusual peers.

"What's more important than killing the bastard?" asked Mikki.

Sharene had been briefed that Mikki could be trusted.

"His records," said Sharene. "I'm to locate and steal his personal drug files, and also his munitions contact information, if possible."

"Wish I looked like Sandy Kroghan," said Mikki. "No offense, but I'm a lot better qualified for the job. I'd get the files, of course, but I'd take out Cablos, too. You should kill the bastard while you're there, Sandy."

Sharene responded, "Bastard or not, Meino Cablos is still a human being."

"My ass, Sandy," barked the smaller of the two. "Cablos has spent his whole life looking to get wasted."

"Isn't that for God to decide?" asked Sharene.

Her words came out muffled around another cough, almost apologetically; as if Sharene Marsena in this weakened state would rather depart and go to sleep than defend her beliefs.

Wasn't she already being tested to her limit by an apparent contradiction between the Ten Commandments and "A time for every season," as written by the Preacher, in Ecclesiastes? Hadn't she endured another weakening bout of coughing only moments before?

Wouldn't she willingly be offering her body to God, in the near future, as a living sacrifice? What was her price?

Mikki then pressed Sharene on the subject of God, as if Sharene Marsena had introduced a troubling topic that needed to be quashed immediately.

Unbeknownst to either of them, at the request of Pastor Dale Hemri, in a steep-roofed church thousands of miles away in rural Alabama, Claudia Bohna was praying. She wasn't praying for a miracle cure for Sharene Marsena, but instead that Sharene would be an effective witness to others.

And Claudia Bohna's prayers, documented by the Word, her faith in it, and verifiable results from her seemingly unending stream of praise and supplications to God, didn't go unheard.

The act of praying was as natural to Claudia Bohna as the act of flying is to a golden eagle. She'd learned at an early age, and never quit.

Aware of her unusual spirituality, leaders in her church in rural Alabama made Claudia Bohna, at barely 20 years of age, the first woman ever seated on their church board. And, at one of her first-ever board meetings, she'd been present behind closed doors when Sharene Marsena's great grandfather had approached the board with what he'd contended was a revelation from God.

Like Claudia, a devout believer in Jesus Christ, Sharene's great grandfather shared during that meeting the contents of a dream he'd had the previous night that he, though not fully understanding its content, felt had eternal implications. The message he'd received in the dream was to build a tall church for God and, in its gables not visible from the ground, place the words of Genesis 28:13 on a small plaque.

That very night, the seven-person church board read the words of Genesis 28:13 aloud, prayed, and committed the congregation to a mammoth church construction project.

Two weeks after the new church's dedication ceremony in 1914, without fanfare, Sharene Marsena's great grandfather had climbed a tall ladder, manually held in place by the church's pastor, carefully traversed the steep roof, and hung a small plaque on one of the church's gables.

Claudia Bohna, more aware than the other board members standing beside her that the infant church would face many future trials, had looked upward that day and smiled at the hope personified in the words on the plaque.

They read, "And, behold, the Lord stood above it, and said, I am the Lord God of Abraham thy father, and the God of Isaac: the land whereon thou liest, to thee will I give it, and to thy seed;" Genesis 28:13.

Time, like many aspects of nature, often transcends human comprehension, and Claudia Bohna's upward-turned vision at that long-ago moment was similar in many ways to the prayers she now projected as an old woman from inside the same tall church in Plateau, Alabama.

Both were laced with trust, faith, and a conviction that His will, focused on the eternal outcome of perfection, would be done.

Sharene Marsena in rural Colombia, far away physically from Claudia and the church in Plateau, didn't know that she and Mikki now were in the presence of God's angels.

Sharene plodded on in exhaustion.

" ... for when I am weak, then am I strong," had said the Apostle Paul nearly two thousand years earlier, and Sharene Marsena, in weakness with the help of a living spirit within her, planted valuable seeds.

By the time Sharene was able to lay her head on a pillow, it nearly was two a.m. Colombian time, and she'd shared her full testimony with a doubting sister. After her breathing smoothed into sleep, Mikki lay awake another two hours pondering what to her were new thoughts regarding the subject of grace.

The hunter was away as the two women talked into the night. He was elsewhere, viewing a nocturnal roadside scene that lacked his blessing.

It was there that three well-trained operatives in black hijacked an armed limousine belonging to Meino Cablos. One of Cablos' guards had the real Sandy Kroghan in his rifle sights when the driver of the limousine turned and killed him at short range with a pistol. The second bodyguard dropped his weapon and pleaded for mercy.

The woman in the vehicle, Sandy Kroghan, stepped outside the limousine alternately laughing and swearing at her liberators. Long months of stress and cocaine abuse found freedom an enigma.

Within minutes, Nadia drove Mikki's car, with Sandy Kroghan in the passenger seat, away from the remote site of the ambush. One of Cablos' two bodyguards on the trip lie dead in the trunk, while the other was bound tightly, gagged, and placed fully conscious beneath a multi-colored blanket on the back seat.

Mike, Cameron, and the driver took the Cablos vehicle in search of another Sandy Kroghan. The entire operation, witnessed by no one except the participants, the hunter, and the hunter's enemy, took less than five minutes.

Mikki was awake when they drove into the driveway and stopped the limousine in front of the two-story house.

"How'd it go?" she asked.

"No real problems," said Mike. "Sherm had to kill one of the bodyguards, but nothing major. Is she ready to go?"

"She's dozing, but dressed," said Mikki. "It only will take a second. I'll go get her."

The three men stood in front of Cablos' white limousine. Two were dressed all in black: the third wore a chauffeur's gray uniform and a stiff black hat traditionally worn by local soldiers when they were on parade.

Sharene stepped from the doorway into the early morning light. She was soft and beautiful. She wore a short gray skirt with pleats, a salmon-colored chiffon blouse, and tan shoes. Her face was tracked with rouge, her ears laden with silver earrings that dangled well below her lobes.

"Do you have my bags?" she asked the chauffeur, as if he were a bellhop or a personal servant. He turned toward her for the first time and smiled, and Sharene only lost composure for a moment.

"Would the lady like her bags beside her as she travels, or in the trunk?" asked Sherm Purcell.

Without a word of explanation, Mike handed Sharene a small pill and a canteen, then watched as she swallowed the pill with chlorine-laced water from the canteen.

He gave final instructions as Sharene and Purcell readied to leave.

"Your accent doesn't have to be perfect. Remember that you are very ill, and don't let that damned doctor put you to sleep."

The limousine began creeping out of the driveway with Mike walking alongside the open rear passenger window, less than two feet from where Sharene was sitting. She listened intently to his final instructions.

"Your bedroom, his bedroom, and then the private study …"

Mike did a surprising thing then, dropping to one knee in the dust and bowing his head. Cameron watched from the doorway of the house with a wondering heart. Mikki, who would have shouted triumphant obscenities the day before, marveled at Mike's action, and longed for another talk with Sharene Marsena some time in the future.

The limousine turned right onto the pavement.

"Why are you here?" asked Sharene as she opened a suitcase filled with light sweaters and scarves, with English-language romance novels and a brass corkscrew.

"I blow with the wind," he said evasively.

"Did you even like me back in Georgia, or was I just another pretty face?" she asked.

"Oh, you'll never be just another pretty face, Sharene. You're enough to haunt a man's dreams."

A man of many conquests, Sherm Purcell spoke those words with earnest conviction.

Sharene never would know about his current misgivings for having brought her into the picture. She'd never know about his drunken pact with Meino Cablos to supply the drug lord with a second Sandy Kroghan, a second toy to taunt and tease and love and abuse. That plan never would have been enacted had Sherm Purcell, in advance, had any inkling about the inner resolve, the life-sustaining force that radiated so naturally out of the soul of Sharene Marsena. He had no foreknowledge that he'd get emotionally involved.

"Did I read you so wrong in Georgia?" she pressed. "Or was I just a simple country girl swept off her feet by the handsome stranger?"

He drove on in his gray uniform and black hat, only occasionally seeking her out in the rear-view mirror. The day was bright, and he protected his eyes with dark, oval sunglasses that could just as well have sat on the noses of John Lennon, a high-ranking officer in the German Reich, or a storied pope.

Sharene, experiencing waves of dizziness, could tell nothing about his inner thoughts.

"For now, Sharene, you'd best become Sandy and prepare yourself for a storm. Try to anticipate any possible situation and how Sandy Kroghan would react. Your life and any possible benefits from this mission are at stake," he said.

The limousine's chrome reflected the sun as the vehicle wound through paved turns and straight stretches, all the time pointing its energies to the southeast, toward a reclusive fortress teeming with unfriendly soldiers.

Sharene wanted to hone her thoughts on Meino Cablos, a man she only knew through photographs and described mannerisms, but the woman in her, the vibrant woman destined soon to die from bodily malfunctions, a bullet, or even a machete, was focused on something else.

"Did you love me, Sherm?" she asked.

The words now were vocalized, and she was glad. She thought it better to ask, risking the possibility of a negative answer, than mutely to refrain from vulnerability.

"I loved you," she continued matter-of-factly.

The driver remained silent. He looked through dark glasses into a day that could have brought tears. He hated himself for an instant, long enough to consider unburdening the truth, but only for an instant. It was too late. The miles that lie before them were too few to explain or confide. And so, Sherm Purcell, a man of many coats, spoke what he thought to be another lie, or at least a partial lie.

"I loved you, too."

The hunter inaudibly thundered his approval.

In spite of nausea triggered by Mike's pill, Sharene got the comfort she needed from those brief words, then let them lie idle like carvings in the bark of a large, Canadian fir, or black paint boldly splashed on an isolated replica of Stonehenge in Washington state. Each would own its message for a season. Satisfied, Sharene brushed aside a thought of Jordan Norton, and, with a subtle smile budding in her heart, began to focus on her immediate situation.

Sherm Purcell alternately tended to the gas feed and the brake, mechanically drawing them nearer to a date with destiny.

Or was it destiny, he pondered as a white sedan sped past in the opposite direction, heading toward Medellin. Surely a factor other than fate had precipitated his greed, had prompted the words to long-time friend and rival Meino Cablos, "What would you pay me to supply you with a second Sandy Kroghan, a look-alike playmate to add to your harem?"

The other's greed for women, rivaling Sherm Purcell's greed for money, had lusted in the possibility, and, assured that such a woman did exist, Meino Cablos had bankrolled and released his munitions ally to search for the holy grail.

But, before Cablos lost patience and sent two of his best soldiers to extradite his conquistador from along a busy Georgia street, several telling events took place. Sherm first renewed acquaintances with a fierce female accomplice from New Orleans, named Mandi, and then made a tactical error in judgment by phoning his mother in Missouri.

Previously alerted that the drug lieutenant might be returning stateside, the CIA took precautionary measures. The tapping of Mrs. Alma Montgomery's phone reaped rewards, and Sherm Purcell had been apprehended, informally detained, and given a list of life options that ranged from betraying Meino Cablos to a lengthy stay in a federal U.S. prison. Swayed by their arguments, he'd shared the unusual nature of his visit to the states, agreed to cooperate, and, with help, was sent to fill a teaching position in Georgia.

Not even the CIA was privy to his purposeful fling with Mandi.

Sherm Purcell relived these events in his mind as he drove onward in the Colombian sunshine.

He knew the road well, knew he'd soon turn left and approach a high gate guarded by sentries. He knew that both his life and the life of his passenger soon would be tested.

"It's time for you to get under the blanket and be as sick as you've ever been," said Purcell. "Good luck."

"God bless," was her retort from the back seat, and Sherm Purcell inexplicably felt a crumbling chink in his armor. He found himself caring for, almost loving, what this brave, beautiful woman stood for.

The limousine stopped at the gate, engine running, and a soldier with a semiautomatic weapon strapped around his neck and shoulders addressed the driver with guarded familiarity.

"Why have you returned now?" the soldier asked in Spanish.

"Cablos' woman became very sick. She needs a doctor," said Purcell.

The soldier tugged without success on the handle of the limousine's door immediately behind where Sherm Purcell was sitting. The vehicle's dark-tinted windows provided no visual access that would have allowed the soldier to learn who, or what was inside.

"Open the door," the soldier barked.

Purcell reached behind his seat and awkwardly lifted the interior locking mechanism on the passenger door. The guard opened the door and peered in, seeing a blanketed form lying prostrate across the wide seat. Sharene peeked out wearily with the sweat and grime of a fever visible on her forehead.

The man tipped his cap toward her, and closed the door.

"Where are the others?" the soldier asked.

"I'll take responsibility," said Purcell. "They already were close to the sea where Cablos had given them assignments in addition to watching the girl. I told them to stay there for a few days."

The guard had Purcell kill the engine, then took the key and checked the limousine's empty trunk. He gave the key back to Sherm Purcell and waved them through the gate.

Smothered by the thick blanket, Sharene felt drops of sweat trickle down her face. The sweat sensitively touched the crease where her nose and cheek met, flowed intact to her smooth upper lip, and ended its journey in her mouth. The taste was like water from one of God's salty, undrinkable oceans, but she swallowed it anyway.

She felt hot, feverish, and didn't care if that sensation came from the heavy blanket, the tension, or the small pill Mike had her swallow just before the white limousine had pulled away from Mikki's driveway. She didn't think about tainted blood relentlessly gnawing away at her young body. Instead, Sharene Marsena focused mental energies on someone she'd known since childhood, a man in white robes who radiated gentleness and authority. She was thinking about one who understood her plight, her purpose, far better than she or anyone else ever would know.

Sharene was praying, and knew, without doubt, that she was being heard.

The vehicle hadn't proceeded fifty yards beyond the gate before the resonant voice of Meino Cablos hailed its driver.

"What have we here, Mr. Purcell? Have you lost your way?"

Any of the sixty-odd persons in the camp knew and responded immediately to that voice, whether it was spoken in English, Spanish, or Mestizo dialect.

Sharene's heart beat erratically as she vacillated from peace to fear, and back to God's unfathomable, all-encompassing peace.

Cablos, unable to see through the limo's dark, smoked windows, gripped the unlatched door handle behind Purcell and yanked open the door.

"Chu-Chu, are you all right?" he asked. "Why are you lying down?"

Sharene hid beneath the blanket and said nothing.

Meino Cablos crawled into the wide back seat, scooted next to Sharene, and pulled the blanketed form into an affectionate hug. He pulled the blanket down and looked eye to eye at a woman he'd never met, a surrogate lover who wanted his ruin, if not his life. She immediately saw a rugged, intimidating man who hadn't shaved for several days. He saw familiarity in her and Sharene saw a frightening power in him.

Cablos kissed her on the mouth and put a hand on her breast.

Sharene abandoned her cloak of silence.

"No," she said, as she turned her face away from him and fought the urge to remove the unwelcome hand from her breast. "I need to go to my room and rest. I'm sick. I'm weak and dizzy."

"OK, Chu-Chu. We'll take you to your room right now," he said. "I'll call Dr. Shotsu. Take it easy. You're very important to Meino, and that makes you very important to everyone here."

He scooted back across the seat, got out of the limousine, shut the door, and spoke quietly to Sherm Purcell who was standing by the vehicle's front fender smoking a cigarette.

Sharene mentally sang a chorus of "Amazing Grace" to calm her soul and, through pursed lips, tasted more sweat under the canopy of blanketed darkness she'd returned to.

Sherm tossed the cigarette in the Colombian dirt, reentered the vehicle, shut the driver's door behind him, and engaged the transmission.

"You passed your first test," he said, while checking the rear-view mirror. "I'm to help you to your room, then the show is up to you. Are you sure you can find the meadow?"

"Yes," from under the blanket, from "… we've no less days to sing God's praise, …" sung earlier in the church choir at age fourteen when Jordan Norton had wanted her back in the pews by his side.

"You've got to be there by five a.m.," said Purcell. "Nothing short of a miracle will make that pilot wait any longer."

He stopped the vehicle and turned off the engine. Without additional words, Purcell stepped outside and walked around the long front-end of the white limousine. He circled to the passenger side of the vehicle next to a door that opened into the cavernous hallway that led to Sandy Kroghan's living quarters, as well as the living quarters of many others. He opened Sharene's car door and had to catch her as she tumbled out of the seat and into the daylight. She began to cough and moan, and Purcell put his hand to her feverish forehead.

"Let me carry your weight," said the man not only responsible for bringing Sharene to Cablos' stronghold, but the one most responsible for her very presence in South America. She coughed some more, swooned momentarily, and Sherm Purcell carried her still form through an outer doorway held open by a woman whose countenance expressed deep concern. The woman wore a dull blue dress that covered her ankles and a white blouse with long sleeves.

"Thank you, Carleta," he mumbled in Spanish.

The hallway that the exterior door entered into was an enclosed miniature of Spanish-looking walkways similar to those at Stanford

University, in California. Supporting the many arches was the wide, beige floor made of smooth imported stone.

Purcell carried Sharene to the first door to the left of where they'd entered the hallway, and lightly placed her on her feet. He turned the door's knob without the use of a key, again picked up Sharene, carried her across a nondescript room, and laid her on the outer covers of a queen-size bed. Sharene opened her eyes and saw a lamp without oil sitting on a wooden table near the head of the bed.

The large door separating Sandy's room from the hallway had clicked sharply on its hinges when they'd entered the room, sending a staccato ringing down the quiet, stone corridor. Still, the door hadn't closed.

"Remember that I love you," Purcell said softly so only Sharene could hear, expressing more purpose than sincerity, and the ears of one belonging to the gender known for intuition heard his subtle change in inflection and understood its meaning.

"Good luck," he said.

He pulled away and was preparing to leave her with a parting smile—almost like Pilate, with his hands washed clean—when Sharene Marsena again chinked his armor with reality.

"God bless," she said.

Somehow touched by what he didn't understand, with strange emotions bubbling up within his soul, Sherm Purcell returned to her bedside and leaned much closer to Sharene than Meino Cablos would have allowed.

"What do you mean when you say that?" he asked.

She smiled then, from the semicamouflage of a feverish, tortured woman, and for the very first time in his life the man of multiple conquests truly knew love. Beauty knows no bounds.

"Galatians 6:18," she said mysteriously with her head on a soft pillow. "Read it. Share it. It's the last verse in the book of Galatians, which is in the Holy Bible of our Lord Jesus Christ."

"Thank you," he said awkwardly, and kissed her on the forehead like a confused Pharisee giving last rights.

Then, Sherm Purcell pulled away and shut the large wooden door behind him as he left the room.

Chapter 11

Inner doubts plagued Nadia as she inserted three different keys into the trio of padlocks protecting the chained driveway entrance to Meino Cablos' cottage by the sea. She'd secured the keys many hours earlier from the front pocket of the dead bodyguard, and carried them across much of Colombia in a zippered tool kit that rested on the front seat between she, and, for much of the trip, an erratically talkative Sandy Kroghan.

Nadia worried about Sharene Marsena, all the time knowing such uncharacteristic emotions within her could hinder her personal effectiveness in a violent war against drugs and munitions. She also worried about an innocent young man from Alabama whom she expected soon to meet at the Cartegena airport. Too, she was concerned about the haggard, yet beautiful young woman who'd spent long months as an abused sex kitten for a powerful South American man whose actions were dictated by lust, cocaine, immorality, and death. As they drove through the sun-drenched countryside, Sandy Kroghan alternately had thanked her for snatching her from "hell," then incoherently screamed for a return to "my Meino."

Yet, the biggest source of doubt and worry for the female agent, as she swung open the massive metal gate with octagonal, vertical bars, had been the afternoon meeting at a small, private airport near Cucuta, when she'd handed Sandy Kroghan off to a CIA operative. The codes of greeting had been met, the site and timing of the meeting kosher, and the woman agent had said nothing wrong. Yet, Nadia felt uneasy. She'd expected almost any operative other than this Creole woman who wore heavy makeup and spoke with a Cajun twang. Only a shortage of time with a dead man in her trunk, coupled with the woman's calm demeanor, had prevented Nadia from exploring her personal suspicions.

The second bodyguard, gagged and barely conscious, moaned meekly from the cramped floorboard of the back seat.

Nadia engaged the automatic transmission of Mikki's car and began the steep, winding descent to the sea.

"Not to worry, my friend, nothing is to be gained from killing you," she said to the man lying behind her. "I just need to keep you quiet for a few more hours."

The Caribbean Sea sparkled in the late afternoon sunshine as Nadia approached Cablos' retreat. She checked her watch, and nodded purposefully like a Cheshire cat puffing a long cigar. She and Jordan Norton would meet Sharene at dawn.

CHAPTER 12

It wasn't fifteen minutes after Sharene's arrival in Sandy Kroghan's quarters that Dr. Shotsu knocked lightly on the door.

Sharene felt feverish and giddy as she waited between the sheets of the room's only bed. She coughed and sneezed, and genuinely was lightheaded.

Sharene wore a silk negligee procured from a bag Sandy Kroghan had packed for her planned trip to the Caribbean seashore.

She didn't respond to the gentle knocks, and Shotsu entered the room on the authority of Meino Cablos, not the authority of the Hippocratic Oath.

"Well, well, Ms. Kroghan, we meet again. You certainly don't look your best," said Shotsu.

He wore baggy white pants and a silk green shirt that was similar in color to wavy stripes on the off-white tile floor. His eyes were alcohol red, and his face pocked as if cigarette torture had been applied shortly after birth.

He touched her forehead and cheeks with the familiarity of a close female friend, then pulled back the sheets and probed her body for answers.

The woman, child, and soldier felt dirty, even betrayed. What was the purpose? What was her purpose? She sought an answer in her mind and landed faithfully on a rock of righteousness. She prayed uneasily, rote like, with her teeth clenched tight and her conscious thoughts centered on foreign hands touching her vulnerability.

Sharene coughed involuntarily, and sensed it was the right thing to do.

Shotsu returned the covers.

"Your fever is small, and the redness in your face and elsewhere is a mystery," he said. "I'd almost expect a spider bite were it not for the coughing. You had none of these symptoms when you left yesterday. Have you eaten anything unusual?"

"No," she replied weakly, then attempted a dry cough triggered by her consciousness.

Shotsu looked at sad, reddish eyes and a smooth, unwashed face that somehow seemed younger, more innocent than it had the previous day. He saw the face Mike, Cameron, Nadia, and now Sharene wanted him to see, yet intuitively perceived a subtle renaissance in Sandy Kroghan's being as if this mysterious illness had rejuvenated her soul.

He'd comment about this to Meino Cablos.

Pills were produced from the doctor's black carrying bag with the smooth leather handle; pills to help the beautiful woman sleep away what was ailing her.

"Sleep from now through the night and I'll return in the morning," he said professionally. "I don't think your strange illness is cause for alarm."

He handed her three pills, all larger than those given to her by Mike, and a glass filled with water drawn from a shiny chrome faucet extending above a curved white sink anchored on the wall opposite the bed. Then he watched, but didn't see, as Sharene tucked the oblong tablets beneath her tongue and swallowed the entire glass of water. She smiled weakly as the doctor let himself out of the room, then spit his prescription for sleep into her hand.

She'd passed her second test.

Young Sharene Marsena silently acknowledged the source of her temporary successes in this hostile environment and, for a brief second, thought about dropping to her knees, burying her forehead into the soft covers of Sandy Kroghan's bed, and praying. But she knew better than to do so. Between she and the adjoining room belonging to Meino Cablos was a door designed to swing only one way, and at the choosing of only one man. And that one man, Meino Cablos, knew the hunter very well. The two harmonized in their objections to prayer. Any sighting of Sharene Marsena kneeling in prayer within the confines of Cablos' world of dominance—whether he knew who she was or not—wouldn't be tolerated. Meino Cablos ruthlessly would squash any known loyalties to another.

In his mind, women were easy to replace.

Sharene had been tutored in such things, and only prayed internally as she explored Sandy Kroghan's room. She tentatively touched the door leading to Cablos' bedroom, a door with only a key-locking mechanism and no doorknob on her side, and familiarized herself with the lock for future reference.

She was inspecting the second drawer from the top of Sandy Kroghan's dresser and finding a cache of expensive jewelry and embroidered silk scarves made in France and Libya when she heard a sharp click behind her. Sharene's heart beat rapidly, accelerating the face-flushing effect of Mike's latest pill, and she turned toward the outside door as the woman Purcell had called Carleta let herself into the room, unannounced, from the outer hallway.

Startled, Sharene began to cough while covering her mouth, then hastily put the scarves back into the drawer as if caught in an act of thievery. With Carleta watching, she closed the drawer, walked back to the bed, and collapsed with her chest heaving in cough-induced spasms. Her face and neck were flushed red, and she yearned to be eons away with a man in white robes.

Carleta approached the bed and the woman lying above its sheets, and kindly pronounced the word "klahowya," obviously offering a salutation in a tongue foreign to Sharene.

Sharene continued to cough.

"I wouldn't have come in had the doctor not said you would be asleep," she said in accented, yet understandable English.

Then Carleta drifted into the Spanish dialect she commonly spoke with Sandy Kroghan. Sharene only understood enough to avert her eyes, clasp a pillow, and cough in weakness. She neither knew or cared if the coughs were contrived, induced, or a natural progression of her illness.

"You do sound sick, Ms. Sandy," continued Carleta as she reverted back to English. "You should be sleeping and not moving about the room. Now get under the covers and go to sleep, or I'll tell Dr. Shotsu you need more medicine."

The Mestizo woman, probably in her forties, next stroked Sharene's hair and gently moved her aside to pull down the covers. Then, as Sharene slid below those outer blankets, Carleta stilled the other's movement with a strong hand, and pondered the presence of a significant mole on Sharene's left ear.

"You don't speak my language, do you my dear?" probed the maid in Spanish dialect, speaking in a soothing, gentle voice that Sharene didn't understand. "That's odd, since you did yesterday."

Sharene smiled in submissive vulnerability, oblivious to yet another element of the danger she faced.

Carleta slowly backed away from the bed. Looking all the time at Sharene Marsena, she fumbled behind her and grasped the door handle leading to the hallway. Then she said in English, "You are not in a good place, my love. May the Father and Mary protect you." Then she crossed herself, exited, and shut the door in her wake.

Voices were heard from the hallway, one male and one female, and Sharene briefly experienced the fear of a nonbeliever at the Second Coming, or a small bird in the visible sights of the hunter. She wanted to run, to close her eyes and hide beneath Sandy Kroghan's bed. She frantically sought an exit from her dilemma, and saw none.

Sharene Marsena's immediate salvation, if it were to come at all, must be triggered by an outside source. She battled her fear with prayer.

What had beeen a faint conversation beyond the door ended abruptly following a pleasant laugh from Carleta. The door handle to Sandy's room again turned, and Sharene didn't know whether to cough or plea for her life. Had she no input on whom entered through that door?

Sherm Purcell stepped inside the room, turned, and inspected the handle where an inside lock normally would be.

"Did you ever think of getting a lock for your door, Sandy?" he asked in a firm tone without looking toward the woman who'd stirred his heart. "It would prevent just anybody from walking in."

He turned toward her for the first time since entering the room with a cautioning finger to his lips and his opposite hand gesturing from Meino's bedroom door to the hallway door, and then toward the ceiling. As he approached the bed from where Sharene was watching him, Sherm offered a quiet shushing sound through the finger on his lips. Too, he wiggled the lobe of his left ear and pointed to himself.

"How do you feel, Sandy?" he said. "Carleta says you can't sleep. You must sleep to get well. Should I ring for Dr. Shotsu?"

"She knows," whispered the concubine of a Colombian drug lord, or at least a sweet replica from Alabama who didn't want to die in the bedroom of another woman. The pace of Sharene's heart continued to flutter at an unnaturally fast rate, and she earnestly coughed until her eyes watered in submission. Then she coughed some more.

"Good," whispered the man who didn't understand why Sharene was offering herself as a living sacrifice. Sherm Purcell then smiled through her misery and whispered, "You can trust Carleta. She loves Sandy Kroghan and secretly hates what Cablos has done to her. She is Catholic, and I told her Galatians 6:18 seconds ago when we parted. Do you think she will understand?"

A spark returned to Sharene's wet eyes, and once again she consciously remembered why she'd come to this hellish place. In a whisper of her own, she responded, "She'll understand far better than you."

Purcell dropped to both knees beside the bed and spoke in hushed tones. She rolled toward him and stifled another cough.

"Cablos and I are to get together in another building at half past nine. I can't promise you any more than two hours. Do your best, but be back in your room by half past eleven whether you have the information or not. Wait. Then leave for the meadow by four a.m. Even in the dark, it shouldn't take any longer than forty-five minutes to get there. I'll see you in the meadow."

Moonlight, coming from a high window on the back wall above Sandy's bed, was yellow and dim as it angled into the room and struck the tile floor near the door to the hallway. Dust particles, invisible to the human eye, danced in the night.

He bent over and kissed her on the forehead.

"Good luck, Sharene Marsena."

"God bless," she whispered back, and smiled.

He saw her white teeth in the hushed closeness and longed to prolong the moment. He wanted to kiss and hold, to do away with both the past and present, to savor one incredibly special moment with one incredibly special woman.

"Can your God give us a repeat of this moment?" he whispered, then looked toward the unlocked door that could open any instant.

"Our God can do anything, Sherm. All we have to do is put Jesus Christ in our hearts, and submit in baptism."

She knew he wanted to respond. It was in his eyes. Yet, uncharacteristically, Sherm Purcell, a man with a level of complexity that even he didn't understand, found himself without words. He felt like a lifelong blind sojourner seeing first light after healing mud had been applied by tender hands. The scales that had long blinded his vision were beginning to fall away.

He felt peace, love, joy, and confusion in an instant, then again put a finger to his lips as footsteps echoed down the stone hallway outside Sandy's door.

Sharene smiled an impish smile with a dimple and a twinkle, and said in a loud voice for all to hear, "And don't forget to let the others know," and laughed aloud as if she didn't have a care in the world. But she did, and her laughter immediately gave way to a wracking, uncontrollable cough that stole her strength for nearly a minute. Purcell hurt at her convulsions, but didn't see the innocent blood she coughed into her right hand.

"You'd better go," she whispered once the coughing ceased.

"Get your rest, Sandy," he responded in a normal voice. "I'll check on you in the morning."

Then he kissed her gently, again on the forehead, and whispered as if he now understood what previously had been a mystery, "Galatians 6:18. And remember, nothing before half past nine."

Sharene watched the door close behind Sherm Purcell and experienced instant panic, as if her own coffin lid was closing or she'd slipped on a mossy shingle atop the steep church roof in Plateau, Alabama, and was dangerously close to falling off its edge. She held back a strong urge to scream.

"Humans are so weak," intoned the hunter from his vantage inside the room. Yet, he saw something in this woman that brought out the survivalist in him. Her course threatened his longevity in a world that, for the most part, acknowledged his reign. He knew that 144,000 was becoming a smaller number. He had no realistic aspirations of denying the inevitable, but damn sure wanted to delay it.

Sharene thought of Jordan Norton and what life could have been. She certainly wouldn't have come to South America to mix with this violence and intrigue. Wouldn't she and Jordan have had beautiful children and attended a white, high-roofed church with fellow followers of the Christ? Wouldn't they have tithed, prospered, and lived in peace? Why was she, Sharene Marsena, chosen to live with an incurable disease and pain while Chiska Sullivan got Jordan and happiness? What was her mission in life?

Sharene hugged the pillow of another woman and cried.

The clock by her bedside wound slowly, second by second drawing her closer to a destiny only God understood. Periodically, she would look at the clock and feel apprehension and, occasionally, fear. Still, it only was a sense of submission that gave her any semblance of the comfort and peace she sought.

As her time neared, Sharene Marsena inevitably turned to the one she loved. She set aside her fears and self-pity, and looked in the only direction that offered hope to her troubled heart. She prayed to Jesus, and an air of freshness touched her soul.

The hunter left the room to visit Meino Cablos.

Sharene thought of her brother, Peter, and wanted to comfort him, to assure him that God would provide all of his needs. She didn't know if she'd ever again get the chance to tell him she loved him, and asked God to do it for her.

The lying down tempered Sharene's cough, and she slipped briefly into a busy dream of angels and prostrate creatures. At ten minutes after nine she woke and stared blankly into the darkness. The light from the moon was still visible through the window above Sandy's bed, but now was dulled by some high clouds. Other than the clock's illuminated face and the moon's reflective presence, a glimmer of artificial light coming beneath the hallway door offered the biggest point of focus for her eyes.

Sharene knew it was thirty minutes after nine before she looked at the clock. Her soul had traveled long to reach the apex of her journey, and now it was time to take the first step down the other side—no matter how steep, no matter how dangerous. Blood within her veins surged like that of innocent virgins sacrificed to pagan gods centuries before. She'd been abandoned to accomplish a difficult mission, but knew she was far from alone.

In the darkness, she probed for, and soon retrieved the large black bag Sherm Purcell had carried into the room upon their arrival. With delicate fingers, she quickly felt the rough surface of a zipper and traced it to the clasp. She unzipped the bag. Inside, among Sandy Kroghan's clothing, was a small leather valise that had been in Sharene's hands many times during her two weeks of training in Paraguay. She opened it, and, with the help of her trained mind's eye, pulled out a small flashlight from an interior pouch, flicked the flashlight's on-switch, and illuminated the contents of the valise. Miniature bars of steel, metal toothpicks, keys, chisels, and tubes of gel were arranged in hard metal clips. There also was a leather-cased ring of graduated metal keys Cameron had called a lock kit.

Sharene walked in bare feet to the door of Meino Cablos' bedroom, the door with no handle on her side, and set the valise on a small stand she'd placed there earlier. Using the flashlight, she studied the lock closely, looking with confidence at the slotted keyhole. She picked through her ring of metal tools like a cat burglar or a hardened felon trained by the best of thieves at San Quentin. She was glad Cameron had made her listen to more than five hours of his instruction, solely on the subtleties of selecting the correct implement to begin picking a lock, before he'd even placed one burglary tool in her hands.

Sharene tried various keys and listened for a possible tumbler as she worked by flashlight in a drug lord's fortress in Central Colombia. Then a loud click signified the release of a lock, but the door still wouldn't open. A dead bolt on the other side would complicate matters, but Sharene suspected it merely was a double lock.

A ring of keys slipped from her fingers and clanged loudly on the cold tile floor.

She paused to listen for a response, but no one seemed to have heard what sounded so loud to her ears. Sharene's heart raced anyway. She reached for the fallen keys and began to cough. She tried to stifle the sound of that first cough, was weakened when one cough led to others muffled by hands held over her mouth, and knelt in the darkness until her brief attack subsided. Nothing to lose from coughing in what supposedly was her own room, but the exertion tired her at a time when she needed to be strong and alert.

Ten minutes more, and the highly trained Sharene Marsena penetrated the second lock and found herself in the bedroom of Meino Cablos. Had he and Sandy Kroghan made love in this room, her room, or both? Sharene felt muddied by her thoughts.

She flashed her small light around a room much larger than Sandy Kroghan's. Sharene checked a cabinet by his bed, then inspected each drawer in a large wooden desk. Nothing seemed important. At the foot of the bed on a rectangular stand were strewn clothes and a duffel bag with an unclenched padlock. Sharene parted the open lock and found within the bag a large plastic pouch filled with a white substance. She unsealed the pouch and put the substance to her lips as she'd been taught to do.

"Very careless, Meino," she said quietly.

Suddenly, Sharene was aware of footsteps coming from the echoing hallway. She left the duffel bag in a compromising position and scampered back into Sandy's room. She shut the door with no time to lock it. Her heart pounded madly, uncontrollably, as the severity of her peril resurfaced once again in her mind. She coughed loudly, and the footsteps continued down the hall.

She felt weak, exhausted in fact, yet saw no viable option other than proceeding with her mission.

Again, Sharene switched on her small flashlight. She walked through the door with the dismantled locks, making certain to close, but not lock the door behind her, placed a bag of cocaine in her valise, and restored the duffel bag, minus that cocaine, to its original location. Next, she proceeded through the bedroom to the locked doorway leading to Meino Cablos' private office.

It was slightly past ten p.m.

Sharene inspected that lock closely. With no patented name on the lock, it initially was a mystery to her. The pin tumbler that needed to be triggered seemed to be in an unusually recessed locale.

She patiently, yet quickly, tried many of her tools, striving to find a penetration angle that would trigger the lock's release. Nothing worked. She sensed the puzzle was solvable, and kept addressing the lock as if it were a New York Times' crossword puzzle with the final solution just out of reach. Her two thin-hooked tools were too short to reach the release.

Cameron had told her he'd found locks that even he couldn't pick. However, Sharene didn't think this was one of them.

She continued to work rapidly, holding the small flashlight in her teeth while trying, with the tools of a burglar, to pick the door of a thief. Time moved on, and the girl from Alabama began to repeat her actions, to suffer from frustration and fatigue.

Near tears, she dropped to a knee and turned off the light. The darkness was intimidating.

"What did He teach about locks?" she thought. "Or, more importantly, what did He teach us about keys?"

Then thoughts turned to prayers.

Sharene knew her time was short. A bag of cocaine might slow Meino Cablos temporarily, but neither his drug operation nor the flow of armaments to a troubled world would be impacted at all unless she gathered more information. And the answer to so many questions was just a few feet away on the other side of the locked door that separated Cablos' bedroom from his office.

Was she betraying mankind by stopping to pray? She sensed she was doing the right thing, and continued to pray as valuable seconds ticked away.

At fifteen minutes until eleven, Sharene got her answer, and knew, as surely as Jesus had instructed Peter to lay aside his sword at Gethsemane, that the gates of hell wouldn't prevail.

Sharene sprang back into action. She used a flat card to locate the bolt between the door and the jam, pulled a fine diamond wire from her valise, crimped one end with tight-fitting gloves on her hands, and looped the bolt. Moments later, metal clips were anchored to the diamond wire, and the cutting of the bolt began.

By ten minutes after eleven, Sharene had severed the bolt and was in the private office of Meino Cablos, yet she was totally unprepared for what she found.

The room was a sea of litter. Papers, small boxes, cigar butts, stale food, exhumed electric pumps, food wrappings, and hundreds of opaque plastic bags were strewn from corner to corner in the small, dank room. Sharene noticed a marked contrast from the litter when she peered more closely into the room with her flashlight. Looking toward the room's true edifice, Cablos' desk, she saw organization and open space around a telephone, file cabinet, computer, and lamp. Like the Red Sea, a parted path led from the hall doorway to the desk, but the analogy ended there.

Intelligence reports had informed Sharene where Cablos' safe would be, and she crossed the room, stepping over discarded banana peels and hand-written promissory notes. She pushed the debris aside and found the subtle outline of a floor safe. She sat in the rubbish created by Meino Cablos, flashlight in her teeth, and began efforts to open the safe.

The lock responded easily, too easily, and in less than two minutes Sharene was reading lists and figures that much of the world would kill for … if they were the real things. Doubts nagged her progress. IF Meino carelessly had told Sherm Purcell the location of the safe, and IF the lock was this simple to pick, then quite possibly the contents inside weren't what they seemed to be. Still, she stuffed what papers she could into her tool valise and closed the safe.

She checked her watch, was acutely aware that time was short, and waded through a sea of rubbish to reach the desk. She started with its drawers. Equally ill kept, their contents haphazardly seemed strewn with business mail and partially completed spreadsheets and letters she didn't have time to peruse. One half-written note, in a foreign script, had an Algiers heading, and she poked it into the valise.

She continued to search with her blood racing. Lives were at stake, and no one previously had ever come this close to unlocking, and hopefully disclosing, the secrets of Meino Cablos. Sharene doubted the validity of the papers in the valise, and looked lightly at the cocaine's legal significance in the country of Colombia.

She needed more. It was seven minutes before Purcell had said she must leave, and she could be discovered any moment.

Then, in the bottom left-hand drawer of the desk, she found what she'd come to retrieve. It was a small metal box, no more than eight-inches square, with the word MASTER engraved on its top. She grabbed it, hoping somehow to squeeze it into her valise, but discovered the box wouldn't move. By further illuminating the master box with her flashlight, she found it to be a fortress unto itself, made of heavy metal and bolted through the bottom of the drawer into solid metal anchored into the floor. Explosives could shatter the desk, even the entire room, but the box most likely would remain intact. At a quick glance, Sharene determined that the lock on the box was beyond her capabilities to undo, maybe even beyond those of Cameron, she thought.

Sharene Marsena experienced the despair of a thoroughly trained, strategically placed army that hadn't foreseen the early onset of winter. Would she now fall inches short of completing her mission?

She abandoned the metal box and alternately shined her light on the telephone, file cabinet, and computer on Cablos' desk. Instinctively, below the level of conscious thought, she reached out in prayer to a God who'd known her every desire and movement from birth to the church pews of Plateau, from behind a tennis court in South Carolina to a training camp in Paraguay. He still knew her needs, and subtly prompted Sharene Marsena to focus on an item she'd read about, but had little personal experience with—the computer.

It read Imsai 8080 on the upper right corner of the computer's face, and Sharene looked at a number of toggle switches whose functions she didn't understand.

She coughed before her hand could muffle the sound, then coughed some more with her hands cupping, but not totally silencing the outburst. Anyone walking down the hallway at that moment couldn't help but hear sounds coming from a room reserved solely for the use of Meino Cablos.

If life had any importance to her, Sharene had to leave now. Maybe the papers and cocaine she'd crammed into the valise would equate to some semblance of justice, yet she wanted something more convincing, more telling. She again focused her tunnel of light on the box-like computer, and prayed for concrete evidence to use against a powerful drug lord who disrupted and took lives by the thousands. Her own unusual life and impending death had to count for something, she thought.

With no experience of any kind with computers, Sharene naively punched a small black button on the right side of the motherboard and was rewarded with a cassette marked MASTER VII.

It was time to go.

"Chu Chu, do you feel better?"

Cablos had heard a cough and quietly entered his office from the hallway.

He switched on the overhead light, and no amount of training could have curbed the terror in Sharene's heart at that instant. She stuffed the interfaced cassette into the valise with the tools, papers, and cocaine, while Meino Cablos, gnawing on an unlit stub of a cigar, watched with interest. He could have reached out and touched her.

Cablos reacted to her fear with a greasy, insincere smile, and tucked the key to the room in his pants pocket.

"Chu Chu, I did not suspect you were capable of such treason," said Cablos. "After all we have been through? I do not like to think of your consequences any more than you do. People should know better than to violate the trust of Meino Cablos."

Sharene, without taking her eyes away from those of Cablos, stepped slowly backwards and sideways until the desk was between them.

"Why move away, pretty one? Do you not know without doubt that I will kill you?"

He thinks I'm the familiar weak woman he's been tormenting for months, thought Sharene, as her terror ebbed into a will to survive. Then, without apparent recourse, her actions filled a time vacuum much like a shoreline along the Pacific Ocean moments before a tsunami. Her actions were peaceable, and her anticipation of what was to come great.

Sharene stepped away from the desk and the menacing drug lord in the direction of the door leading to his bedroom. He followed her at the same slow pace, tossing his unlit cigar butt among the debris. His masculinity was kindled as she approached the bedroom, and he didn't want to stop her quite yet.

"I agree with you, Chu Chu," he said. "Why don't we share some pleasure before parting for good?"

He undid the copper clasp on his leather belt and, in one swift motion, yanked the belt free from around his waist. He snapped it tautly inches away from her face.

She backed into the bedroom, a room that obviously held memories for Sandy Kroghan and not Sharene Marsena.

Meino Cablos still didn't know whom he was with.

He closed the distance between them near the bed, and Sharene suddenly kicked him with as much force as she could muster. The blow hit squarely on the assailant's thigh, only his trained reflexes preventing a crippling, possible lethal blow to the groin. Cablos fell to a knee, gasping for breath, and positioned his hands to better defend the next kick.

Sharene knew that a whirl and a kick to the face would crash Meino Cablos to the floor, yet for some reason hesitated to deliver the deciding blow that would have bloodied Cablos' face, and maybe broken his neck.

"You should kill the bastard while you are there," had said Mikki.

"To every time there is a season ..."

Cablos was vulnerable for only two seconds, maybe less. Then he stood again and pulled a pistol from a deep pocket in his French leather vest. He held the gun at a low level, pointing the weapon upward at the heart of the beauty from Alabama.

"You are not Chu Chu," he said menacingly. "Chu Chu would have struck me much sooner if she possessed such skills. You are the one Purcell searched for. The bastard told me how much you two look alike. Maybe I should believe him sometimes."

Cablos had her pinned by the bed and was mesmerized by her beauty.

With his free left hand, he thrust her backwards, and Sharene fell on the bed of her attacker. She stared at the gun, then at the sweaty face of greed and cruelty inches above her. She remembered South Carolina, and wished she could will herself to death.

Meino Cablos discarded his vest, then unbuttoned and removed his flannel shirt without once removing his eyes, or the pistol, away from Sharene Marsena.

"Our Father, who art in heaven, hallowed be thy name ..." she said aloud in self-defense, defiantly challenging the drug lord on grounds she knew would bring ultimate victory.

Cablos reached out and touched Sharene's forehead with the barrel of the gun.

Sharene's prayer went silent.

"This is the way it will be, my fake Chu Chu," Cablos said. "I will tell you what to do and you will do it. And, maybe, if I like your spirit, you will live through the night."

He crawled roughly upon the terrorized woman, straddling her just above the waist; his gun poised inches from her face.

"If Meino likes your spirit ..."

With his free hand, he ripped her bathrobe down the front. A second motion and her young breasts were exposed.

The hunter, nearby, relished in the lust of the moment.

Tears rolling down her face, Sharene resumed her defense. "All power, glory, honor, thanksgiving, and might be to our God," she said aloud in defiance of an enemy who transcends flesh and blood. The savage then bolted forcefully upon her, reaching his eager lips to hers, and in doing so, rendered the pistol harmless, its muzzle pointing aimlessly to the side.

The explosion of Sherm Purcell's pistol stopped time. Meino Cablos' lust returned to dust, and Sharene Marsena was numbed.

Blood came to the drug lord's mouth, but no words. Purcell toppled Cablos' lifeless body off of Sharene and onto the cold floor. The woman instinctively covered her nakedness, and in that one motion forever blocked Sherm Purcell from seeing a bullet wound to her abdomen.

"Are you all right?" Purcell asked with genuine concern. "I came in through your door and had to wait until the gun was out of your face. Are you all right?"

"A little out of breath," she said in shock and pain. "I must get some clothes on."

Adrenaline aided her journey back to Sandy Kroghan's adjacent bedroom to gather clothes to wear. She walked to the sink along the wall to wash her face and arms, and felt faint. She rallied. Sharene looked to see that Sherm Purcell still was in the other bedroom with the body of Meino Cablos, then checked the wound to her stomach. The same bullet that killed Cablos had entered the sanctity of her body, and hadn't come out. Sharene hurt when she moved, but the pain was less than what she would have expected.

She thanked God for life.

"Are you dressed?" asked the man who'd just killed Meino Cablos, the complex man of mystery who subtly had been changed since crossing paths with a college student in Georgia named Sharene Marsena.

"We'll have to move fast," said Purcell, stepping into Sandy's bedroom. "If Cablos is discovered missing, dozens of soldiers have orders to shoot first and ask questions later. We need to get you out of the compound, and that won't be an easy task. You're a marked woman, Sharene. Every person here thinks they know you by sight, and that you're sick and confined to this room."

Sharene coughed, and winced from the pain caused by the bullet. She leaned forward in temporary anguish, and with her hands hid fresh bloodstains appearing on Sandy Kroghan's clothing.

She shielded Sherm Purcell from the news of her wound like a mother protecting her infant from the neighbor's pit bull. To Sharene, Purcell had absolutely nothing to gain and much to lose if news of her wound were to alter his own plans of escape.

He acted like the man he was. He clasped her by the shoulders, causing her additional pain he didn't see, and instructed her to be strong.

"You've got to put this suffering behind you for a few more hours," he said. "Go into survival mode if you have to, but you must be strong enough to hide yourself, get off the compound, and meet the helicopter at five a.m. Get your head on straight, Sharene."

"I'm dizzy," she said. "Let me sit for another minute. I'll be all right."

"You're damn right you will be. You've got some stories to tell," Purcell said convincingly. Then his voice softened. "Do you know I still don't know what Galatians 6:18 is about?"

"Many people can tell you that," she said with a weak smile, and an angel shed a tear.

Speaking much like Mike, or even a domineering drill sergeant, Purcell said, "Do you remember how these buildings are laid out?"

"Meino! Meino! Are you all right? We heard a shot. Are you all right?"

The voices came seconds before a loud pounding on the nearby door leading from the hallway into Meino Cablos' bedroom. More concerned queries were made in Spanish, then Mestizo, and a general cacophony of excited voices ensued. Then the dreaded knock on Sharene's door was heard.

"You haven't seen him," whispered Purcell.

A second loud pounding followed the first knock, and Sharene walked across the room and opened the door partway.

With God's grace, one of the guards spoke to her in English. "Have you seen Meino?"

Sharene, looking and feeling the part of a very sick woman, counted four men in the hallway. "No," she said. "I've been asleep."

"Did you hear a shot?" the same man asked through the slim space in the partially opened doorway.

"No, I heard no shot," she responded laboriously. "Now please, take your fantasies somewhere else. I need to rest."

She closed the door, and she and Purcell listened as footsteps echoed down the stone hallway. One voice could be heard above the departing footsteps, saying, "He said he was going to his room."

Sherm Purcell said in a whisper, "I put the body in his office and made sure the doors were locked. They won't find him tonight.

But within minutes they likely will put the entire grounds on a lock down."

He paused to think.

"Do you remember where the laundry room is?" he asked. "I'm sure Mike taught you that. I'll help you get there. Go to the broom closet in the northwest corner and wait. For some reason, it has a low window inside it with spaced metal bars. Use the tools you brought with you and hack through the middle bar. Slide through the bars and make your way through the tennis courts and into the woods. Nothing should be lit up there unless they suspect the truth and are more organized than I think. Even then, it's your best bet, Sharene."

They'd been sitting close to each other on Sandy Kroghan's bed, speaking in whispers. Impulsively, Sherm Purcell leaned toward her and gently kissed her on the mouth.

"I love you, Sharene Marsena," he said.

Sharene smiled and shook her head in wonder, her right hand reaching to her stomach, covering the blood that rightfully should have belonged to Sandy Kroghan, Stephen of Acts 7, or even Jesus Christ.

Maybe it did.

"Galatians 6:18," she said.

He chuckled inwardly, then said, "Let's go before they come back."

Sharene found that walking wasn't as painful as the simple act of rising to her feet. Purcell noticed her extreme discomfort when she stood up, but didn't suspect the cause or extent of her pain.

"Get through this night and you'll be knocking on heaven's door," said a man who didn't understand the significance of his own words.

He opened the door leading from Sandy Kroghan's bedroom to the hallway, looked both directions, then pulled Sharene through it into yet one more phase of her self-willed vulnerability, her sacrificial offering to her Lord. She was covered by a colorful shawl she'd taken from Sandy Kroghan's dresser, supposedly to conceal her identity, and held a lower corner of the shawl to the wound below her rib cage.

Her blood soon would seep through the thin outer garment, but be camouflaged by its bright patterns and designs.

They walked away from the dead body of a drug lord, away from Sandy Kroghan's untold past months of anguish, and toward the center of the long, narrow Spanish building that was paralleled by a second arched edifice about forty feet away. Between the buildings was a well-lit rectangular section of green grass.

Purcell hugged the shawl-covered form of Sharene Marsena as they walked past doorways, some with light peeking beneath them and others without any trace of light. He spoke soft condolences to her, thinking in his mind that the opposing medicines of Mike and Dr. Shotsu soon would wear off.

Sherm Purcell wore the khaki of a Cablos soldier; it was the uniform denoting the corporeal power and authority granted by the man he'd just killed.

Voices approached, and Purcell pulled Sharene to the inside wall of the hallway and into an intimate embrace.

"Put your arms around me," he said with authority, and, as she lifted the shawl to allow him inside, their lips met and blood from her wound stained his shirt.

Sharene was numb, weary, and frightened, and got little comfort from the kiss.

The same four men who'd been outside Sharene's door, plus a lieutenant of Cablos who'd always opposed Meino Cablos' odd friendship with Sherm Purcell, walked past the apparent lovers without taking notice. One said, "I think she's lying," as they marched away from them in the direction of Sandy Kroghan's bedroom.

"Hurry," said Purcell in a hushed tone. "They won't let us pass a second time as a soldier with a whore."

Later, much later, Sherm Purcell would remember how gingerly Sharene Marsena had proceeded on this forced march to the laundry room, but only much later. Now, he was a military general in command of one soldier, and, for her own good, she must be compelled to move quickly.

Her fingers, still grasping her midsection where the flow of blood had slowed considerably, were red and sticky. Her option, other than lying down to die or allowing herself to be captured, was one and the same. Keep going.

They saw no one else on the remainder of their flight to the laundry room. Purcell took her to the far corner, to the broom closet, and sat her down among the brooms and dustpans and mops and mop buckets. She rudely fell from his arms and onto the floor, and he apologized for his insensitivity.

Again, he urged her to be strong.

The dull radiance of the half moon, no longer behind clouds, poked through the three metal bars protecting the ground-level closet window. Purcell focused as best he could on Sharene's silhouetted face and hair, which now were outside the confines of the shawl.

"When this is all over, I'll come see you in Plateau," he said in earnest. "Maybe our lives have crossed for a purpose."

He could imagine better than he could see Sharene's smile in response.

"Anyway," he continued, "cut through the bar and get into the woods as quickly as possible. In the confusion, I should still be able to drive through the main gate."

Then, there was absolute silence, the silence that occurs when two good friends sense they're destined to part for a long time.

"Don't forget our verse," she said bravely.

"What does it say?" he asked sheepishly, like the shyest boy in a grade-school classroom who's finally mustered the courage to ask the one burning question that's long been tantalizing his boyish curiosity.

She coughed, and he waited. He couldn't see her smile clearly because of the low positioning of the moonlit window, the room's only source of light. Yet, he sensed he knew what it looked like at that moment—big and beautiful and radiating that special love she had for all.

"It's brief, but carries the complete message," she said with renewed strength in her voice. "It says, 'Brethren, the grace of our Lord Jesus Christ be with your spirit. Amen.' "

And then they hugged tenderly, painlessly, but only for a short while.

"Good luck," he said.

"God bless."

And Sherm Purcell stood up and walked out, shutting the broom-closet door behind him. Sharene, yet again, was left with only one realistic direction in which to proceed.

By the time Purcell emerged from the laundry room, his thoughts were focused on his own survival. He thought once again as the drug lord's confidant, about where he could have been since Meino Cablos had left their meeting to check on Sandy Kroghan. He needed an alibi to tell Cablos' lieutenant where he'd been when a shot was heard, and where he'd been since Cablos mysteriously had disappeared. He checked his pocket watch. It was late, the beginning of another day.

He walked directly toward the center of commotion in the hallway outside Sandy Kroghan's room. Two excited soldiers were questioning Carleta, who was wearing a robe and a nightgown.

"I left Ms. Kroghan to sleep several hours ago and have not seen her since," she said. "How many times do I have to tell you?"

"What's the problem?" asked Purcell as he approached the two soldiers and Carleta.

"Ah-h, Mr. Purcell. Where have you been?" asked one of the soldiers, who was wearing a beret and carrying a pistol in a holster at his side. "We've been looking for you. A shot was heard and we haven't been able to find Meino," he said.

The second soldier, with exposed, short-cropped hair, added, "We tried to find you in your room. Do you know where Meino is?"

Purcell started to respond, to tell a lie about snorting cocaine with Cablos and walking in different directions to be alone, but stopped short. The soldiers were staring at blood on his shirt that he had no way to explain to their satisfaction, or even his own. Hadn't he been careful while dragging Cablos' body from the bedroom to the study?

The first soldier reached for his pistol, and Sherm Purcell felled him, like cut timber, with a whirling kick to the ear. The second soldier reacted slowly, in apparent shock, then went to the stone hallway floor himself when Purcell kicked strongly with his left leg and swept that soldier's feet out from under him. Purcell silenced the latter with fists to his face, leaving the two of them quiet, but still breathing, on the cold floor. Midway between the two fallen soldiers, like an island unto itself, lay the one beret.

Carleta watched what transpired and said nothing.

Miraculously, none of the dozens of soldiers searching for Cablos at that very moment came upon that short scene.

"Come on, Carleta," said Purcell. "Help me drag them into Sandy's room."

He grabbed legs, and she grabbed the door. The unconscious soldiers soon were out of sight, and the maid and the man primarily concerned with saving his own life were left standing in the darkness of Sandy Kroghan's bedroom.

"Where is she?" asked Carleta of the woman she'd grown to love.

"She'll be home soon," he responded. "You'd better come with me and leave this place. You know too much. Gather your essentials and meet me at the vehicle barn in thirty minutes," he said. "Don't talk to anyone."

The middle-aged maid then exited the room and slowly walked down the hallway, as if she had much more than thirty minutes to pay lasting respects to her home of more than a decade.

Purcell shook his right fist, trying to shake away the sting of smashing the smaller soldier's face and eyeglasses. His own blood already was drying from small glass cuts on his knuckles. He looked at his shirt, and, with thumb and forefinger, felt the large red stain that he couldn't explain. He thought about Sharene, who had to leave the compound as quickly as possible.

The bloods of Sharene Marsena and Sherm Purcell did not touch.

He went directly to his own room across the triangular piece of green grass, and retrieved a waterproof pouch from the tank of his archaic toilet which flushed quietly, and with little force, whenever the slim chain extending through the lid was tugged. Clipped inside the pouch, in separate cellophane bags, were complete identifications for four different people. He selected the driver's license, credit cards, passport, and social security information for a man from Delta, New Hampshire, and arranged them in the wallet he almost always carried with him in a leather ankle wrap. Identification papers proving Sherm

Purcell was who he claimed to be were placed in the cellophane bag vacated by the New Hampshire I.D. He retrieved a long, manila envelope, scissors, and a chunk of medium-sized cardboard from a small desk and cut from it two pieces of cardboard slightly smaller than the envelope. Grabbing a pen, he next addressed the envelope with his left hand, in big, block-like childish script. With the pieces of cardboard inserted in the envelope as a buffer to shield the shape and contents of what was inside, he stuffed the four opaque bags between the pieces of cardboard and sealed the envelope. He next pasted more than enough postage on its upper right-hand corner.

The envelope was addressed to Mandi Ciene at a particular box number at a downtown post office in New Orleans.

He placed the envelope by the door, then, making as little sound as possible, proceeded to destroy his own residence. Clothing and papers from every drawer, including coveted munitions information from his personal desk, were tossed in a pile in the middle of the living room. The only damning information remaining about Sherm Purcell, or who he chose to be next, would be on his body or in the envelope when he left the room.

He wadded paper, lit a match, and made certain the pile was engulfed in flames before grabbing the envelope and stepping back into the Colombian night.

The vehicle barn and petrol bank stood to one side of the driveway that led from the elongated housing complexes toward the outer gate, and Purcell walked in that direction.

Animated voices were heard coming from Sandy Kroghan and Meino Cablos' adjacent sleeping quarters, but no one hailed Purcell as he calmly walked in the opposing shadows.

Those voices grew to frenzied proportions seconds later when the two unconscious soldiers were discovered in Sandy Kroghan's bedroom.

"Warn them at the gate," yelled the lieutenant who disliked Sherm Purcell.

Because of his relationship with the drug lord, Purcell almost had as many keys to locks in the bastioned stronghold as did his dead friend, and used one of them to enter the office adjacent to the building that housed most of the compound's vehicles, and next to it, its petroleum.

Inside that office, he switched on a flashlight he'd saved from his now-flaming quarters, and slipped the New Orleans-bound envelope in the middle of a stack of outgoing mail.

Wasting no time, Purcell grabbed a vehicle key from a nail on the wall, and, with hammer and large spike retrieved from a mechanic's tool box, flattened every front tire on nine of the ten vehicles in the vehicle barn.

Voices were heard again, loud and coming closer, and Sherm Purcell crawled under the limousine he intended to use for his escape, the only one with healthy front tires.

Lights in the vehicle barn were turned on, and the sound of soldiers' boots on the building's concrete floor was deafening to Purcell's ears.

He was pinned beneath a white limousine, and felt surges of fear and claustrophobia. So much reward money to collect, and he was going to die here? His pulse quickened and he began to sweat. Voices in more than one language, along with the staccato ringing of militant boots, approached the vehicle under which he was hiding.

Purcell fought the urge to panic, and tried to control his own thoughts. Without premeditation, he asked himself what Sharene Marsena might do in a similar situation. Then, Sherm Purcell, a hard-core survivalist who rarely put anything ahead of self, found himself in prayer to the one God he needed to know.

"Dear God of Sharene, help me," he thought. "I don't want to die like this. Get me out of here and I'll try to be a good man. Honest."

By now, the soldiers in khaki uniforms had discovered the flat tires and were yelling to other soldiers outside the building. The sound of boots approached the vehicle he was under, and the air in the enclosed room stifled his breathing. Purcell continued to sweat profusely, as if his prayer, lacking faith, left him perched on the periphery of hell.

Then a door opened, sweet freshness, and a woman's voice drew the boots away from the limousine Purcell was under like sharks to blood.

"Mother Mary, what do you want with me?" asked Carleta. "I have no reason for being here, really. Mother Mary. Why are you angry with me? Am I suddenly a dog? Why do you question me so? Mother Mary. I am the personal maid to Ms. Kroghan. Why do you stare at me as if I had leprosy? Go find another to kick around. I personally will go tell Meino Cablos of your accusations. Mother Mary."

Purcell freed himself from under the vehicle, and, with the soldiers concentrating on Carleta, eased into the driver's seat of the white limousine.

"Mother Mary," she continued, "each one of you will pay for such rudeness to a woman such as me."

"Let her go," boomed the lieutenant who now disliked Sherm Purcell more than ever, this time speaking in Spanish. "She'll be here when we need her. But now we have more important fish to catch."

Carleta elicited an additional "Mother Mary" as she exited the vehicle barn, then hastily walked in the direction of the main gate.

The drug lord's soldiers in the vehicle barn, now maybe ten in number, refocused their attentions to the interior of the large garage. Like the lieutenant, they drew their pistols and slowly advanced toward the white limousine.

With a smile and an audible, "Thank you, God of Sharene," Sherm Purcell turned the ignition of the only vehicle in the garage with operable front tires, Cablos' personal limousine, and dropped the shifter into D2. Tires squealed in the tight quarters of the metal building and soldiers fired round after round of bullets at the bulletproof glass and body of the car. The well-fortified limousine smashed through the closed aluminum door of the garage like Rocky Mountain elk through a farmer's fence. One burst of power, and Purcell and Cablos' limousine were outside the vehicle barn.

Only the intervention of a higher power kept the lieutenant and his men from piercing or disabling tires on the vehicle.

Carleta had used her newfound freedom to march toward the lights of the main gate. Purcell spotted her along the driveway, skidded to a halt, slid over to open the passenger door, and welcomed her into the dark interior of the limousine.

"Mother Mary thanks you," she said breathlessly.

"We're not home yet," said Purcell as he punched the gas pedal on the floorboard. "The outside gate is made of stiffer stuff."

Purcell knew Cablos' soldiers at the entrance to the fortress would be alerted by now, and was amazed when he and Carleta approached it to see the heavily barred gate swung wide open. An older car with single headlights was being granted admittance to the compound.

"Hang on," said Purcell to the Spanish-Mestizo maid.

He veered Cablos' limousine to the right, banged the approaching car along its left side, and the unscratched limousine bounced onward into the night, leaving the compound behind.

Sherm Purcell laughed.

"Shotsu must have been drunk and raised hell for them to let him in. Whoever's in charge after tonight will make life unbearable for many of Cablos' men."

The big, white car sped away, quickly putting distance between it and the centerpiece of Cablos' empire.

"It certainly was lucky I convinced Cablos to bulletproof his limousine," said Purcell. Then Carleta, by lights radiating from the dashboard, saw Sherm Purcell's face sour, as if he'd once more eaten a forbidden fruit. "Or maybe lucky isn't the right word," he mumbled.

"Mother Mary," beamed Carleta.

The remainder of their drive was spent in silence. The half moon was visible in the sky, and Purcell's thoughts drifted to a woman trying to free herself from a broom closet. Carleta, on the other hand, pondered where life would take her next. Each, though not yet for the same reason, trusted for the best.

Mikki expected a car to arrive late at night and was on the porch to greet its occupants. Her first words to Purcell were, "Did you kill the bastard?"

He nodded in moonlight that now was supplemented by illumination from a light fixture above Mikki's doorway.

"Did she have to do it?" she asked.

"No. I did," he said.

"Good."

"This woman is named Carleta, and she needs your help," said Purcell. "She requires everything from clothing to shelter and food, and needs a new start in life."

"No problem," said Mikki.

"I'm going to take your car. I have to go back," Purcell said.

"Is she in danger?" asked the young girl who wished she'd been the one who'd killed Cablos, instead of Purcell.

Purcell laughed a laugh that eased tension for all three of them as they stood in the moonlight in front of Mikki's temporary quarters.

"Sharene Marsena has been in danger since she left Georgia, and maybe long before that," he said, turning his eyes toward the ground.

"Mother Mary," said Carleta.

CHAPTER 13

Sharene wasn't small enough to squeeze through the opening after cutting through the window's middle metal bar, and cutting the second bar took much longer. It was nearly three a.m. when that second bar fell free.

Only once during her hours of tedious sawing had she been forced to halt because of a nearby commotion. Many times she'd stopped because of fatigue.

The blood had stopped flowing from her gunshot wound, but the pain was getting worse.

During her hours by the broom-closet window, Sharene had spotted only one solitary soldier walking across the field ahead of her. He'd guided himself by the moon and a flashlight, and never crossed the tennis courts.

Hours spent with a small hacksaw dismantling two of the window's three vertical bars provided time for Sharene to ponder her immediate future. Cutting the bars only would free her to face yet another round of peril. Light from the moon would make her visible from a distance as she crossed open terrain, and her wound would make progress slow. Crawling might reduce her exposure to soldiers seeking to find her, but by doing so she'd never make it to the helicopter by five a.m.

Yet, other options remained. She could step away from the broom-closet window, flash her small light in the night, and hope to be mistaken for a Cablos' soldier. Or, instead, she simply could abandon all thoughts of subterfuge and openly stumble across the moonlit opening like the wounded warrior for the Lord she was.

Acting on faith, she chose the latter option.

From her temporary cubicle of safety in the broom closet, Sharene looked beyond the searing pain and the enemies behind her in hopes of one day finding peace and comfort. With the most basic of survival instincts rising to the surface of her being, she crawled through the opening she'd made through the barred window, and, without the use of her flashlight, stepped forward into the unknown. She hummed Amazing Grace and carried in her right hand the valise filled with cocaine, some papers from the drug lord's safe, and the MASTER VII cassette she hoped would crumble Cablos' empire.

The walk was surprisingly easy, uneventful, and no human being witnessed her painful journey in faith. No human witnessed that journey, yet Sharene, seemingly alone, was under constant surveillance as she moved across the open field and neared the tennis courts. The hunter, like his prey, remembered another tennis court in South Carolina, and decided it was time to capitalize on Sharene's fears. It was time, he thought, to pay a personal visit to one Sharene Marsena.

She was too close to getting away.

It wasn't her possible escape that bothered the hunter, but the manner in which it was being accomplished. She was putting total faith in the only one he feared. Her death now could shorten his personal time clock. For time, to the hunter, was only measured in the number of pure souls who went directly from life on earth to heaven. Minutes and seconds meant nothing. What mattered was the inevitable toll toward that magical number of saints that would trigger cataclysmic events and a Second Coming of the Christ. At that time, the hunter—also known as Satan—would be thrown into a fiery pit of damnation where he, and many others, would wish for, and not receive, an end to their existence.

The hunter had read The Book and knew he'd be released a second time far into the future, but damnit, one thousand years of anguish was something to be postponed at all costs.

Sharene Marsena, weakened from an incurable blood disease, an induced cough, and a bullet lodged below her rib cage, was still armed with a shield of faith the hunter would never grasp. And, aware of her pain, but not the strength of her armor, he determined that she'd earned his immediate and undivided attention.

Sharene experienced a sense of euphoria as she safely stepped off of the open field and on to the tennis courts, but only briefly. She looked closely at the moonlit courts and the nearby woods, and was pierced by a painful memory. She held one hand on her wound and kept walking beneath the bright, bloodstained shawl.

Her prayers were behind her as she proceeded in a brief shroud of comfort.

The hunter, only a few feet away, stalked her mercilessly, patiently waiting for his moment to effectively give succor to her weakness like a black hole sucking reality out of space.

He needed to remove any chink he could find … truth, righteousness, faith, preparation of the gospel. He chose to attack the strength of God's grace by usurping her physical weakness.

"Why do you suffer so?" asked the hunter.

Sharene heard a smooth, soothing voice near at hand, and cringed at its closeness. She was too weak to run.

"You are too beautiful of a creature to be in such pain," the voice continued.

Then he materialized in the night, handsome and radiating a warm light. He reached out a hand to Sharene. "Come, and we will fly with the wind."

Sharene felt a lifting of her burden and dropped to her knees. She was too humbled to look, to speak, and pulled the bloody shawl over her head. The pain wasn't as bad now. Even the hard playing surface of the tennis court she knelt on felt gentle to her knees.

"Who are you?" she said from beneath the shawl.

"Woman," he said, and then his smooth, soothing voice changed dramatically. It became cold, like ice, and he spoke in a rote pattern as if he'd been practicing from the graves for nearly two thousand years. He said, "Cast thyself down: for it is written, He shall give his angels charge concerning thee: and in their hands they shall bear thee up, lest at any time thou dash thy foot against a stone."

Sharene's pain suddenly was gone. She felt healthier than at any time since Sherm Purcell's errant bullet had entered her body, since before Mike's small pills. She dropped the shawl, which now was clean, and looked directly at the radiant prince. Her weaknesses had been stripped.

"Who are you?" she asked a second time.

And the silky, soothing voice returned. "Come with me," he said, "and I will make my kingdom, your kingdom. This world and all of its riches will be yours."

He again extended a hand.

Even in her seemingly new body, Sharene Marsena, probably from long-ago teachings from Pastor Dale Hemri, doubted her good fortune. She asked one more time, "Who are you?"

The radiant prince smiled and stepped closer.

Then Sharene remembered what she needed to say.

"Do you confess that Jesus Christ is come in the flesh and is of God?"

The hunter cringed, backed up, and lost his glorious façade. In seconds, he metamorphosed into a scaly, upright, snakelike creature.

"You will suffer for that," he said cruelly. "Die alone in the dirt if that is your choosing. You will bleed for me, woman."

Sharene crumpled back onto the unyielding, hard surface beneath her with all of her wounds restored. She pulled the shawl over her body to cover her weakness.

Tense angels watched from a distance, and the hunter disappeared from view.

Sharene wanted to succumb to fatigue, to pray herself to sleep, but was aware of the hour. It was four a.m., and she needed to reach the meadow. She didn't want to die on the outback near a drug lord's haunt in Colombia.

She struggled to her feet once again, and began plodding on in the darkness, proceeding solely on faith that her weary body somehow would find Nadia and the others. She stumbled in the faint light and fell repeatedly, drawing new blood from her knees. Yet, she maintained a slow, but steady course toward a meadow she'd never seen.

Her prayers were choppy, but constant.

"Dear Lord," she said, "Please don't make me die alone. I need to see Jordan one more time. He doesn't understand."

CHAPTER 14

"Who the hell is he?" barked Sherm Purcell.

He'd parked Mikki's car beyond the meadow and silently crept upon three people sitting in the midsize helicopter. All three jumped in surprise at his proximity and the harshness of his words, especially the Latin pilot who desired an uneventful takeoff, a palatable payoff, and a return to his warm wife in Cartegena.

"You aren't supposed to be here!" stated Nadia with authority. "Don't think for one second that we're taking you with us. Just why are you here, Mr. Purcell?"

"Just say that I got emotionally involved, OK? And who the hell is he?" Purcell asked once more, pointing to Jordan Norton sitting in the seat directly behind the pilot.

"Sherm Purcell, meet special agent Jordan Norton," said Nadia.

Jordan scooted to his right, and the two men shook hands through the open door of the silent chopper.

"What's your specialty?" asked Purcell.

Jordan Norton didn't respond.

"Sharene Marsena," said Nadia with a smile.

Less than a mile away in the compound, the lieutenant was seeing events getting out of hand. No sign had been found of Meino Cablos' whereabouts, the damned traitor Purcell had set fire to his bungalow and escaped, and the concubine was missing. A thorough search of the premises had discovered bloodstains and severed retention bars in a closet off the laundry room, and guards, armed with guns and flashlights, had traced a sometimes-bloody trail to the tennis courts. It was there where the angry lieutenant joined the early morning search, convinced that Sandy Kroghan had answers to the mayhem arising everywhere around him.

Dawn wasn't far away, and Sharene's bullet wound was sapping her strength, once again leaving a trail of red in the dirt and grasses of rural Colombia.

The half moon seemed brighter as she plodded forward in semidarkness. She saw no angels or more demons, only her own slow-moving feet and the uneven, dark rocks beneath them that caused her to fall over and over again. To fall and bleed, then fall and bleed some more seemed to be her plight. Sharene had no idea how many times she fell, just knew she repeatedly had to revive her energies and rise again.

She prayed a little, but hardly could get past "Our Father" or "Amazing Grace" before she'd fall in the dirt once more and lose the thought.

It wasn't love of God that repeatedly drew Sharene Marsena back to her feet—for she knew in her soul that He always would be there for her, regardless of what happened that morning—but rather a primeval need to right a wrong with one she loved.

"Jordan," she cried aloud to her lost lover who was closer than she knew. Then she'd fall again among the rocks and boulders that seemed to be everywhere. "Please, God," she continued, and tears of frustration usurped her tears of pain.

The bullet wound had reopened since her encounter with the hunter, worse than before, and the blood of a woman from a tiny burg in Alabama stained God's earth like an Old Testament sacrifice before an altar.

Cablos' men in khaki relentlessly closed ground on the wounded woman. They knew she was close.

Soon to be purified in the refiner's fire, Sharene's blood fell to the earth guiltless, like that of a sacrificial Mayan virgin. She was an innocent refugee from life's ugliness. A heinous incident in South Carolina had ripped her away from America's populous ranks of beauty and simplicity, away from the secure world she'd both known and accepted. Now, she was cast into a strange land of danger and intrigue, where ambassadors of God's grace, like her, were few.

Yet, she'd touched many.

Sharene fell and rose one more time. She looked around and saw no trees. She couldn't remember the last time she'd seen a tree.

"There she is," said Nadia from the helicopter.

A human form in the semidarkness, already one-third of the way across the heart of the meadow, was moving slowly towards them.

The soldiers' khaki uniforms were murky in the pre-dawn light as the men following the lieutenant popped upon the perimeter of the meadow. One, two, three, and up to nine soldiers lined up at the edge of the timber, then pointed toward their prey, maybe eighty yards distance from them in the meadow.

"Ms. Sandy, you forgot to tell us about Meino," yelled the lieutenant, and two of Cablos' men, thinking of her beauty, laughed eagerly.

Unaware of the partially obscured, dark-painted helicopter less than three hundred yards away at the far side of the meadow, something he and Cablos' other soldiers had no reason to look for, the lieutenant gave instructions to close the search slowly, methodically, for the sole purpose of prolonging the woman's agony.

"She will feel our touch in complete daylight," he said.

Nadia, Purcell, Jordan, and the pilot heard the lieutenant's taunt before they saw soldiers directly beyond Sharene in the dawn's dim light.

"Give me every weapon you have, but one," Purcell stated in a voice even Nadia couldn't refute. "When I have their attention, pick her up and get her the hell out of here."

Still standing outside the helicopter, Purcell collected two rifles and two pistols through the chopper door, said, "Give me five minutes at most," and, because of the many armaments he was carrying, clumsily ran northward through trees at the meadow's edge. He dropped one weapon, then another as he ran around the perimeter of the meadow, intentionally slowing to quiet his footsteps and his breath as he came closer to Meino Cablos' soldiers.

"Those men have guns. I'm not flying over there," stated the pilot in a hushed, but strained voice to Nadia and Jordan.

Nadia, sitting in the front along with the pilot, put the remaining pistol to the pilot's head.

"Does this make you think differently?" she asked.

"Don't be stupid, lady. There's a whole army out there. This woman can't be worth all of our lives," he said. "I have a wife and family to think of."

Only Nadia and the one who knows all knew her intentions as she cocked the hammer of the pistol.

Filing into the meadow, the soldiers looked with confidence and shades of lust at Sharene Marsena.

Sherm Purcell shattered the deceptive quiet of the early dawn by firing the contents of one pistol as rapidly as he could, then ran and scrambled over boulders and bushes that blocked his path en route to his next weapon. Cablos' soldiers, not knowing from what direction the shots had come, were huddled and confused when Purcell reached where he'd stashed a rifle, then sent a second volley of gunfire their general direction.

The pilot nearly fainted when Purcell's initial barrage pierced the stillness. An instant later, the temple of his forehead bumped against the barrel of Nadia's pistol when Jordan Norton dove over his left shoulder, tumbled through the open door, and fell face first in the Colombian dirt.

"What the hell," exclaimed Nadia, but Jordan Norton already was on his feet running in the direction of Sharene Marsena.

"One big break for you, buckaroo," said Nadia to the pilot as she lowered the gun from his face. "Be ready to take off when they get here."

The soldiers, now hidden among the meadow's many large rocks, were more prepared when Purcell got to where he'd stashed the third weapon, another rifle. They caught glimpses of him as he stood among the rocks and trees, firing bullet after bullet to draw their attention away from Sharene. This time the soldiers returned a many-bulleted volley of their own.

Although daylight was breaking, Cablos' men saw neither Jordan Norton running into the meadow, nor the helicopter directly beyond him. Sherm Purcell, however, did see Jordan heading toward Sharene, and wished he had more weapons to provide a longer-lasting distraction.

The lieutenant and his men, still unaware only one man was shooting at them, began crawling off of the open space.

Sharene heard gunshots from her personal haze and harbored no thoughts other than to keep going and achieve her mission. She attempted to pray from her weakness.

Then, she felt surprisingly gentle arms sweep her off her feet and on to the uneven ground. She offered no resistance, and, in reality, had no more resistance to offer. She bit a corner of her shawl, clutched the valise, and waited for her future to unfold.

"Sharene, Sharene. It's me, Jordan," he said with a loving, concerned smile crossing his handsome face. "It's almost over now. You'll be home soon. I promise. Come with me and everything will be all right."

He took the valise from her hand.

She looked up then, and it was Jordan. Yet, she doubted her good fortune.

"Tell me, Jordan, if you are real, do you confess that Jesus Christ is come in the flesh and is of God?"

"You know I do, Sharene Marsena," he said with an incredulous smile. "I do confess it over and over again. And I love you very much."

Then he picked her up, and soil from a foreign country, as well as sacrificial blood from a well-used shawl, smeared his face.

Seeing the beginnings of a new day from the arms of Jordan Norton, Sharene said, "Thank you, God. You really are here."

"Don't talk, Sharene," he said. "Be still and know that nothing but the best lies ahead."

"Jordan," she said as he carried her into the light of a new day, he being careful not to fall on the many rocks that still impeded their path, "I always have loved you, and didn't want you to know I have an incurable blood disease."

And her burden of guilt was gone as if the hunter's heel finally had been removed from her upward-turned hand.

Sharene sobbed like a baby and held tightly to Jordan Norton, and to love, as he lifted her past an astonished pilot and into the waiting helicopter.

PART III

"You got a locker to rent?"

"Yeah," said the young man behind the counter at the Greyhound bus depot. "But you don't have to use one if you don't want. Just give me what you got and the name of who's to pick it up, and I'll see that they get it. Save you a couple bucks."

"I'll take the locker," said the man from up north.

"Suit yourself."

After the man from up north had been assigned a locker and divvied up the exact amount to pay one month's rent for it, he asked the man behind the counter where locker number seventy-seven was. He was given verbal directions to a locker around the corner, well away from both the front counter and the clerk. He walked to locker number seventy-seven, tested the key the clerk had given him, found that it worked, shut the locker door that had an automatic lock on it, and strolled into the dust-laden men's room.

Two flies were caught helplessly in a crimped overhead screen, and buzzed in rebellion as if their plight mattered.

The man walked into the third and final toilet stall away from the door, closed the swinging, metal door behind him, and put his left foot on the toilet seat. He pulled up his pant leg, tugged down his sock, and exposed an ankle belt filled with money and a passport. He drew out a big wad of large American currency, and carefully counted out $150,000. He jammed the $150,000 into a six- by-nine-inch manila envelope he'd carried with him when he'd entered the bus depot, and sealed it with moisture from his tongue. Then he exited the toilet stall and the restroom, unlocked and placed the envelope in locker number seventy-seven, made sure it again was locked, and returned to the counter.

"Got an envelope?" asked the man to the clerk, who was busy reading a dated issue of Popular Mechanics magazine.

"What?"

"It's Sunday, and your stores are closed. I just need one envelope," the man said.

"Not supposed to," said the clerk matter-of-factly.

"It's Sunday," said the man from up north.

"Yeah," said the clerk, and went back to reading his magazine. After a few moments of silence he looked up from the magazine and saw the man staring at him. "OK," he said. "You need a stamp, too?"

"Yeah," said the man with the locker key marked seventy-seven grasped in his right hand.

"Tell you what I'm gonna do," said the Greyhound clerk. "Beings it's Sunday, I'm gonna give you the envelope and the stamp for free."

"Thanks."

The man from up north took the stamped envelope to a pay phone on the premises and grabbed a slim telephone book dangling by a string below the phone. He searched through the pages, found the name and address he was looking for, and wrote that information left-handed, in big script, on the letter-size envelope. Outside the clerk's view, he fished into a nearby trash can and pulled out the first flyer he found. It was an advertisement for an upcoming Christian youth rally. He wrapped the flyer tightly around the key, and put the small wad he'd just made into the stamped envelope that now had a destination, but included no return address. Then, he sealed the envelope as he had the first one, with moisture from his tongue.

"Where's the nearest drop box?" he asked loudly.

"The what?" asked the clerk.

"...the closest place to mail a letter on Sunday."

"That would be at the Drive Inn just up the street."

"Thanks."

As the man from up north opened the Greyhound depot door to step into a warm spring day, the clerk called out to him, "Don't tell anyone about that envelope, OK?"

Sherm Purcell stepped into the sunshine and fished a soiled map from his pants pocket. A boy who'd never met Sharene, but admired her, had given it to him after that young man had attended Sharene's funeral. From what he'd told Purcell, Nadia probably had been there, too.

But that was three years ago.

He double-checked the street sign to make certain he was on Summit Street, and headed south. The thought that he was beginning a two-mile stroll, with a detour to post the envelope, gave him pleasure. The world mostly was springtime green, and very few cars passed his way. After he crossed Topu Avenue by the school and before he reached the Drive Inn, Purcell noticed a huge church directly in front of him. It looked old.

He saw men working on the roof.

The Drive Inn obviously was the small town's focal point of activity. Many cars, teenagers, sodas, and banana splits radiated an aura of American 1980's innocence. He found no drop box, and the white, stamped envelope remained in his hand.

He could see the men working on the steep church roof clearly when he turned a hard right on to South Street.

"Just turn on South, and the cemetery is at the end of the road," the boy had said.

South Street had few residences along it, and was flat. An old Chevy with fresh paint and white-wall tires cruised past at a slow speed. The occupants in it, a boy and an equally aged teenage girl, stared at him unabashedly. He carefully picked his way along the sometimes dirt, sometimes broken sidewalk route along South Street, pausing to look east when it ended at Johnson Road—at what obviously was the poor part of town. That was where Mrs. Newton's son, Richard, had just returned home to live, hoping for a fresh start after more than three years in prison.

Where South met Johnson, which ran east and west, Purcell looked across the junction and saw a large overhead sign that read PLATEAU CEMETERY ENTRANCE.

He walked through an open gate, and within twenty minutes was standing by the gravesite of Sharene Marsena. He still held the envelope in his hand, with the key to locker number seventy-seven inside it.

"Hello, Sharene," he said in a hushed voice. "Guess I'm a little late. I've got something to give you," he said, and waved the envelope apologetically, listlessly, like a cheerleader waving pompons in the final seconds of a monumental defeat. "It's part of the reward for returning the Kroghan girl."

He waited, as if expecting a response from the grave of Sharene Marsena.

Silence.

"Shit," he mumbled to himself. "Mandi was right. This isn't going to work."

Seconds went by, troubling seconds for the man who'd spent much of his life chasing monetary wealth, a fraction of which was in the envelope he held in his hand. It hadn't come as an immediate recognition, but after receiving the huge cash reward for returning Sandy Kroghan, Sherm Purcell realized over a span of three years that there was much more to life than money. The closest living representation of what he thought he now wanted had been Sharene Marsena, whose source of strength still was a mystery to him.

"I looked it up, Sharene. I even memorized it. Galatians 6:18 is just like you said. 'The grace of our Lord Jesus Christ be with your spirit brethren, amen.' I understand the words, sort of, but for the life of me, I can't grasp the peace and comfort you got out of them. Can you teach me a little more, Sharene?"

And the man from up north bowed his head out of respect for one whom he'd loved, not for the Lord and Savior she'd died for.

He didn't hear the footsteps until they were upon him. They approached quickly, yet quietly, and Sherm Purcell looked up late to see a teenage boy who needed to catch his breath from a run. He wore jogging shorts and a light gray sweatshirt.

"Hi. My name is Peter. Did you know my sister?" the boy asked in a friendly, upbeat voice between deep drafts of life-giving air.

Sherm Purcell's self-protective guard remained down. He nodded and smiled. "She was one of the most beautiful people I have ever known," he said.

"Where did you know her?" asked the youth. "I mean, did you know her in South America? We hardly know anything about that part of her life. We're not even clear why she was there."

"Yes," said the man, standing up in the Alabama sunlight next to the grave of one he'd loved. "I knew her in South America. She saved my life."

"Wow! Can you stay long enough to meet my Father?" asked the boy.

The man from up north seemed in a daze, as if he'd just experienced a revelation from his own lips. "Yes, Sharene did save my life. Or, at least she started the process."

"Where is your car, mister?" asked Peter Marsena.

"I walked," said Sherm Purcell.

"Can I walk back with you?" asked the boy, offering a hand of friendship to the grown man he didn't know.

"Sure."

"Can you wait a minute?" asked Peter. "I have a few things to tell Sharene."

The man walked a polite distance away, but still could hear the teenage boy talk to his deceased sister.

"I like the flowers, Sis," he said of a small pot of fresh, tight-budded daisies placed next to the headstone. "Did you hear the news? Jordan and Chiska had a baby! It's a little girl. Be happy for them, Sis, because they're such a neat couple."

Peter paused for a moment, and, as if receiving fresh input from a higher source, said, "Somehow, I think you already knew." His voice reflected traces of adolescent disappointment.

Then, he beamed in resilience, as if all previous comments paled in comparison with what he now had to share.

"Something I bet you don't know, though. Where do you think your and my father is at this very moment? Don't know? He's on top of the church working on the roof. He told Mom it was one thing he knew he had to do before he died. He said he knew, without doubt, that the view from up there would change him for life."

Peter puffed proud as if his news was unparalleled.

"See you, Sis. I love you a bunch."

The man and the boy walked from the gravesite in silence, only speaking once they'd removed themselves from the cemetery and put the PLATEAU CEMETERY ENTRANCE sign behind them.

"Is your dad working on top of that huge church on Summit Street?" asked Sherm Purcell.

"Yep," said the boy with a tinge of pride.

Then Sherm Purcell asked a question, an involvement-type question he normally wouldn't have asked. "Do you think I could go up on the roof?"

"Sure," said Peter. "The ladders are all in place."

THE END